I0818090

The Godfather President 2

By

Bobby Legend

The Godfather President 2

Published through Legend Publishing Company
This is a work of fiction. Names, characters, places, and incidents are the product of the author's imagination or are used fictitiously. Any resemblance to actual persons, living or dead, events, or locales is entirely coincidental.

 Book Design and Layout by Mickey Strange: ISBN 978-0-9991813-1-7.

Introduction

Mobster Jack Cotti, elected by the voters to become the forty-fifth President of the United States, has been put down by an assassin's bullet. He wanted only to get things done and bring both sides of the aisle together. But now his life is in the hands of New York City's finest surgeons. The doctors believe there is little hope for recovery. The question remains: Will Jack Cotti make it into the Oval Office or will his Vice President, Underboss Johnny Napolie, take control of the White House. Only time will tell!

Chapter 1

Bobby Legend and other reporters were waiting in the halls of the hospital for word on President-elect Jack Cotti's surgery. Legend and his cameraman began filming.

"Independent news reporter Bobby Legend here," he said, speaking into the camera. "President-elect Jack Cotti will be undergoing surgery to remove bullet fragments from his back and chest. The doctors here give very little hope of a full recovery, if any. It'll be touch and go."

As the reporters and Cotti's family waited patiently for good news, the surgeons in the operating room were trying desperately to save Cotti's life. Just after surgery began, he quit breathing. After two tries to revive him, the doctors called it.

"What's the time?" asked Dr. Haig, the head surgeon.

"Two fifteen pm," replied Mrs. Laurie Petty, the head nurse.

"Well, we tried," said Dr. Gloss, second in command.

"Thank God he's dead," remarked Nurse Judy Gladstone. "We don't need a gangster as President."

"Aren't you forgetting something, Judy?" said Dr. Gloss. "Johnny Napolie will now be President. He's a mobster too. Maybe even worse than Cotti."

They all nodded.

"Well, let me go speak with the family and reporters," said a dejected Dr. Haig.

He walked to the waiting room to give Cotti's family members and friends the bad news. The reporters followed him but were kept from entering the room. A few minutes later, he went back into the hallway and stood in front of a slew of microphones.

"May I have your attention, please?" After getting the reporters to quiet down, he gave them the bad news. "I have some news on President-elect Jack Cotti. At two fifteen pm, Jack Cotti was pronounced dead. We tried reviving him twice before giving up. We did our best."

As Doctor Haig was about to answer a reporter's question, Nurse Gladstone, still in the operating room, suddenly heard a beep, then another. It was the heart machine going off.

Gladstone looked at her dead patient and saw his chest rise. She checked for a pulse. "I got a pulse," she shouted. "He's breathing. Cotti's breathing." She looked for Doctor Gloss, but he had already left the room. "Someone go get Doctor Haig!"

But no one in the room moved. It was as though they were in shock.

So, Nurse Gladstone ran out of the operating room, into the hallway, and through a crowd of reporters to get to Doctor Haig. "Dr. Haig, Dr. Haig, come quick. Jack Cotti is alive and breathing."

They both ran down the long corridor and into the O.R.

Nurse Gladstone, standing over the patient, told Haig, "We've got a strong pulse."

"How?" asked Haig.

"Who knows?" replied Gladstone. "He came back less than a minute after you left the room."

"Well, let's get to work. Somebody get me Doctor Gloss," Haig demanded. "We have to operate. Pronto!"

A few minutes later, Doctor Gloss returned to the O.R. to assist Doctor Haig.

"Well, let's get to work!" Haig told his crew, leaving the room for a few minutes.

After scrubbing his hands and donning gloves and a mask, Haig reentered the O.R. "Scalpel," he barked to Nurse Gladstone, who was handling the tools.

When she didn't move fast enough, he yelled out, "Scalpel!"

She finally placed a scalpel into his hand.

After nearly four hours on the operating table, Haig had removed the bullet and fragments and sewed Cotti up. The patient was breathing steadily, with a good, strong pulse.

"Thank God," said Haig. "I think he's going to make it."

"Why do you care, Doc?" asked Nurse Petty.

"Hell, I voted for him."

"Me, too," added Dr. Gloss.

Three others in the room also admitted that they, too, had voted for the patient. Only one out of the team voted for a different candidate, and Haig wouldn't say which one.

***

While the patient was wheeled into the recovery room, Doctor Haig first went to Cotti's family to tell them the good news and then returned to the bank of microphones and told the reporters.

"President-elect Jack Cotti is doing well after surgery. We removed fragments from the assassin's bullet… and the bullet that found its mark… then cleaned and stitched up the wounds. Mr. Cotti is now in the recovery room. If things go as we hope, he should be on his feet in less than a month."

"When will he be able to leave the hospital?" Bobby Legend asked.

"Whoa. We're getting a little ahead of ourselves. Mr. Cotti will have a long rehabilitation process to go through before we can discharge him. But we will keep you reporters and the media informed of his progress. Now if you'll excuse me, I'd like to speak with the family."

As Haig left the podium, the reporters followed, barking questions until they lost sight when he went into the family's waiting room.

Visiting with the family members once again and assuring them that their loved-one would make it with flying colors, he let it be known that there was still a long way to go on the road to recovery.

"If nothing out of the ordinary happens, your husband should be up and out of here in a month or so," Haig promised Cotti's wife, Maria.

Maria suddenly broke down and began crying over the good news. Her children surrounded and comforted her with their love.

"Now why don't you go home and get some rest?" said Haig. "We'll call you when he's strong enough for visitation."

She straightened up and nodded. "Come, children. It's time to go home. We can give our thanks and pray there."

***

A few minutes after the doctor walked out of the room, so did Cotti's family and friends.

Doctor Haig went to the recovery room to see how his patient was doing while the Secret Service had all entrances, exits and hallways guarded.

The FBI had handed over the protection of the President-elect to the Secret Service soon after Cotti was shot. However, the Feds still had the job of investigating the assassination attempt, and they sometimes butted heads with Secret Service agents.

When it concerned the President-elect, the Secret Service had complete control over his safety and security and didn't care whose toes were stepped on.

***

Over the next few weeks, Cotti's health progressed rapidly.

A young and pretty female orderly was in his room cleaning and told him, "Mr. President, you're as strong as a bull. You'll be out of here in no time."

"I hope so, dear. I need some female company."

"Mr. President," she said, blushing. "I'm flattered."

"No, honey. I didn't mean you. I meant my girlfriend."

"Oh, you're not married then?"

"Oh, no. I'm married with kids."

"What does your wife think about you having a girlfriend?"

"I don't bring it up. ***Forget about it***!"

"OK. I won't say another word," she promised.

Just before she left the room he asked her for a favor. "Hey honey, can you bring me some good cigars when you come back tomorrow?"

"Mr. President, you know there's no smoking in here. Shame on you," she said, shaking her finger at him.

"I know, dear. I'm just getting restless and need something to settle my nerves."

"I'll tell the nurse you need something for your nervousness."

"Forget about it! I'm getting tired of that crap too. I just need to get out of here."

"Just hang in there, Mr. President. You'll be out soon."

She turned and left the room. As she was leaving, she passed a doctor who was at the door speaking with the guards.

"I'm Doctor Nubel," he told them. "I'm filling in for Doctor Haig. He was called into emergency surgery, so I'm taking his rounds."

"Okay, go ahead," said Agent Anderson and waved him through.

Cotti was resting and had his eyes closed when the doctor came over to the bed and stood over him.

As Nubel looked around the room and then at the door to make sure the guards wouldn't interfere with his next order of business, he slowly and quietly pulled an eight-inch knife out from the inside of his waistband. He was ready to plunge it into Cotti's chest, but a nurse came into the room unexpectedly to give Cotti his pain shot. She interrupted the doctor's criminal act.

When she saw the blade, she screamed, "He's got a knife!"

Seconds later, the two guards entered the room with guns drawn and fired a total of seventeen rounds. Nearly all of the bullets hit the assassin square in the head and chest, knocking him into the wall next to the headboard of Cotti's bed. Blood splattered all over the walls, the bed, and Cotti. As he slowly crumpled to the floor, the blood turned the beige tiles to a crimson red. It poured out of him like a raging running faucet that wouldn't shut off.

The guards then ordered staff to remove the President-elect from the room and into another secure and safe room. Within minutes, the staff whisked Cotti to another secure location on the floor above, picked by the Secret Service, who were busy investigating the doctor they had just killed.

The first thing they noticed was that he had no hospital identification or badge pinned to his shirt or on his person. He had no identification of any kind: no wallet, no credit cards, and no social security card. The agents were baffled as to who this person was. They would have to hope that his fingerprints would yield some reason as to why this guy wanted Cotti dead.

But the investigation was the least of the Secret Service's worries. They would have to answer to higher-ups for their security lapse. Not just the two agents guarding Cotti's room but everyone on the security team who had allowed the assassin to enter the hospital in the first place, all the while not carrying any identification.

The FBI was also called in to investigate the assassination attempt. They were to determine whether it was in any way connected to the last assassination attempt on Cotti's life—the one that had landed him in the hospital. They still had no clues in that case other than finding a thirty-thirty caliber rifle with scope in the bell tower of a church just a half block away, which gave the shooter a clear shot at his target. In any case, the agents had very little to go on.

Meanwhile, a previous assassination attempt on Cotti's life, the case of the AIG airliner engine failure was being closed, with one arrest and conviction: that of twenty-year-old Danny Angelo, whose father is Anthony Angelo, Capo with the Lucchese Family and enemy of Cotti.

However, the kid, whose job was to refuel AIG's aircraft, had proclaimed his innocence from the beginning and throughout his trial. He claimed that a man dressed in a black suit had flashed a badge, given him a gallon can of liquid, and ordered him to add it to the fuel. Danny obeyed and returned the empty can to the man in black. Minutes later, the plane suddenly came to an abrupt stop just seconds before going airborne due to acid being mixed in with the fuel. But the jury believed Danny had added the acid to the fuel for the Mafia, hoping to end Cotti's life from a plane crash instead of a bullet and found him guilty of attempted murder. Soon after, Danny was sentenced to ten years in a maximum-security prison called Dannemora in upstate New York.

***

While the FBI was concentrating on their investigations concerning the President-elect, the Secret Service was concentrating on protecting him. But Jack Cotti wanted none of it and said so to the man in charge, Secret Service Agent Bill Owen, in no uncertain words the following morning. Owen was hoping to smooth things over with his boss. However, nothing he said helped. Cotti had other ideas.

"Okay, William, I've had just about enough with your clowns in your circus. I want my own men in here guarding me. Your boys aren't very good at it. And you better check if they were drinking on the job. I'm told they do that a lot."

"Mr. Cotti, my men are professionals," said Owen matter-of-factly. "They know their business. They killed the assassin, didn't they?"

"Hey, ***fuck you***, Bill! The guy shouldn't have gotten into my room, let alone the hospital. I was shot while the FBI was protecting me, and nearly shot a few other times. Damn near was killed by a sabotaged airplane. All while the Feds were protecting me. Hey, Bill, not for nuthin, but, No! You guys don't do a very good job. So, I'm bringing in my guys, and I don't give a ***fuck*** what you have to say about it. ***Forget about it!***"

As Cotti was about to spew more venom at the Secret Service agent, two FBI agents entered the room to interrogate the next President of the United States about the most recent assassination attempt. But they got nowhere.

"You're not ratting anybody out, Mr. Cotti," said Agent Alex Crum. "We just want to know if you have any idea who this guy was, or who he worked for? Or maybe who in the hell wants you dead?"

Cotti remained silent. Even if he did know, he wasn't saying: not to the Feds, anyway. But the agents weren't stupid. They could tell from Cotti's eye movement and facial expressions that he was withholding information of some sort. They left frustrated and scratching their heads. Their peers listening in on many wiretaps concerning the Mafia had heard nothing that was related to this attempted hit, if that's what it had been. Hell, it could have been some nut that wandered in off the street and wanted to get his name in the paper. Who knows? But they were sure to find out, one way or another.

***

A few hours later, Cotti was on the phone talking with his number two man, Underboss and now Vice President, Johnny Napolie.

"Johnny. Jack. How ya doin?"

"Jack! What the ***fuck*** have you gotten us into? I got Feds all around me and my family. ***It's driving me fucking crazy***! I can't make a move without these guys following me and pestering me. I don't know how long I can take this."

"Well, I might have that problem solved. That's what I wanted to talk with you about. I need you to bring me twelve of our best guys to protect me. If you haven't already heard, some guy was shot and killed in my room when he tried to ***stab*** me while I was resting in my bed. Can you believe that shit! Somebody tried to hit me in my bed. In the FUCKING HOSPITAL! So, I need my guys to protect me. I think all these Secret Service guys are a bunch of drunks. They allowed this guy into my room. So, do it, now."

"But, Jack, we got Tommy Valoppi running the Family now. I thought the grandson of our Family's Founding Father was a good choice. In fact, all the Capos voted for him."

"Good. But we'll talk about that later. You know we shouldn't talk about that stuff over the phone. What the fuck is wrong with you?" Cotti barked.

"I'm sorry, Boss. My head's so screwed up lately with all the Feds around me that it's driving me batty. I'm actually going out of my mind. I can't breathe. I can't, Jack."

"Don't worry, Johnny, I'll handle it. Just get those guys as soon as possible. Capiche?"

"Sure, Jack. I'll get right on it."

The conversation ended on that note.

But the Feds, listening in on Cotti's conversation, were delighted to hear the agony in their voices.

"Hell, who knows?" quipped Agent Greg Meadows. "With all the agents around them twenty-four/seven, that's torture to them Goombas."

"Yeah, maybe they'll commit suicide and take the easy way out," added Agent Keith Brunson.

"If those two Goombas can't handle the security now," argued Agent Ken Lundy, "they'll never last if they make it to Washington, D.C."

"Okay, guys," replied their supervisor, Agent Dennis Arms. "Break it up and get back to work."

But the Feds weren't the only ones talking about President-elect Jack Cotti. The media, and especially the McLaughlin Group's John McLaughlin, had something to add on the Cotti escapade.

That Sunday, a few days after the assassination attempt, McLaughlin held in front of the cameras the front page of the ***New York Times*** from right after Cotti's surgery for his viewers. It read: "President-Elect Jack Cotti, DEAD! NOT!"

"A few weeks ago," McLaughlin told his pundits and viewers, "a daring and excellent surgeon tried removing a bullet and some fragments from Cotti's body when Cotti quit breathing. According to the doctor, he twice tried to revive the President-elect and failed to bring him back. As he's telling the media reporters that the President-elect is dead, Jack Cotti suddenly resuscitates himself and begins breathing on his own. And now, there has been an assassination attempt right in his hospital room. I guess you could say the Secret Service dropped the ball again. They've been doing that a lot lately. So, I ask you, Pat, Buchanan: Do you think President-elect Jack Cotti will make it to his inauguration?"

"You can take a breath now, John," joked Buchanan. "But seriously. Are you asking me if he'll be strong enough and healthy enough to take the oath, or are you asking me if someone will whack him before then?"

"The latter," the other pundits said in unison.

"I ask you the same question, Eleanor Clift," said McLaughlin.

"Wait a minute, John," said Buchanan. "I didn't get to answer."

"Okay, Pat. Shoot."

"I think the new President will be sworn in as President—if he doesn't get killed first."

The other pundits laughed.

McLaughlin asked Clift again for her opinion. "Will the President-elect make it to his inauguration?"

She nodded. "John, Cotti's got about eight weeks before inauguration day. If he can stay out of trouble for that length of time, he should make it into the Oval Office. On the other hand," she snickered, "someone definitely doesn't want him in the White House."

Mort Zuckerman jumped into the conversation. "But why would the mob want to whack him now? Once he's in the White House, he'll control the DOJ, the DEA, and every other department investigating the mob. He can order those departments to cease and desist from harassing the Families and end all surveillance."

"That's right, John," interjected Tom Rogan. "Cotti can get all surveillance, including wiretaps, pulled from the field. And if those department heads don't play ball, he can have them transferred to Homeland Security in a town where the weather is thirty below zero all year round. I think it is someone other than the mob that's trying to kill him now."

"Are you talking about someone in government?" Buchanan asked Rogan.

McLaughlin interrupted the conversation. "I'm sure we'll be talking more about President-elect Jack Cotti in the weeks to come."

"I'm sure we will," quipped Buchanan.

"Okay, we have enough time left to ask for predictions," McLaughlin told the pundits and viewers. "I ask you, Pat Buchanan. What is your prediction?"

"I predict the deal with Iran will fail even before it starts."

"Eleanor Clift," McLaughlin barked. "Prediction."

"John, I say Putin will fold before Cotti's inauguration."

"Mort Zuckerman: prediction."

"I believe the New York Stock Exchange will make a negative three-thousand-point adjustment before the end of the year."

"Tom Rogan: prediction," McLaughlin said.

"I say the Supreme Court will find in favor of the states suing Colorado over legalized pot. It might even make medical marijuana illegal."

"I predict Jack Cotti will never make it to his inauguration," McLaughlin added. "Bye, Bye."

***

Once Cotti had all twelve bodyguards in place, he finally felt secure—at least, secure enough to continue his rehab. He desperately wanted to leave the hospital for his home and figured that, the faster he finished his rehab, the quicker he'd get home and take care of business. He didn't seem to mind the bodyguards surrounding his chair when he was wheeled to rehab. He knew his guys would take good care of him and not let anything happen that was detrimental to his health. And that confidence made him into his old self: a healthy, vibrant seventy-four-year-old who acted fifty.

And in less than three weeks, the day finally came; the doctors released him.

The Secret Service was stepping all over themselves trying to decide the best way to transport their client to his home. It seemed to Cotti that they weren't ready for this. They acted as though they hadn't expected him to leave the hospital... alive, anyway!

Cotti told them that they should have thought about that problem weeks ago. He scolded them like children. He was livid and beyond himself with their incompetence. His loud, guttural, cave-man-like voice echoed throughout the hallways.

"Hey," he snapped, "I'm waiting to leave this hell hole, and you guys are holding me up. Hell, I'll have my boys take me home. ***Forget about it!***"

"Mr. Cotti, we're rounding up cars and personnel as we speak," Agent Owen promised.

Cotti shook his head in disgust. "I'll give you fifteen minutes to get your shit together, or I'll have my boys get me home. Better get it together. Time's ticking away." He tapped the glass face on his watch.

Agent Owen waited for word through his radio. Twelve minutes later, it came. They would whisk Cotti out through the rear entrance and into a bullet- and grenade-proof limousine.

***

Cotti entered the limo surrounded by his bodyguards, who had to push Secret Service agents out of the way to get him in safely. Cotti's soldiers weren't taking any chances.

Two cars carrying four agents apiece rode with the limo, one in front and one in back. Cotti's bodyguards followed behind in three cars, along with a few military vehicles carrying armed soldiers.

***

When they arrived at Cotti's home, Cotti's soldiers were the first to exit their vehicles with guns drawn. They were alarmed because, as the convoy stopped, the vehicles driven by the Secret Service agents had been involved in a slight collision. The car following the limo had crashed into its rear end, which pushed the limo into the car in front of it, which in turn pushed that car onto a curb and into a fire hydrant. The hydrant exploded, spurting water thirty feet into the air. It wasn't a happy sight at all. And to make matters worse, President-elect Cotti developed whiplash from the incident.

Once things calmed down a bit, bodyguards of many persuasions—Secret Service, the military, and Cotti's soldiers—surrounded the area. Soon they were all over the neighborhood: on rooftops, in cars along the adjacent streets, around Cotti's home. They ranged up to three blocks away in all four directions. This time, the Secret Service pulled out all the stops—they might even have overdone it. But they were leaving no stone unturned and taking no chances after their screw-up at the hospital.

As Cotti stepped out of the limo, he wasn't at all happy. He looked the situation over: first, at all the Feds surrounding the area, and then to the three banged-up cars. Then, suddenly, while rubbing his sore neck, he stomped his feet and hurled a tirade of insults to his Federal protectors.

"You fucking incompetent sons-of-bitches," Cotti bellowed to all around him, but then directed his wrath at Agent Owen. "How in the fuck did you guys get your jobs? I bet you have to hire someone to protect your families. If our government is run the way you guys do your job, I got a lot of work to do to get things in order."

"And Owen," added Cotti. "I want those three drivers to have their blood drawn to see if they've been using drugs or alcohol. And even if they haven't, I want them fired for incompetence. Get me?"

Agent Owen was beyond himself and found it hard to speak. All he could do was meekly nod his head. What else could he do? Or say? He definitely didn't want Jack Cotti as an enemy. The President-elect held Owen's future in his criminal hands. No siree, Bob. Owen would kiss Jack Cotti's ass for as long as necessary to keep in good graces with his soon-to-be boss.

Chapter 2

Cotti and six of his men slowly walked through the throng of Federal Agents and into his abode. He refused to allow any of the G-Men to follow. He was beside himself and finding it hard to breathe. The G-Men were smothering him with their protection.

"Johnny was right," Cotti thought. "These guys are already driving me crazy! What the hell have I gotten us into?"

***

Waiting for him at the front door with open arms was his loving wife. She seemed to be very happy to see him. But behind closed doors, she was anything but! She let him have it with both barrels.

Before Cotti could say "hello" to his kids and give them a hug, his wife started in on him.

Everyone in the room cowered away from her torrid outburst. Even Cotti hurried away to his office, but his wife followed. He couldn't hide from her, so he had to sit and listen.

"You just had to do it, didn't you? You stupid fuck! You just had to run for President. It was a bad idea when you first brought it up. How many times are your enemies gonna come after you?"

Before he could answer, she continued: "I'll tell you, Mister. They'll keep coming until they kill you. Somebody wants to keep you from running the country. Haven't you figured that out yet? So, you better find out who it is and do it quick before it's too late!"

"Okay, honey. Calm down. I just got home, for Christ's sake. With all the G-Men out there, I don't think anyone's stupid enough to try anything."

She shook her head in disgust and quipped, "Yeah, that's what you thought before you got shot. You got lucky that time. Next time, that bullet might be fatal."

"***Forget about it!*** And quit worrying. I have. And now, if you'll excuse me, I have to call Johnny. We need to talk over business."

She told him to be discreet and "watch what you say, Jack. These days, you definitely know whose listening."

He nodded and then got on the phone with his Underboss.

"Johnny, Jack. You gotta get over here, so we can talk."

"How can I? These G-Men will be with me."

"Let them. They won't get into the house."

Cotti ended the phone call and waited for his number two to arrive. He lit up a fine Gurkha cigar and poured himself a glass of brandy then laid back in his chair and pondered his future.

Johnny Napolie arrived an hour later with four agents of the Secret Service tied to his hip. While he walked toward the front door, the four agents joined their peers in the front yard.

When Johnny reached the porch, two of Maria's girlfriends, one short and stocky, the other big and burly, wearing gaudy, flowered dresses and matching hats, were being searched before entering Cotti's abode. After a few minutes, all three were allowed through the front door. Upon entering, they were met by Cotti's wife. As they were yacking and making small talk, Jack heard the noise and wondered what all the commotion was about. He walked to the foyer.

Cotti, at first, only saw the two women. One, was the size and shape of Napolie, and the other was just about the size and shape of Cotti. But when Cotti shouted Napolie's name, he was surprised to see Johnny peek out from behind the women. Sheepishly, Johnny went to Jack's side and followed him into the den.

After lighting Gurkhas, they talked about the insanity controlling their lives. Cotti thought it would be "easy sailing" once he had won the Presidency, but right now he would have to live with the G-Men sticking to his every move.

Napolie was even more outraged. "Jack, what the hell are we doing?" he bellowed. "With all the Feds swarming all over me, I can't make a move."

"***Forget about it!*** You're the next Vice President of the United States. And don't worry about these G-Men. I'll take care of them when I'm President."

"Yeah, but what the fuck do we do until then?"

Cotti thought for a few seconds. "You said Tommy is now in charge, right?"

"Yeah. So?"

"Well, you call him and tell him to meet me here at two pm tomorrow afternoon. He can be our go-to guy."

"Yeah, he doesn't have as many Feds on his back. I don't think he'll like being put into the spotlight, though. What do you need him for?"

"We gotta have a meeting with the heads of the other Families, and I want him to set it up. I want to speak with them about the hit that put me into the hospital. I want to look into their eyes and see who the guilty one is. If it was Talluchi, this problem must be solved. Capiche, Johnny?"

"Jack, we can't have another war. Not now! You're going to be the President of the United States, for Christ sakes. We don't need the aggravation. ***Forget about it!***"

"Johnny, if I don't take care of the problem now, we might not make it to Washington. Something has got to be done!"

"Let the FBI handle it, Jack. We got other shit to worry about."

"You're right. We gotta worry about the People now. They need our help more than ever. But we still gotta have that meeting. So, fix it!"

"Will do, Jack. But Talluchi and them guys ain't gonna show up with all the Feds and Secret Service around. How we gonna lose them?"

"I think I got it figured. We'll wear disguises. We'll leave here wearing women's clothing, and the G-Men won't be none the wiser."

"Jack, I think you're losing your mind. Dress up as women? You gotta be kidding."

"Those two women that you came in with. They are about our size. Let's see if their clothes fit us."

"You've lost your mind!"

"Do you have another idea? If so, let's hear it."

Napolie just shrugged and continued to smoke his cigar.

***

Jack went into the living room to speak with his wife. He took her into the kitchen and told her about his idea. After a few minutes of bickering and arguing, she agreed with his reasoning and returned to the living room to speak with her girlfriends and see if she could convince them to go along with the outrageous request. At first, they completely refused. But then Jack intervened, handed them each five crisp one-hundred-dollar bills, and walked back to the den. The two women instantaneously changed their minds at the feel of those bills and began peeling off their clothes. They were left in their bras and panties and quite satisfied with their new-found wealth while Maria took the clothes to her husband. She walked into the den and threw them onto his lap.

"There you go," she said. "Don't ruin them. The girls still have to wear them home."

"Yeah, but if they fit, they'll have to come back and let us use them for a few hours. In fact, I'll give them money to buy a new outfit or maybe two."

"When?" she asked.

"When I tell you! I'll let you know."

Cotti looked at each dress and handed the shorter one to Napolie. "Put it on!" he snapped.

Then he told his wife to leave the room. As she was leaving, he barked, "Honey, bring me the hats and shoes."

She nodded and left the room, bringing each woman a blanket to cover up with.

While she was out of the room, the two wiseguys undressed down to their boxer shorts then tried on the gaudy, flowered dresses.

Soon after, Maria returned with the hats and shoes. She threw them at her husband's feet, laughing at the ridiculous sight in front of her; two tough guys dressed as women in flowered dresses that actually fit them rather well.

"I gotta take a picture," she said, still laughing.

"***Forget about it!***" Jack yelled.

Cotti picked up the apparel and handed a flowered hat and the smaller pair of two-inch heels to Napolie. When Cotti tried on his hat, he found that it had a black facial netting that would hide his face from gawkers. Napolie's hat had one also. Cotti believed the hats could put them over the top. The G-Men wouldn't be able to clearly see the faces behind the veils.

Now if only the shoes fit. Cotti seemed to have no trouble fitting into his pair. Napolie, on the other hand, fought to get into his. He huffed and puffed, pounded his feet into the ground and finally, after nearly three minutes, was standing on his feet and trying to walk in shoes that his feet weren't made for. Cotti too. They needed to walk without bringing any suspicion to their cause. They needed to talk, walk, and have the same mannerisms as the women they were portraying. It would take a lot of luck to pull it off, but they were determined to go through with it.

They practiced their walking, which actually looked like waddling, while Maria watched and laughed uncontrollably. She thought they looked like two dimwitted and spastic women.

"You guys will never get away with it," she said, still laughing.

"Honey, will you please get the hell out of here!" Cotti shouted.

The two tough guys needed to practice for as long as it took to fool the G-Men and not draw attention to themselves.

Maria did as ordered, and returned to speak with her two friends.

After nearly two hours of walking in those crazy outfits and tight shoes, their feet began to swell, so they had to put an end to their mischievous ways.

They quickly stepped out of the women's outfits, and after trading the dresses for their suits, Cotti called for his wife to return the apparel to the women.

"I'll come out in a few minutes to thank them," he told her.

Cotti did as promised. "Thank you, ladies," he said.

The two women nodded.

Cotti then told them of his plan and asked if they'd participate.

They agreed.

Cotti then gave each woman ten crisp one-hundred-dollar bills and promised an additional ten the day of the meeting.

"I'll have Maria call you and tell you when to come," he told them. "I want you to go out and buy another identical outfit just like the one you have on. Two identical hats and shoes. Wear one dress over the other. Same with the hat. And you can hide the extra pair of shoes in your purse. Don't ask me why. Just do it! You'll see why after the meeting. Any questions?"

"I don't have any," they said in unison.

Everyone laughed.

"Okay, then. Me and Johnny have things to talk over, so if you'll excuse us, ladies," Cotti politely told the women.

Cotti and Napolie returned to the den to relax and rub their aching feet. They couldn't believe what they had just done.

"Jack, we must be crazy," Napolie said.

"Yeah, crazy like a fox," Cotti retorted. "This is the only way we can have this meeting. Either that or let the Secret Service fucks follow us, and then the others will refuse the request. No! Disguises are the way to go. And what better disguise than that of a woman."

"I still think you're crazy! Why not tell Tommy what needs to be said and send him to the meeting? I mean, ***not for nuthin***, Jack, he is the boss of the Family now. We should let him do his job."

"Yeah, but they're trying to kill ***me***!" Cotti ranted. "I gotta talk to them and set them straight. Anyway, I haven't met the new guys yet that took over for Scarfino and Parrissi."

"You mean Sal Craveno and Bobby Cantano? Craveno was Parrissi's Consiglieri. Cantano was an up-and-coming Capo for Scarfino. They've been around for a while."

"Johnny, I'll tell you what. I promise that if we get to the meeting without any problems, I'll tell the Commission that Tommy will handle all Family business for the Valoppi Family. And then me and you can concentrate on the job at hand."

"Are you talking about when we get to Washington?"

"Yeah. We only have six weeks to inauguration day."

"So, what do you have in mind?"

"We gotta get the economy going again," Cotti replied enthusiastically. "And get the People back to work with good paying jobs. That's gonna be our first priority."

"Forget about that now, Jack. I wanna know why you think the other Families will listen to us? They're pissed off as it is!"

"'Cause I'll tell them what they want to hear."

"And what is that?" Napolie asked, not really wanting to hear the answer.

"That they'll be first in line for billion-dollar government contracts. Which will be worth ten times more than any scam they've ever run. I'll tell them that all they have to do is sit back and watch the money roll in."

At that moment, the front door opened and shut rather loudly. Cotti went to the window to see who had left. It was Maria's two girlfriends. He watched as the two walked away and hopped into a cab. He chuckled when he thought how their waddle resembled his and Napolie's.

"Heck," he thought. "We mimic their waddle damn near to a T. We got it down!"

"Who was that, Jack?" Napolie asked.

"Oh, it's just the two women who lent us their clothes."

"Yeah, if we're done here, I need to get back home before my wife calls Missing Persons," kidded Napolie.

Cotti reminded him to contact Tommy Valoppi and relay his message. "I want him here tomorrow by two. No excuses! Get me?"

"No problem! I'll get right on it."

Napolie said his goodbyes and left for home, along with his bodyguards, the Siamese quadruplets.

***

The next afternoon, precisely at two pm, Tommy Valoppi was at Cotti's front door being frisked by two burly Secret Service agents and wasn't too thrilled with the treatment. He reluctantly put up with it but vented his anger to his mentor when he was allowed to enter.

Cotti met Valoppi in the foyer and wasn't very pleased with the vulgarity spewing from his mouth.

"Fuck, Jack. Am I the boss of this Borgata, or not? I felt violated having those fucks frisk me."

"Hey. Don't disrespect me, you little fuck!" Cotti snapped. "You watch your mouth. My wife is in the kitchen. You get an attitude with me, and it'll be your last. And as far as you running Family business, I ***let*** you be the new boss. That could change at any time. But one thing you will remember is that I'm to be the next President of the United States."

Valoppi cowered in fear and was apologetic over the words he had used. "I'm sorry, Don Cotti. I apologize if I've offended you in any way. My anger got the best of me. It won't happen again."

"Apology accepted."

After shaking hands, Cotti led him into his den and let him in on his plan.

"Let me tell you why I asked you here," Cotti said.

"Johnny mentioned something about a meeting with the other Families but didn't expand on the subject. He just told me to meet you here at two." Tommy just shrugged his shoulders.

Jack lit a cigar and handed one to his guest. As Tommy lit his cigar, Cotti explained the problem. "I called you here to set up a meeting."

"What meeting?"

Jack became a little annoyed with the guy's ignorance. He exhaled his cigar smoke and answered, "Like Johnny told you. The meeting with the Heads of the Four Families." Then he whispered, "But we gotta do it without the Feds watching."

"Why?" Tommy asked.

Cotti told him, "Someone doesn't want me in the White House. As you know, they've tried to kill me more times than I can count, and I want it to stop."

"Do you know who's doing it?"

Cotti shook his head. "No. But I have a gut feeling. I think Talluchi… or somebody from the Lucchese Family has got it in for me. They still think I had something to do with Parrissi's murder."

Maria entered the room with a tray of coffee and cannolis. She set it down on the table and left the room.

Jack poured his guest a cup of coffee before pouring himself one and, between sips, explained his plan.

"I want you to contact the Heads of the Families and tell them to be at our meeting place on the same date and time as before. They'll know where and when."

"What about the new guys, Craveno and Cantano?" asked Valoppi as he puffed on his cigar. "Do they know where and when?"

Cotti shrugged his shoulders. "If not, tell them to get the info from Talluchi. He'll know."

"What if they refuse?"

"Tell them that the next President of the United States insists on their indulgence, and it would be wise and in their best interest to show up. Just tell them that!"

***

Two days later, Napolie contacted Cotti and informed him that the meeting was on. It would take place in three days at two pm in the conference room at the Selsor Hotel.

When that day finally rolled around, Napolie was none too happy. It was bad enough that he had to dress up as a woman in a gaudy, flowered dress, of all things. But then he and Cotti had to fool the G-Men into believing they were two old women wobbling down the sidewalk. He didn't think it would work but did as ordered.

***

The women involved in the plan came to Cotti's home two hours before the meeting was to start. They had no problem on this day with the Secret Service agents, who allowed them entry without a body search and never noticed that they each had on an extra set of clothing.

As soon as the women were in the foyer, they began peeling off the extra clothing. They handed it to Maria, who in turn gave the clothes, including hat and shoes, to her husband. Cotti then threw one set of clothes to Napolie.

"Put them on, Johnny," Cotti demanded. "This is the big day!"

Napolie looked saddened at the prospect. "Do I gotta?"

"Yeah, you gotta!" Cotti answered. "***Forget about it!***"

It took each wiseguy nearly twenty minutes to get into the women's clothing. Same ugly dress, hat, and torturous four-inch heels.

Once dressed, Maria came into the room and put fresh makeup on each Goomba's face; they were whining like little boys while she did it, especially about the lipstick.

"That shit tastes terrible! Don't put so much on!" whined Napolie, as he was the first to experience this degradation.

"Quit being such a cry baby," she quipped and gave him a light smack on the cheek.

Her husband was even worse in the whining category. "Honey, I don't need that shit on my face," Cotti said. He swiped his wife's hand away as she tried to apply some rouge on his cheeks.

She gave him a light tap on the top of his head. "You want to fool the Secret Service agents, don't you?"

Cotti nodded.

"Well then, let me finish with the make-up."

Within a few minutes, she had finished her task. Before leaving the room, she wished the two Goombas good luck.

***

While they waited nervously for the cab to arrive, Napolie began to doubt the plan would work and told Cotti so.

"Jack, we're gonna make fools out of ourselves if this plan of yours doesn't work. If we go out there and the G-Men see right through us, we're cooked. We'll be watched like hawks for the rest of our lives."

Cotti tried to answer, but Napolie continued with his little tirade.

"And how do you know the Feds don't know about what we're doing? They could be listening to us right now," he added.

"That's a chance we're gonna have to take, Johnny. ***Forget about it!***"

"Yeah, I'd like to '***Forget about it!***'" Napolie quipped.

"You worry too much! The Feds aren't about to bug me now that I'm the next President."

"Are you sure about that, Jack? Remember, you're still a gangster," Napolie reminded him.

But Cotti was right… to a point. The Feds had taken the bugs out of Cotti's home while he was in the hospital. They had no idea about Cotti's plan or the meeting or what he and friends were strategizing and conniving about. But they still had bugs set up in the conference room at the Selsor Hotel.

***

Napolie went to light a cigar and was reprimanded by Cotti. "Hey, don't smoke that. You'll mess up your make-up. And you'll get our dresses full of smoke."

"Jesus Christ, Jack. Are you serious? I can't smoke because I'll mess up my make-up. Give me a break! What has gotten into you lately?"

"I just want to pull this off. I'm tired of ducking bullets! ***Forget about it!***"

"What are we gonna do about suit clothes? We can't go into the meeting wearing these," Napolie said, holding out the skirt of the dress.

Cotti had the answer for him. "I got the guys to bring our clothes with them. They'll follow behind our cab and be our security at the hotel. We'll change clothes in the hotel john, go to the meeting, and then we'll go back to the house and make asses out of the SS Agents."

"Why rub it in their faces?"

"Why not? I'd rather not have their presence around my house and neighborhood. I'd rather have our soldiers guarding me. I can trust ***them***."

"Jack, we don't have much time before the cab gets here, and I need a smoke to calm my nerves."

"***Forget about it!***"

Just then, a horn honked outside the house. Cotti looked out the window, and the time had come. The cab was waiting to take the two wiseguys to the hotel.

"Fuck!" Napolie whined, trying to stand straight in his tight-fitting high heels.

***

The two Goombas wobbled to the front door, said a short prayer while crossing themselves, and put their veils over their faces before leaving. Before Cotti could open the door, the two women handed them their purses. That was the one thing Cotti had forgotten about. Close call!

Before stepping out onto the porch, they each took a deep breath and hoped they wouldn't fall down on their way to the cab.

It was an unusually warm December day. The two Secret Service agents guarding the door parted ways as the two "women" fixed their dresses and hats before walking down the steps. It was a short three steps, but to the two wiseguys, who hadn't practiced walking down a set of stairs in high heels, it seemed like thirteen—the number they use for the gallows.

As Cotti coaxed Napolie down the stairs, Napolie held onto Cotti's elbow to steady himself, which actually worked. They made it down the stairs without much of a problem. So far, they had fooled the G-Men. But a few feet from the cab, Napolie's heel got caught in the crack of the sidewalk and tripped him. He fell onto the grass. Two G-

Men quickly helped him up, wiped off the back of the dress, and then the taller one opened the cab door for them.

"Take care, ladies," said the agent, none the wiser.

The cabbie took off… with a car full of Valoppi soldiers following.

The agents noticed the car full of hoods but thought nothing about it other than to stay alert. Boy, was that a joke; the agents couldn't have stayed alert if their lives depended on it.

Cotti believed them to be a bunch of drunks and losers. He wanted nothing to do with them. Truthfully, he despised them and all of the other G-Men. He let Napolie know his thoughts.

"Well, I guess we fooled them," Cotti said as the cab stopped in front of the Selsor Hotel. "We got outta there without anyone the wiser. Those fucking Secret Service agents are fucking stupid."

"Yeah! We got through that obstacle. But now we got the meeting to contend with."

Just as Napolie was about to open the car's door, one of the half-dozen Cotti bodyguards opened it for him.

"So, who's got our suit clothes?" Cotti asked the bodyguards as he stepped out of the cab.

They looked at each other in disbelief, shrugging their shoulders, and then each mumbled, "I don't have them."

Cotti was livid.

As the cab drove away, Cotti gave it to his bodyguards with both barrels. "How in the FUCK could you forget our clothes? We can't go to the meeting with the Heads of the other Families wearing dresses with matching hats. Someone better go and get our clothes… and quick."

The bodyguards tripped over each other trying to get back into their car to retrieve their boss's clothes. When all six got back into the car, ready to leave Cotti and Napolie without any protection, Cotti gave it to them again.

"Are you fuckin' guys stupid or what?" he yelled. "One guy can go get our clothes and the others can stay here and protect us… and keep us from harm."

The thugs slowly exited the vehicle, embarrassed.

"What do we do in the meantime?" Napolie asked Cotti as their protection surrounded them.

"We'll go inside and wait in the lobby," he replied. "No one will be able to recognize us. Not in this getup."

"Well, let's hope not," quipped Napolie as they walked into the lobby of the hotel and sat down on a couch across from the reservation desk.

Their bodyguards followed them inside but stayed away, not wanting to attract attention.

Napolie immediately took off his heels and rubbed his feet.

"Don't take those off," Cotti snapped. "Your feet are gonna swell, and you won't be able to put them back on."

Napolie did as ordered; as he was struggling to get his feet back into the shoes, Don Talluchi walked through the lobby and went directly to the men's room.

Napolie looked up at the clock on the wall behind the desk. According to the time, the meeting was to start in less than twelve minutes… and he was worried.

"Jack, when is that fuckin' guy gonna get back with our clothes?" Napolie asked, nervously. "We got about ten minutes until the meeting starts, and we still have to change."

"Don't worry about it," Cotti retorted. "We got plenty of time. ***Forget about it!***"

"Yeah, but those guys will be pissed off if we're late to a meeting that we asked for."

Just then, Talluchi came out of the men's room and walked right past the two wiseguys. He looked at the two as though he recognized them from somewhere but couldn't put a finger on it. He was about to say something to them but then decided against it and walked away toward the conference room.

Cotti and Napolie waited impatiently for their clothes to show up. The clock ticked away those remaining ten minutes in record time. They could wait no longer.

Both stood up, straightened their dresses, fixed their hats and wobbled into the conference room with heads held high.

Chapter 3

As the two wiseguys walked into the room, the others sitting around the table were quite perplexed over the fact that two old broads had come into the room uninvited.

"Excuse me, ladies," Talluchi chimed. "The women's john is through the lobby and to the right."

The dozen men in the room laughed, not at Talluchi's joke but at the two ugly and burly women. But the last laugh was on them.

Cotti and Napolie took off the hats and veils and showed their faces to the Men of Power.

"What the fuck is this!" shouted Talluchi in his deep, gruff voice.

"What the hell is going on here?" Farcano snapped.

"Hey, easy guys," answered Cotti, as he and Napolie sat down at the table. "Don't get your titties in an uproar. I can explain."

"Oh, I gotta hear this," quipped the new Don of the Bonnano Family, Bobby Cantano.

"And who in the fuck are you?" Cotti asked the new kid on the block.

"I'm Bobby Cantano, head of the Bonnano Family. I'm glad to meet you, Don Cotti. Or should I say President

Cotti?" Cantano leaned across the table and shook Cotti's hand.

Cotti smiled. "Smart kid!" replied Cotti. "He should go far in our world. And I suppose this other good-looking guy sitting across the way is Sal Craveno?"

Napolie reminded Cotti: "Jack, watch what the fuck you're saying. You're wearing a woman's dress, for Christ sake."

Cotti nodded and remembered why he had called the meeting. But first, he had to explain to them why he and his Vice-President-to-Be were wearing disguises.

"I know you all are wondering why Napolie and me are wearing women's clothes."

Everyone around the table nodded.

"We wanted to come here without tipping off the G-Men. I didn't want them following us to this meeting. And this is what we came up with." Cotti pointed to his outfit.

"You look like a fuckin' faggot," Talluchi blurted.

Cotti took that as an insult, especially after explaining his reasoning. He reached across the table and popped Talluchi in the nose with his open palm.

"That's enough of that kind of talk," snapped Cotti. "Don't ever speak to me like that again, Don Talluchi. You must learn to respect me. I am the next President."

"I'm sorry, Don Cotti," said Talluchi.

"Now let's get down to business," Cotti told them. "I called you all here to talk about my health."

"Your health, Don Cotti?" asked Craveno in a high-pitched voice.

Cotti looked at the other new boss and said, "And I take it you're Salvatore Craveno, the new boss of the Lucchese Family."

Craveno nodded.

Cotti continued, "Now, all of you sitting here know that someone at this table continues to hold a grudge against me for one reason or another, and that person is trying to kill me despite the truce that we all gave our word to. I want to look each and every one of you in the eyes when I ask the sixty-four-thousand-dollar question."

"And what question is that?" asked Talluchi, holding a handkerchief to his bleeding nose.

"Which one of you is still trying to kill me? Or are you all in it together?"

Cotti eyed each and every man sitting at the table. Usually, he had a gut instinct in these matters. But today, his gut instinct left a sour taste in his mouth. They all seemed to be carrying a grudge.

"You know, Don Cotti," said Farcano, "It's hard to take you seriously in all that makeup and that crazy getup. But I, for one, had nothing to do with your unfortunate accident."

"Don Cotti," interjected Talluchi, "I can speak for everyone here. We are not the ones who are trying to kill you. We are abiding by the truce. We are not happy with the way things are going—you being the next President and bringing all this attention our way. It is not good for our Families. But it's not us who are trying to kill you. It must be an enemy from outside the Families."

Cotti shot back, "I don't believe that. And I see, Don Talluchi that you are still trying to run the Commission. The others may allow you to speak for them. But you do not speak for me or the Valoppi Family."

Craveno jumped into the fray. "Why are you so hostile, Cotti?"

"Why? 'Cause someone doesn't want me in fucking Washington," he shouted. Cotti wagged his finger at the Goombas. "But I'm telling you guys, whoever it is, STOP! Unless you want a war that you won't win—in that case, keep ***fuckin' with me***. We already had one war. You want another?"

"Who in the fuck are you to threaten this Commission?" Talluchi bellowed. "Who in the fuck are you to order us to do anything?"

Cotti smiled. "I'm the next goddamn President of the United States. And you better learn to respect that. Without me, the Feds will put each and every one of you sitting at this table out of business, plus a thousand!"

"But Mr. Cotti," interjected Cantano, in a deep, guttural voice. "Talluchi promised you that none of us here had anything to do with your recent assassination attempts. But you don't believe him. You're not gonna believe anything we say anyway."

"You have not lost the respect of any of us, Don Cotti," said Farcano. "But it seems you have lost your respect for us."

"Yes, Don Farcano," Cotti replied, "I am no longer the Head of the Valoppi Family. I have taken a sabbatical. And for those of you who haven't heard, Tommy Valoppi is, now and forever, the new Head of the Valoppi Family. Or until I say different."

"So why should we listen to anything you have to say?" Talluchi growled.

"Because, Talluchi, when I get to the White House, the world is ours! Luciano organized the mob nationally. I'll take it international. I'll organize the Russians, Chinese, Colombians, Japanese, and Mexicans and bring all the criminal factions around the world into one global Mafia."

"I disagree," snapped Talluchi, puffing on his cigar. "We don't need no other ethnic group in Cosa Nostra. That's sacrilegious."

"But Tommy," replied Cotti, "more factions mean more money and more deals. And that is just one suggestion. I have others."

"You have others?" asked Craveno, who actually seemed interested.

Cotti nodded. "Once I take over the government, the Families will be the first in line for the big government contracts. Billion-dollar contracts. We'll even rig the bidding so you'll be the lowest bid. All you guys will have to do is sit back and collect the money. Ah, that reminds me: money. I'll be in control of the biggest bank in the world. Imagine what we could skim from three trillion dollars. All this is within your grasp, gentlemen. And I can make it happen. I only want to know who in this room ordered my demise. I'm tired of looking over my shoulder. I've been lucky so far. But one day my luck may run out. So, I gotta know! I promise no repercussions or revenge. You have my word. But for the good of all the Families, it's got to stop. If it happens again, I'll put so many Feds around you twenty-four/seven that none of you will be able to breathe. And I won't stop them until you're all out of business. Get me? I'm gonna be President of the United States, and don't you forget it!"

Talluchi spoke up. "Jack, we told you that none of us here is guilty of the crimes you suggest. But if you'll give us a minute so we can talk, maybe we can come up with an answer that will satisfy you."

Cotti nodded. He and Napolie wobbled to the other side of the room and lit cigars while waiting for an answer.

"Okay, guys. Who ordered the hits?" Talluchi asked the others.

Each and every man sitting at the table denied involvement.

"Let's tell Cotti that Parrissi ordered the hits," interjected Craveno.

"It can't hurt!" added Cantano, puffing away on his cigar.

Farcano just shook his head, not wanting to give his opinion. But he finally gave in when the others voted to blame the assassination attempts on the deceased boss, Angelo Parrissi.

Talluchi caught Cotti's attention and motioned for him to return to the table.

Cotti and Napolie wobbled back to listen to their answer.

But they weren't the only ones listening. The Feds had been listening from the beginning.

In the surveillance room at FBI Headquarters, Agent Lundy noticed a light come on over a tape recorder that was voice activated, which came on automatically when tripped by voices. The recorder had a label on the front of it with the words ***Conference room, Selsor Hotel***. Lundy placed the headphones over his ears and listened. He was giddy over the Commission's conversation.

But Cotti was perplexed at the words that came out of Talluchi's mouth. Talluchi blamed Parrissi for the hits. Cotti, however, didn't believe that for a minute. Parrissi had already been dead for months when the attempts occurred.

Cotti was angry but kept it inside. He didn't want to show contempt for his fellow wiseguys. Not yet, anyhow. So, he thanked them for their time and reminded them that there were "good times ahead." Then he and Napolie waddled out of the room.

When they entered the lobby, Cotti was livid that their suit clothes had not shown up yet. Neither had the Valoppi soldier who was sent to retrieve them. Cotti questioned the other soldiers concerning the health of their pal.

"Where's your friend with our clothes?" an angry Cotti asked Partelli, his number-one bodyguard.

The soldier explained that phone calls to his buddie's cellphone had gone unanswered.

"I even had to call an old friend to pick us up because of our lack of transportation," admitted Partelli.

Cotti and Napolie couldn't believe it. They wanted to get out of those ugly dresses. They looked at their bodyguards' clothes, which they had thought about donning before the meeting. But they rejected the idea. The soldiers' clothes wouldn't fit.

So, it was decided that the two wiseguys would return to Cotti's home as they had left: dressed as two old women in matching flowered outfits. They hoped once again that the G-Men wouldn't see through their disguises.

***

Their cab arrived at about the same time as his soldiers' new ride.

Before leaving the hotel, the two placed their hats on their heads and veils over their faces. As soon as they stepped into the cab, Napolie began complaining.

"Jack, this shit is getting old! I'm the next Vice President, and I'm in a dress carrying a purse, for Christ sakes. What are you doing to me?"

"Easy, Johnny. We'll be home in a few minutes. Once we get out of these clothes, we can sit back and relax."

"You might be able to rest, but I can't. This shit we're doing is just fucking crazy!"

"Hey, ***forget about it***!" Cotti barked. "We made it to the meeting, and the G-Men were none the wiser. Whether it was worth it, we'll soon find out."

The cab dropped Cotti and Napolie off in front of Cotti's abode twenty minutes after the meeting ended. Before they could get out of the vehicle, a Secret Service agent opened the door for them.

"There you go, ladies," said the agent. "You look lovely on this beautiful day."

Napolie gave him a disgusted look. Cotti just nodded as they wobbled down the sidewalk, up the stairs, and into the house.

***

The Secret Service agents were still in the dark about the meeting. And they definitely had no idea that the next President and Vice President had left the house wearing women's clothing without Secret Service protection.

The FBI, however, was well aware of the meeting of the Commission. Agent Lundy played the conversation to his fellow workers, who really got a kick out of it.

"Can you believe it?" he remarked to his buddies. "The next President of the United States wearing a dress."

"Boy," interjected Agent Brunson, "if that ever leaked out, Cotti would probably die from embarrassment. A wiseguy wearing a dress. Unfucking believable!"

"You want to leak this tape?" Agent Lundy asked his Supervisor, Dennis Arms.

"I'm not sure. I'll have to speak to my boss."

Arms was concerned about the tape. He believed it could bury the next President, a guy that he had voted for. He needed time to think.

***

While Arms was thinking over his dilemma, Cotti and Napolie were out of their outfits and back into their street clothes, relaxing with a cigar and glass of cognac on the couch in Cotti's den while trying to figure out their next step.

"We gotta find the fucking people responsible for ordering my demise," Cotti demanded.

"You got any leads?" Napolie asked, puffing on his cigar. "I'll tell you one thing, Jack. You ain't never getting me to put on a dress and high heels again. You'll have to kill me."

Cotti laughed. "It was pretty disgusting, wasn't it?"

***

After three days, Agent Arms had made his decision. He decided to give a heads up to Cotti. He thought it was his duty to warn the next President about the damaging tape recording. He had placed the tape into the safe in his office to keep it out of harm's way. But nothing would keep his "boys" from singing the song, unless he ordered them not to. He would need some type of incentive to do that—he was sure Jack Cotti would be most grateful and reward him well.

That morning, Agent Arms decided to visit Cotti's home and give him the bad news. He had been there before a few times to speak with Cotti about a number of subjects, mostly unsolved murders.

After showing his identification to the two Secret Service agents guarding the door, he was allowed in.

Cotti met Arms at the door and recognized him immediately.

"Where is your little buddy?" Cotti asked him.

"Oh, I thought it best to come alone. I need to speak with you concerning a taped conversation of a recent meeting that you and the VP were at."

Cotti seemed not only surprised but shocked. He invited the Fed into his office. "Take a seat. Arms, is it?"

"Yes, sir. Agent Dennis Arms."

"So, Agent Arms. What's this mysterious tape concerning?"

"Let's just say that a couple of wiseguys were caught with their skirts down," Arms quipped. "In fact, the other Family Heads weren't too fond of your outfits."

"So, you must have had that conference room bugged. ***Motherfucker!***" Cotti shouted, but then calmed down. "Well, I guess we'll have to find another place to get together."

"Yeah, one that we don't know about," Arms retorted, sarcastically.

"So, why exactly are you here?" Cotti asked him, lighting a cigar. He offered one to Arms. The agent accepted and allowed Cotti to light it for him.

"Mr. President, I feel I owe it to you to give you a heads up about the tape. If it should leak out for some reason, it could be hurtful not only to your administration but to your friends on the Commission."

"And why in the fuck wouldn't you leak it? You guys don't want me in the White House. You're afraid of me. I just might do some good."

"You're wrong, Mr. President. Hell, I voted for you. I just figured you were a hell of a lot better than the other two candidates. I mean, sure, I wanted to throw your ass in jail. And we did. We just couldn't hold you."

"So, what can I do to ensure that that tape gets lost?" Cotti smiled.

"Well, to be on the safe side," Arms explained, "not only would the tape have to be misplaced, but I would have to order my underlings not to discuss the conversation with anyone."

Cotti looked him directly in the eyes when he asked his next question. "So, what's all this gonna cost me?"

"I don't know," Arms said as he looked down at the floor.

"What if I made you the new FBI Director in my administration? You think my problem could disappear?"

Arms eyes glistened at the thought: FBI Director. He loved the idea. "Mr. President, it's done!"

They shook hands.

"Good!" said Cotti. "I want you to keep me abreast of this thing we just talked about. You're working for me now."

"Oh, by the way, Mr. President: I had the crew take the bugs out of your house and phones. We're not allowed to bug the President unless we get a warrant."

"Great!" Cotti quipped.

"Oh, and let me just say: I thought your disguises were ingenious. You fooled those stupid Secret Service guys right out of their socks. They knew nothing of your meeting."

"Well, let it stay that way for now," Cotti ordered. "One day, I may want that tape released to show what incompetent fucks those G-Men are."

"I'm a G-Man," Arms reminded him.

"I meant those other assholes."

Cotti walked Arms to the door and thanked him as he left. Cotti returned to his room and congratulated himself for having a top Fed in his pocket. Arms was now on the Valoppi Family payroll. Just a little extra to help his family with the hardships of life. Now that Arms was on his side,

Cotti believed the agent would do as he ordered. How wrong he was.

Arms didn't lose the tape; instead, he edited it. He deleted many minutes of the conversation, especially the part concerning Cotti's apparel. As a result, the tape had one twelve-minute gap. This was blamed on a recorder malfunction.

***

Fifteen minutes after Arms had exited Cotti's abode, Tommy Partelli showed up. After confronting the Secret Service agents, he was reluctantly allowed in. Maria met him in the foyer, then walked him to the den to speak with her husband.

Cotti seemed surprised by his visit. "What's up, Tommy?"

"Bad news, Boss. We just found out Joey Talli's body is at the morgue. He was found in his car, riddled with bullets, a half-block from the tailor shop on the same day he went to get your clothes."

"Who did it?" Cotti asked angrily.

Partelli shrugged his shoulders. "We don't know yet."

"We find out who killed him, we find out who's trying to kill me."

"Right, Boss. I'll see what I can find out. At least we know why Joey didn't show up with your suit clothes."

"Get your crew together and have them find out who was behind Joey's murder. I gotta nip this shit in the bud! And fast!"

Partelli promised Cotti he would get to the bottom of it, then left.

Cotti was disgusted by the news. He couldn't figure it out: who would kill the kid, and why? Was it just by coincidence that this murder had happened when he went to retrieve the clothes for his boss? Cotti was mystified, although he still believed Talluchi or someone from the Lucchese Family had something to do with it. He just hoped that Partelli could come up with some answers. He was tired of worrying about his health.

One thing after another kept piling up, complicating his life. He not only worried about his health and whether he'd ever make it to the Oval Office alive, but now he had to think about his newest employee, FBI Agent Dennis Arms. Would he stay true to his word? Unfortunately, he found out that answer sooner rather than later.

Chapter 4

Agent Arms kept his promise to Cotti—to a point. He deleted parts of the tape that would have embarrassed Cotti. He then was going to place it back into his safe and forget about it, as he had told his "boys" to do. But then something happened to change his mind.

He and Agent Lundy went to visit Secret Service Supervisor Bill Owen, who was in charge the day of Cotti's assassination attempt, to coordinate the information collected so far. But Owen refused to cooperate, which started an argument between him and Arms.

Arms threatened to expose Owen's team of ineffective and incompetent buffoons.

"If you refuse to share any of the information you may have learned with us," said Arms, "then we won't share our information with you. It's as simple as that!"

"Why? What have you got?" Owen asked, suddenly interested.

Arms smiled and bragged, "I've got some news that would shock the ***shit*** out of you. And your team."

"Yeah, like what?"

"Don't cooperate and find out," Arms warned him.

"Fuck off!" Owen snapped. "And get the fuck out of my office!"

Arms and Lundy turned to leave, but before exiting Arms cried out, "You'll be sorry!" and laughed.

***

Arms wrestled with his conscience over the threat made to Owen. The match, however, went in Arms' favor.

A few days after the meeting between the G-Men, the story was leaked to the ***New York Times***. Their headlines read: "SS DROPS BALL AGAIN! LEAVES NEXT PRESIDENT UNPROTECTED!"

When Secret Service Supervisor Owen was asked about the incident by a ***New York Times*** reporter, he denied the story, saying it "didn't happen."

Agent Arms heard Owen's denial and knew he had the Secret Service agent by the balls. Now he would put the squeeze on even more and stick the knife even deeper.

***

Just two days after the denial, the tape recording that Cotti had told Arms to lose was leaked to the ***Times***. Once the story broke, the media ran with it, especially the McLaughlin Group.

John McLaughlin showed the ***New York Times*** headlines to his viewers and his pundits and said,

"According to the Press, the Secret Service messed up again. How many black eyes can they accumulate before heads will roll? Pat, I ask you: "How did President-elect Cotti and Vice President-elect Napolie allegedly leave the house without the Secret Service agents noticing? How did this happen?"

"I don't know, John," he said. "Houdini couldn't have done a better job."

All the pundits snickered at that one.

"Yes, John," interjected Eleanor Clift. "Heads should roll if this is true."

"You've heard the tape recording of the meeting with Mr. Cotti and the other Four Heads on the Commission," McLaughlin reminded them.

"Yes, John," said Mort Zuckerman. "But we only have the press and their unnamed source to go by. I think we need to have a name as to who leaked the tape. Otherwise, it's a '***he said, she said.***' It's as simple as that."

"And has it been doctored?" wondered Tom Rogan.

"You think the tape has been edited?" McLaughlin asked Rogan.

"Could be," he replied.

"But, John," interjected Zuckerman, "how do we know that the meeting didn't take place last year?"

"Because," McLaughlin retorted, "the unnamed source was said to be an agent that worked on surveillance of the

Mafia; but the source wasn't authorized to leak it and won't give a name."

"Oh, he's a whistleblower, huh, John?" said Zuckerman sarcastically.

"I wouldn't say that," McLaughlin replied. "Usually a whistleblower gives out his name because there's money involved. The ***Times*** reporter, however, claims the FBI did not know about the meeting but got lucky when the voice-activated bug picked it up."

"John, I'll say this," interjected Rogan. "If this story is true, then it sounds to me like someone at FBI Headquarters has it in for the Secret Service. It might just have to do with the investigation of Cotti's hospital assassination attempt. But whatever the case, the Secret Service has a lot of soul searching to do, and the sitting President will have a decision to make."

"Heck," said Buchanan, "the President-elect only has one and a half weeks before his inauguration. Maybe it'll be up to President Cotti to discipline his Secret Service personnel."

"John, do we know what the meeting was about?" asked Clift. "I mean, what was so important that Cotti had to sneak out of the house without his protection?"

"I don't know, Eleanor," replied McLaughlin. "But I'd bet that, if he didn't have Secret Service protecting him from harm, he somehow managed to have his own Mafia soldiers tag along. I mean, there's been so many assassination attempts against his life lately that I'm sure he was taking no chances, with or without protection."

"You could be right, John," said Buchanan. "But I'm wondering who called the meeting. Did Cotti call it or did one of the other Families? That's the sixty-four-thousand-dollar question," he added.

"I don't know, John," interjected Zuckerman. "There's just too much mystery to this story."

"Well," said McLaughlin, "until we hear from the President-elect concerning these events, it'll continue to be a mystery. Predictions: Pat:"

"I say ISIS will fall. The President will get the job done."

"Eleanor Clift:"

"On inauguration day, President Cotti will have the highest favorable rating of any President."

"Mort!"

"John, I say Secret Service heads will roll soon after Cotti becomes President."

"Tom Rogan, your prediction."

"I predict the Supreme Court will rule that recreational marijuana is illegal and warn Congress to change the laws."

"I predict Cotti will never make it into the Oval Office," said McLaughlin. "Bye, Bye."

***

The next morning, a female spokesman and representative from the Secret Service went in front of the reporters' cameras and claimed that an investigation into the matter was well at hand and there would be answers forthcoming.

"If the allegations are true," said the representative, "the Agency will take swift action against those involved. We in Secret Service take such allegations, which involve leaving the President-elect unprotected, very seriously. Such negligence is unacceptable, no matter the reason!" she added.

The Secret Service representative wasn't sure if the allegations were true, but President-elect Jack Cotti knew they were and didn't give a shit. He ***was*** angry, however, that his new FBI connection, Dennis Arms, hadn't lived up to his agreement. Now all bets were off.

If he was going to keep his word to Arms concerning Arms' new Directorship, Cotti wanted to know why the tape was leaked. And he would find out, come hell or high water.

***

Not long after the statement from the Agency, Secret Supervisor Bill Owen stopped by the Cotti residence to have a sit-down with the President-elect concerning this crazy story. He had spoken with the agents involved and been told that only a few people had shown up and only two women had come and gone more than once on that day.

"Unless you and Napolie were dressed up as those women," acknowledged Owen, "I don't see how those allegations could be true. Or the tape, for that matter."

Cotti took a long puff from his cigar before answering. He looked Owen directly in the eyes and snapped, "You guys figure it out. I ain't saying one way or another."

"But Mr. Cotti, this story has placed the Secret Service in a precarious situation," replied Owen. "We're taking ***shit*** from every direction. We're here to help and protect you. We don't deserve all the criticism we're getting."

"Hey, ***fuck you***!" Cotti barked, and then stood up and loomed over his nemesis. "I don't like you," he told Owen. "And I don't like your guys protecting me. I told you that before! I can fend for myself, and my guys do a better job of protecting me than your guys."

"But Mr. Cotti, that's our mandate," Owen answered. "This is what our job dictates. We will die for you."

"Bullshit!" snarled Cotti. "And when I get into Office, there's gonna be major changes happening. ***Forget about it***!"

Owen left Cotti's home much angrier than when he had entered. In fact, he was so angry that he left the house cursing under his breath.

A day later, a story was leaked, once again to the ***New York Times***. This time, however, the readers were told that Cotti and Napolie had possibly fooled the Secret Service agents by dressing as the two women who had visited Cotti's wife.

The tenacious reporters who were covering the story tried in vain to find the two women in question but were told they were on vacation somewhere far, far away. Cotti wasn't talking, nor Napolie. The reporters were frustrated with the lack of information.

And Cotti wasn't sure if Owen or Arms had leaked the story. Whether true or not, the media was having fun talking about the President-elect and Vice President-elect wearing dresses to a meeting with the Commission and wondering how they got out alive.

The McLaughlin Group was once more having their fair share of commentary and fun at Cotti's expense.

"You heard the story on our next President," McLaughlin told his viewers and political pundits. "Now we're told that he and our next Vice President were disguised as women. Dressed in flowered dresses and matching hats. That, supposedly, is how the two mobsters fooled the Secret Service."

"Yeah, but John," interjected Pat Buchanan, "did they wear them to the meeting with the other Family Heads? Or did they change into street garb?"

"Women's clothing is street garb," blurted Eleanor Clift.

"You know what I mean, Eleanor," retorted Buchanan.

Zuckerman jumped into the conversation. "I can't believe they wore their dresses to the meeting. That would have ended badly."

"They must have changed into street clothes," surmised Tom Rogan.

"Well, I'm sure we'll have more on this story in the days and weeks to come," said McLaughlin.

"I wonder if Cotti and Napolie will be wearing dresses to the inauguration," Zuckerman joked.

"I wouldn't say that too loud," interjected Rogan. "Those guys are still mobsters."

"That's all for today. Bye, Bye," said McLaughlin.

Cotti's Rock and Roll nemesis was also mocking and bad mouthing the President-elect.

"Jack Cotti once called me a sissy," exclaimed Ted Nugent on his hunting show. "Now I hear he's got a thing for dresses. And I hear he looks pretty hot in them." Nugent looked directly into the camera and threatened Cotti. "Jack Cotti once sucker punched me and got the best of me. Next time we meet, and I don't give a fuck if he's President or not, I'll be ready and waiting for him. Jack Cotti, I owe you one and next time I see you, I'm going to collect." Nugent pulled his vest to one side and showed the audience his holstered pistol, as if to say, "Next time we meet, I'll use it!"

When Cotti heard Nugent's diatribe, he let out an evil laugh, then became livid and angry. "The next time I see that punk," Cotti bellowed, "I'll break him in two and stuff a donkey dick down his throat. We'll see how well he sings then. I'll break his fingers and hands."

***

With only three days to the inauguration and the story still fresh in everyone's minds, reporters visited Cotti's home to get an interview. All were turned down. All but one, that is: independent investigative news reporter, Bobby Legend.

Cotti was actually happy to see the kid and allowed him to ask questions, off the record of course. He also had a job offer for the kid concerning a place in his new administration. If Legend accepted, he would be Cotti's Press Secretary.

"How ya doin, Bobby?" Cotti asked him as they shook hands in the foyer.

The kid looked in awe at the person standing in front of him. "The Godfather President," said a nervous Legend. "It's good to see you again; I thank you for this time with you. I know you're busy. I just have a few questions."

"Off the record, of course," Cotti replied, smiling and chomping on his cigar.

"If that's the way you want it."

Cotti nodded.

"Okay then. Let me ask you—"

"Hold on there, kid. In due time. Let's go into my den and have some coffee and cannolis. I also have something I want to talk with ***you*** about."

Maria brought in a tray of coffee and cannolis, set it on the table in front of them, and then turned and left the room.

Cotti poured them each a cup, and each grabbed some cannoli before getting down to the nitty-gritty.

Once they had eaten their cannolis, Cotti sat back and allowed Legend to ask his questions.

"Go ahead, kid. Ask away."

"Well the big question everyone wants to know is, did that meeting take place on the date that the FBI stated? And if so, how did you leave your home without the Secret Service agents' knowledge?"

"What do ***you*** think?"

"I think you and the Vice President disguised yourselves as women," Legend surmised. "That's how you left the house undetected. Am I right?"

Cotti just smiled and continued to puff away on his cigar. "I'll never tell. You'll just have to figure that out for yourself."

"Let me just add, Mr. President, if what I think is true, it was a brilliant maneuver. But you were taking a chance, going to that meeting unprotected."

"I never go anywhere unprotected. I got ***my boys*** for protection. They're the best in the business. In fact, they'll be protecting me at my inauguration and thereafter. The Secret Service protecting me will be a thing of the past."

"Can I quote you on that, Mr. President?" Legend asked.

"Off the record, remember?" Cotti retorted.

"Well, if it's off the record, please tell me that you didn't go into that meeting dressed as a woman. Please tell me that."

Again, a big smile crossed Cotti's face as he chomped on that snub of a cigar. "I'll take the fifth. ***Forget about it!***"

Cotti gave him nothing. This story would stay an enigma as far as he was concerned. If anything, he just wanted it to go away. So, he changed the subject.

"Now let's get down to the real business at hand, Mr. Bobby Legend. How do you like Washington, D.C.?"

"It's okay, I guess. I wouldn't want to live there."

"I'm sure you'd get used to it."

"I'm sorry. I like living in New York City. This is my home."

"It's my home too," Cotti acknowledged. "But in two days, I'll be living in D.C. I'm making a sacrifice. But it's for the great people of this country. I have to think now of the whole Borgata. And I want you to be part of my administration, as my Press Secretary. You think you can handle that?"

"Mr. President, I'm only thirty years old. I don't think I'm qualified for that position."

"Oh, you'll do fine. Now, no more about it. You be ready to fly with me and my entourage on Air Force One in two days. Secret Service will be in touch and give you the low down. They'll take care of everything, including the ride to the aircraft."

Chapter 5

Cotti was true to his word. Bobby legend was chauffeured in a limousine by Secret Service directly to the departing gate and was standing there alone when Cotti and entourage arrived.

As the Secret Service agents and others from various government agencies, including the military, spread out to protect the next President, Air Force One rolled up to the gate and stopped.

Suddenly, the forward passenger door opened, and standing there was Cotti's buddy, Karl Rove. Big smiles showed on both their faces.

The Secret Service escorted Cotti and Napolie through that door while the rest of the group entered a door farther to the rear.

Cotti's entourage included his wife, his ninety-six-year-old mother, and three of his kids. (Petey wasn't invited. His father was still angry at him for being ***made*** into the Lucchese Family.) Napolie came alone; his wife was too sickly to travel. The others included Benny "the brain" Bartolo (Cotti was to make him Secretary of State), two of Cotti's most trusted bodyguards (Tommy Partelli and Louie DeNato), and three Heads of the Commission (excluding Talluchi. Cotti hated him but hoped to keep peace and harmony among the others).

The Secret Service tried their very best to keep the Mafia members from tagging along but lost the argument with their new boss.

"Those guys are my friends," Cotti told Owen. "And some will be in my new administration. ***Forget about it***!"

"I don't think Congress will allow that, sir."

Cotti let out a sly laugh. "This is a new day, Agent Owen. I believe all those politicians in Congress will go along with everything I suggest." He smiled.

Agent Owen tried in vain to change Cotti's mind, but Cotti was adamant.

"Not only that," Cotti added, "but my bodyguard, Parelli, will be standing right next to me on stage while I'm giving my inauguration speech."

"But sir, that's ***my*** job," Owen whined.

"Not today, it's not!"

***

Rove was also disgusted that his "***boy***" would consort with those thugs, and he told Cotti this in no uncertain terms.

"Jack, what are you doing?" Rove asked. "You're going to be President in a few hours. You can't be associating with the Mafia."

"Fuck you, Karl! The People who voted for me know I was a member of the Mafia. I'm not gonna change who I am. EVER!"

"Okay, Jack. I mean, sir. Don't get upset. I still need to

go over some things with you and Napolie."

A few minutes after takeoff, Cotti, Napolie, and Rove went to a large conference room and listened to Rove as he explained formalities concerning the inauguration and other important issues following the event.

"Jack," said Rove, "you will be escorted by the Secret Service to the stage near the podium, where you will stand and take the oath from the Chief Justice. Afterwards, you shake a few hands: the ex-President, his wife, and anyone nearby. You will then give your speech, and soon after you will be driven down Pennsylvania Avenue, where you can wave to the crowd. Secret Service doesn't want you to get out of the car due to possible assassination attempts."

"We're using the convertible, aren't we?" Cotti asked Rove.

"I'm not sure," he answered. "That will be up to the Secret Service."

"Well, I say we use it," Cotti retorted. "***Forget about it!***"

"What do I do?" Napolie asked Rove.

"You'll be sworn in too. And you'll be following the President in the third car."

"I'll need a car or two for my friends," Cotti said.

"Sir," Rove replied, "the Secret Service has your entire entourage under their wing. But please, Jack, don't associate with those Mafia guys. I understand about Benny but, please, not the guys on the Commission."

"Karl, I can't just ignore them. Hell, I invited them," Cotti exclaimed.

***

Rove suddenly excused himself to use the restroom, which left Cotti and Napolie to talk over the new life they were about to partake.

"The perks are great, hey, Jack!" Napolie said.

Cotti looked around the room and couldn't believe this was happening to him.

"Johnny, can you believe this shit? I just realized: In a few hours, I'm gonna be President of the United States."

"And I'm gonna be the Vice President!" Napolie added.

"I guess this plane will be my new toy," Cotti quipped. "My new taxi."

Rove came back into the room and said, "Yeah, this will be yours to use, at least for the next four years. But after today, they'll use the helicopter to ferry you between New York and D.C. and from D.C. to Camp David."

"I don't like camping," Cotti remarked.

"Sir, that's your home away from the White House," Rove said.

"But I told you; I don't like camping. And I don't like staying in tents."

Rove just shook his head in disbelief. He knew Cotti was serious about the "camping" thing.

Just then, the captain's voice came over the intercom, telling the passengers to return to their seats. "We will be landing at Andrews Air Force Base shortly."

The plane landed on the runway and rolled up to the gate, where limousines were waiting for the President and Vice President-elect, and SUVs were waiting for Cotti's entourage.

***

Secret Service agents were everywhere, protecting their clients. However, before Cotti would get into the limo, he said that he wanted his two bodyguards to ride along with him and his family.

Agent Owen refused the request. Cotti argued with him over the matter. Owen tried to compromise, telling Cotti that the bodyguards would have to disarm and turn their guns over to the Secret Service.

Cotti was livid and refused. "***Forget about it!***" he bellowed. So, he took it upon himself and ordered an armed Partelli and DeNato into the limo. Owen relinquished and didn't stop him. Cotti had gotten his way again.

***

The parade of cars numbered fifteen, which was nothing new to Cotti. Most times he went driving, he had at least that many cars following him, between the Feds, the ATF, and his bodyguards. Now they were slowly being escorted by Washington D.C.'s Finest to the White House, where President-elect Cotti would meet the outgoing President, Barack Obama.

After nearly fifteen minutes, they reached their destination. Cotti and family were swiftly taken into the foyer of the White House, where the President and his family were waiting to meet them.

The two men shook hands. Cotti was greeted warmly by the "old guard."

"I'm glad to meet you, Mr. President," Cotti said in his deep, gruff voice.

The President just smiled. "You're quite the character, Mr. Cotti. I wish you all the luck in the world. With this Congress… you'll need it."

"Don't worry, Mr. President. I'll get those politicians in line. Or else!"

The President laughed and shook his head. He hoped the best for Cotti, but after eight years in office, butting heads every day with ***those*** politicians and trying to get something done for the good of the country, he knew Cotti wouldn't have an easy time of it—unless, somehow, he had a magic bullet.

Cotti had a bullet, all right. One for every politician that didn't do as he ordered. And wasn't afraid to use them.

***

Soon after, Napolie was also introduced to the President and his family while the others, including Rove, were escorted by the Secret Service to the stage area where the inauguration was to take place.

After all the guests were seated, the President, Cotti

and family, and Napolie were escorted to the stage. All were seated except the two Goombas, who were placed at the side of the podium. Cotti's bodyguards were standing nearby; Partelli was just off to Cotti's right side while DeNato was standing a few feet to the rear and left of his boss.

It was an unnaturally warm and sunny fifty-five degree January day. Perfect for an inauguration.

Chief Justice Roberts first gave the oath of office to Napolie. Once finished, Napolie went to his seat.

Just as the President-elect began taking the oath, what sounded like a shot rang out in the distance.

Cotti didn't flinch. But Partelli and the Secret Service reacted without hesitation, pulling their weapons. After a few seconds, everyone realized that the sound had been just a fire cracker going off or a car's backfire. The agents had begun holstering their weapons when, suddenly, a loud bang rang out. Partelli's weapon had gone off, hitting the President-elect in the back of the head. Partelli stood still, shocked at what had occurred.

As Cotti crumpled to the stage floor, three Secret Service agents, thinking Partelli would fire again, emptied their clips into Partelli's body.

When DeNato saw his fellow Goomba go down, he instinctively fired at the people who had shot his friend. The agents shot back as the guests scrambled and jumped off the stage to get out of the line of fire. It was chaotic to say the least.

The scene was surreal. The President-to-Be was on the floor, laying in a pool of blood mingled with that of Parelli.

The Secret Service had blown it again.

A few of the agents went over to the fallen shooters to check their pulse for any signs of life. There were none. Other agents had gone over to Cotti to check his vitals. They found a pulse.

"We got a pulse," yelled Agent Owen. "Get me a stretcher and the ambulance over here. ***Pronto***!"

The White House physician came running over. He placed an oxygen mask over Cotti's nose and mouth and checked his vitals. Even though Cotti had lost a lot of blood, his heartbeat and pulse were strong. However, Cotti was unconscious and in very bad shape.

The President-elect was placed in the ambulance and rushed to Bethesda Naval Hospital, where he was taken into surgery immediately.

First, X-rays were taken, which showed the bullet just at the edge of his brain. Evidently, Cotti had a very tough skull—it had been hard enough to keep the bullet from splattering his brain like oatmeal. However, though Cotti's vitals were strong and steady when he was wheeled into the hospital, over a short period of time his heartbeat and pulse became weaker and his breathing, shallow.

The surgeons had to operate immediately. They had no time to waste if they wanted their next President to stay alive.

While the surgeons were operating, a hospital

spokesmen came out to speak to Cotti's family: to keep them calm, to give them hope at the very least, and to keep them abreast of any news of their loved one's condition.

Afterwards, the hospital spokesman talked about Cotti's current condition to the horde of reporters waiting for any news concerning the health of their President-to-Be. The media once again couldn't get enough of Jack Cotti. He'd been a major story since he began his run for the Presidency.

And then, he'd won it all. An impossibility for anyone else, but not for mobster Jack Cotti.

Now Cotti was again fighting for his life, a life that the Secret Service couldn't protect. But if anybody could pull through after this dastardly act, Cotti could. He was as cunning as a cat and seemed to have nine lives. He would have to call on one of those lives to live through this. Or had he used them all up? Only time would tell.

***

A few hours later, the chief surgeon, Dr. Mary White, came out. She spoke first to the family and then to the reporters.

"The President is holding his own, but he is in a coma. We did not induce it; he just hasn't come out of it yet. We're doing everything that can possibly be done. Please, keep the President in your prayers. He'll need them."

Then Dr. Mary White walked away without answering any more questions from the reporters. She wanted to wait until she had better news.

While Cotti's family waited nervously in the visitor's room, Acting President Napolie was at the White House partying with Cotti's guests. Johnny Napolie would be President for the time being. Someone had to run the country, and it would now be up to Johnny Napolie. He seemed to want it that way.

***

The media jumped all over the shooting. They wrote story after story about Jack Cotti, how this street thug came to be not only the most powerful Don of the Mafia but also the most powerful politician in the world. Now they wondered if he'd live. The ***New York Times*** headline read: "PRESIDENT COTTI, DYING?" The ***Detroit News*** headline read: "WILL COTTI LIVE?" The ***LA Times*** headline read: "WHO KEEPS TRYING TO KILL COTTI?"

Even the McLaughlin Group was talking about anything that pertained to Jack Cotti.

"Another foul up by Secret Service!" remarked John McLaughlin. "They seem to be poison for President Cotti."

"But, John," interjected Pat Buchanan, "Jack Cotti never finished the oath of office. So, in reality, he's not, as of yet, the President."

"He is in name, Pat," whined Eleanor Clift.

"I don't think Cotti has to take the oath to be President," remarked McLaughlin.

"That point is moot, John. Napolie is now Acting President," replied Tom Rogan.

"Yeah, and how convenient?" quipped Mort Zuckerman. "Some say Napolie was behind the hit."

"You know what they say, John," interjected Buchanan. "The man behind the throne is usually the one behind the hit."

"You guys better watch what you say," Rogan warned them. "Napolie might just send some hitman your way and whack the both of you."

"You better make that the ***President***!" quipped Clift. "Johnny Napolie is now the Acting President of the United States, and people better respect him. Or he just might get upset."

"Like you said before, John," Zuckerman acknowledged, "somebody doesn't want Cotti to run the country. I wonder who it is."

"I wonder if Jack Cotti will ever become President Cotti," said McLaughlin.

"He has to come out of his coma first, John," replied Buchanan.

"Will they try again at the hospital?" McLaughlin asked his pundits. "I mean, Cotti just got out of the hospital a few months ago from a shooting, then there was another assassination attempt while he was there recuperating, and now this. When will it all end? I ask you, Pat."

"John, your guess is as good as mine," he replied. "I have no idea."

"Well, we know it would end if he dies," quipped Zuckerman.

"Mort, that isn't funny," said Clift.

"Will Secret Service or the FBI come up with any answers?" asked McLaughlin.

"They haven't yet, John," said Rogan. "Although they did put that kid in prison for the aircraft debacle."

"Well, that's all the time we have for today," said McLaughlin. "I'm sure we'll be talking more about President Cotti in the near future. Bye, Bye."

It wasn't only the media talking about the Cotti situation. The FBI's Valoppi Family surveillance crew back in New York City were talking about it too.

"Man, I swear," exclaimed Agent Keith Brunson, "Jack Cotti must have nine lives."

"Hey, it's President Cotti," snapped Agent Dennis Arms. "Don't disrespect him. He's still our President."

"Damn, Dennis, whose side are you on?" asked a perturbed Agent Ken Lundy. "I hope Cotti never comes out of his coma. He's nothing but a thug!"

"Yeah, but now we have another thug in Cotti's place," interjected Agent Greg Meadows. "Johnny Napolie. Once the Underboss of the Valoppi Family. And I'm sure the guy isn't as smart as Cotti."

"Of course not," replied Lundy. "That's why he was Underboss."

"Some say he ordered Cotti's hit to get where he is now," quipped Brunson.

"What do our agents in DC think?" asked Meadows.

Agent Arms answered, "They have their suspicions, but nothing concrete. They've even asked us to check our wiretaps and tape recordings to see if there was anything that we might have overlooked that might shine some light on President Cotti's assassination attempt."

"I take it they have nothing," surmised Meadows.

"That pretty much sums it up," Arms replied. "The two suspects can't talk. And nobody else is talking either."

"I'd bet my life that Napolie was behind it," interjected Brunson. "That's the only thing that makes any sense."

"You might be right," quipped Arms. "But we need evidence. And we need it fast. Shit, Cotti was shot in the back of the head as hundreds of millions of people watched. He didn't even make it through the oath of office, for Christ Sakes."

***

All intelligence agencies were on the case. They pulled out all the stops. No stone would be left unturned.

The Feds began interviewing and interrogating anyone and everyone involved with the Mafia to find the answers to President Cotti's assassination attempt. They harassed all Family Heads on the Commission, including the new Don of the Valoppi Family, Tommy Valoppi.

The only person unwilling to cooperate in the investigation was Acting President Johnny Napolie. His refusal was of great concern to the Department of Justice.

The Attorney General could ask for a Congressional hearing and have Napolie testify under oath, but that would take time, and with the explosive atmosphere amongst Congressional politicians, the two sides probably couldn't find common ground to make it happen.

Finally, the Attorney General gave up the idea. He figured that, if it did happen, Napolie would most likely plead the fifth or just refuse to participate altogether, and that would cause more problems and most likely would make things worse. She would let the incoming Attorney General make those decisions. Her tenure would soon be up as soon as her replacement was appointed.

And so far, the investigation had turned up nothing. A big zero. No one was talking. Not one mobster had revealed a sliver of evidence. Their lips were sealed. Not even threats of long prison sentences could sway them. They all knew that important phrase: "I plead the fifth."

Then one day, out of the blue, a very intelligent FBI agent from the New York City office came up with an idea.

"Hey," said Agent Ken Lundy to his supervisor, "why don't we give Napolie immunity from prosecution? That way we could ask him whatever we wanted about the mob or any of the Cotti assassination attempts, and he'd have to tell us everything he knew. If not, we could throw his ass in prison for contempt. That's one way to get rid of the guy."

"Shit, he would just run the country from his jail cell," replied Supervisor Arms sarcastically.

"Yeah, he'd be like Lucky Luciano," quipped Meadows.

They all let out a sickly laugh over that prospect. Whatever the answer, nothing short of getting Napolie out of Office would suffice.

"I'll relay that idea," Arms told Lundy.

Arms would relay the message, all right. But not to the Attorney General. He would take it to the highest authority: Acting President Napolie himself. Arms figured this would be a good way to get back in the good graces of the Valoppi Family and its top dogs. He had promised Cotti a trade: to lose a tape recording of a Commission meeting for a place in Cotti's administration. Now he wanted to make that trade with Acting President Napolie, to give him a "heads up" of what to expect if the FBI's plan was to go forward.

Two days later, Arms made that call, and Napolie answered. He knew of Arms' arrangement with Cotti, having been told by Cotti about an FBI agent that was newly on the Family payroll.

"Mr. President, Special FBI Agent Dennis Arms here. I'd like to speak with you concerning a very important and urgent matter, but not over the phone. You never know who's listening in. I could be at the White House within three hours. I'll be there by three pm at the latest."

Arms was true to his word and showed up five minutes before three, having taken the corporate jet from New York City. He was led into the Oval Office, where Napolie was sitting behind his desk—the same one that John Kennedy had used during his tenure as President.

"Take a seat, kid," said Napolie. "What's on your mind?"

Arms sat directly across from the Acting President. They had met before, but under completely different circumstances. When Napolie had been shot outside a Cotti hideout nearly a year before, Arms was the Officer in charge.

Napolie suddenly recognized him. "Oh, now I remember you. You're the son-of-a-bitch that almost got me killed."

Arms let out a nervous snicker. "Well, today we meet under better circumstances."

"Why are you here?" Napolie asked.

"I have a proposition for you."

"So, let's hear it!"

"I have some information that would help you immensely. If you'd give me the same deal that Cotti made me—making me FBI Director in your administration—I could be very useful and quash the investigation into Cotti's assassination attempts."

"What do Cotti's assassination attempts have to do with me?" Napolie replied as he ate salted peanuts from a bowl on his desk.

"Sir, you are the main suspect in this latest attempt. You must know that. The FBI is outraged that you refuse to give them an interview to tell them what you do or don't know."

Just then, the White House butler came in carrying a tray of coffee and cannolis. He poured each man a cup of coffee and handed it to them before leaving the room.

"Have some cannoli," said Napolie, grabbing one from the tray. "As you were saying."

"Yes, sir," continued Arms. "The Attorney General is thinking about giving you immunity, so you'd have to testify or be held in contempt. You can do something about it before it gets that far."

Napolie took a bite of his cannoli, then answered, "Why should I trust you now, when you didn't keep your promise about losing that tape? You're lucky you're still a healthy guy, 'cause just like that (he snapped his fingers), you could be unhealthy."

Arms' face turned a beet red, knowing exactly what Napolie meant.

"I did that," Arms answered, "to make fools of the Secret Service, not you and Cotti. They refused to work with us on certain investigations. I did, however, delete the parts about the dresses."

"You stupid fuck! The Secret Service was still able to figure out how we got out of the house without being noticed. Had you lost the tape, no one would have been the wiser."

"Yeah, you're right."

"I guess you guys learned your criminal behavior from your old boss, J. Edgar," Napolie surmised. "He was a bigger crook than anyone in the mob. I just wish he was still alive. I could use him."

"Well, sir," responded Arms, "I hope I have been helpful to you. I hope you will think about me for your administration. I know I could be very useful. You'd have the FBI in your pocket."

"I'll take it under advisement," answered the Acting President.

With that, the conversation ended and, after shaking hands, Arms left the White House and returned to New York City the way he had come.

***

Napolie was enraged at the thought that the Attorney General would pull a stunt like Arms had suggested. But he was way ahead of the game. Just eight days as Acting President and he had already placed informants in high places. He had eyes and ears everywhere.

Napolie had his "guys" seek out and pay big bucks to secretaries and other low-salaried employees in nearly every department of government that was overseeing the Cotti investigation. And they, in turn, gave any pertinent information and a "heads up" to their Mafia contacts, who they thought were legitimate employees of the President.

***

When word came down that a subpoena for the Acting President's testimony would soon be written up and signed, Napolie made his decision. He fired the Attorney General and her Deputy, without cause, before they had a chance to put their plan in play. He then chose Special Agent Dennis Arms as her replacement and sent his name to Congress for approval.

To say the least, Arms was overjoyed. He had expected to possibly be in the running for Director of the FBI, not Attorney General. He accepted the appointment immediately.

Congress, however, was slow to move. They were angry over the firing and used Cotti's predicament as an excuse not to accept the Acting President's choice for Attorney General.

One politician said to another: "Cotti is still alive, even though he's in a coma. If he comes out of it soon, then Napolie's choice for Attorney General is moot. Cotti will be able to choose for himself the Attorney General that he wants. So why act on the choice now?"

That was the excuse Congress used to delay the inevitable. They also asked for more information on President Cotti's condition before voting, and they sent the attending physician a letter asking for an update on the new President's condition.

Chapter 6

The Acting President went one step further. He ordered Cotti's attending physician to the White House to update him in person.

When Doctor Mary White arrived, she took her seat and was then offered coffee and cannolis, which were now a staple on the White House menu. She accepted both as she nervously awaited the Acting President's questions.

"So, what can you tell me, Doctor White, about the President's condition?" Napolie asked her.

"I don't know what I can tell you," she replied. "His breathing has improved, as have his vitals. His brain wave activity and his heartbeat are much stronger now. We just don't know if he'll ever awaken from his coma. The brain was badly bruised. But it could have been much worse. The President is very lucky to be alive."

"If it's all right with you, Doc, I'd like to come to the hospital tomorrow and look in on Jack and his family. I've been so busy I haven't had the chance to visit. His wife is still by his side, isn't she?"

"Yes, she has a room across the hall from his. She is literally by his side from morning to night, combing his hair, washing his face, putting lotion on his body. She definitely has a deep love for him. I wish mine—" She caught herself before she blabbed about her relationship to the Acting President.

"Yes, Maria puts up with a lot, but she definitely loves her man," said Napolie.

Doctor White smiled at that thought.

Napolie continued: "The Secret Service will contact you with my schedule. I'll give you plenty of warning before I appear at the hospital. I don't want any reporters around when I visit. I'm not ready to face the media yet."

"I know just how you feel, Mr. President," she replied.

They shook hands, and then the doctor was escorted to her car and given the President's schedule for the following day.

***

The following morning, the Acting President had the Speaker of the House, Paul Ryan, brought to the Oval Office to ask him a very important question.

After some small talk while drinking coffee and eating cannolis, Napolie didn't mince words.

"Mr. Ryan," Napolie said with conviction, "I called you here to see if you'd like to be Vice President. I know you were the Vice-Presidential candidate for Romney. But you were on a losing team. Now you can be on a winning team. If President Cotti dies, I'll need to fill the Vice President position. Would you be interested? You'd be the second most powerful person in the world!"

Ryan didn't mince words either and told Napolie exactly how he felt. "Are you serious? I'd be out of my mind if I joined the Mobster Party. I am a Republican, pal!" he snapped as he leaned across the President's desk and wagged a finger in his face. "And don't you forget it!"

Nobody wags their finger in the face of a former Underboss with the Mafia and lives to tell about it. Not some crooked politician, anyway.

"Don't be so disrespectful, 'pal!'" Napolie barked, and then lit a cigar. After blowing out a big cloud of smoke, he continued. "You can be my friend or my enemy. It's your choice." He gave Ryan a cold, murderous look. "And you don't want to be my enemy."

Ryan gave out a nervous laugh before leaving the room without shaking the Acting President's hand.

The Acting President then called Senator John McCain to the White House.

McCain seemed happy to see him, shaking his hand and congratulating him for winning the election.

Napolie explained to McCain the need to name a Vice President as soon as possible if the worst occurred concerning the President.

McCain's answer was similar to Ryan's.

"I can't do it, Mr. President. Remember, I belong to the Republican Party."

"***Fuck*** the Republican Party!" bellowed Napolie. "You guys are all alike. You don't give a ***fuck*** about this country. All you care about is yourselves." He looked deep into McCain's eyes, his face distorted, then he spewed the words: "I can make you take the position."

Those last words left a bad taste in McCain's mouth and brought back horrific memories of decades past. He jumped out of his seat, stood in front of the Acting President, and spewed a few choice words himself.

"Mr. President," McCain snapped, "I know who you are and what you are. You don't scare me. You can threaten me all you want. You can even torture me. I can take it! I'm tough!" McCain then turned and stormed out of the room.

Napolie had angered the two most powerful politicians in Congress. They were two people who he really didn't want as enemies. If needed, he would smooth over their ruffled feathers at a later date.

***

Napolie knew then that he needed a mouthpiece to speak to the media concerning the firing of the Attorney General. But he also knew that reporters would be asking questions about the assassination attempt. He needed someone who would, for propaganda purposes, put out stories that would help the Acting President in his endeavors, whatever they may be. So, he called upon Bobby Legend, Cotti's pick for Press Secretary.

"Hey, Bobby," said Napolie over the phone. "This is Acting President Napolie. How are you doing?"

"Fine, Mr. President."

"Bobby, I'm calling you today because I need your help, and the country needs you. I know President Cotti wanted you as his Press Secretary. But now I would like you to be mine. I'm sure, if and when the President comes out of his coma, he would still keep you on as ***his*** Press Secretary. I mean, he invited you to his inauguration, and he was the one who suggested, right after he won the election, that I find you. So, what do you say, Bobby boy?"

Legend didn't hesitate. "Of course, Mr. President. When do you want me?"

"Pack a bag. I'll send a plane and car to pick you up later today. You're part of the Family now! ***Forget about it!***"

"Thank you, Mr. President. I'm honored!" Legend exclaimed excitedly.

The conversation ended; within just a few hours, Bobby Legend was at the White House standing in front the Acting President waiting for orders.

"Bobby," said Napolie, "I need you to be my front man for the media. With the assassination attempt and the firing of the Attorney General, they'll be looking for blood. You're to extinguish that fire for me."

"Yes, sir. Whatever you need, Mr. President."

"Tomorrow, we go to the hospital to see how my Goomba is doing, and you gotta protect me from any reporters. You tell them what they want to hear. I plead the fifth. ***Forget about it!***"

"That's fine. But where am I sleeping tonight?" Legend asked.

"You'll stay here tonight in one of the guest bedrooms. Thomas, the butler, will show you where to go."

***

The next morning, Napolie and Legend, along with a dozen Secret Service agents, traveled to Bethesda Naval Hospital. Napolie wanted the bodyguards from his Family to guard and protect him, but the Secret Service was having none of it after the Cotti assassination attempt.

When they arrived, there was a mob of reporters waiting for the Acting President. They surrounded him, shouting questions from every direction.

Evidently, news of the trip had been leaked by someone in the White House.

Napolie went directly inside without answering any questions. He left Legend to handle it.

The reporters wanted their questions answered concerning the assassination attempt. It was leaked that the ***powers that be*** believed Napolie to be the main suspect.

"How can President Napolie be a suspect?" Legend asked the reporters. "Secret Service killed the guy that shot President Cotti. So, how can the Acting President be a suspect? I just don't get it."

"Yeah," shouted a female reporter with Fox News, "but isn't it true that the man who shot President Cotti was a trusted soldier in the Valoppi Crime Family? And wasn't he President Cotti's number one bodyguard?"

"That is true. So, what? If you look at the video of the shooting," explained Legend, "it looks to me like Tommy Partelli shot the President by accident. He did not mean to discharge the weapon. Just from Partelli's facial expression, it looks as though he's shocked by the gun misfiring, and by the thought that he has just shot his boss. He was the President's most trusted bodyguard, for Christ Sakes."

"We also heard," said a reporter from the ***New York Times***, "that President Napolie fired the Attorney General because they were going to subpoena him to testify in front of the Grand Jury. Is that true?"

"That's just not true. The Attorney General was left over from the last administration. President Napolie appointed Special Agent Dennis Arms for that position, and Congress, for whatever reason, has failed to act upon it. With everything that has happened, President Napolie's schedule has been hectic. He has just started making his list of appointments for his Cabinet, which will soon be sent to Congress for approval."

"When is the President going to pick his Vice President?" asked a reporter from CNN.

"Only when President Cotti's condition worsens or the doctors determine that he will never regain consciousness. But let's not think about that right now, please!"

"When will we be able to question President Napolie?" asked a reporter from the ***Detroit News***.

"In due time. I'm sure when his schedule is a little less frantic, he'll make time for all of you. Now if you'll excuse me, I have to check in with my boss."

As Legend fought his way through the horde of

reporters, he was satisfied with the answers he had given. Even though he didn't have or know the real answers, he had given them a story that would hopefully fulfill their obsession for news and would satisfy their editors.

***

On the twelfth floor, where President Cotti was managing to stay alive, Napolie was telling a different story. He believed Cotti would never come out of his coma—that he would go the way of Joe Colombo.

After giving his condolences to Cotti's wife, Napolie went to look in on his old pal. He ordered all Secret Service out of the room, so he could be alone with Cotti. And while Napolie was leaning over Cotti's comatose body, he began talking to his old friend. Not in a good way, but in an evil way. Napolie began spewing hateful words and, then, a confession.

"You stupid motherfucker!" Napolie whispered angrily into Cotti's ear. "Look what you've done." He looked over Cotti's lifeless body and continued, "I think ***you*** got yourself killed. And why? Because you had to run for fuckin' President! Now, I'm President! And I'm gonna keep it that way."

Napolie grabbed a pillow from behind Cotti's head, held it to his chest, and continued with his tirade.

"Remember when you said that I could be Head of the Family? Now I am. And you didn't even see it coming! I had Partelli hit you, you ***strunz!*** The Commission sanctioned the hit and ordered me to take care of it. I had to do it, Jack. But I also ***wanted*** to do it! You stupid fuck! It was me, Johnny Napolie, who put you in this coma. Now I'm gonna take you out of your misery. For old times' sake."

Napolie placed the pillow over Cotti's nose and mouth to suffocate him. Just as he began putting pressure on it, Cotti's wife walked into the room. Napolie immediately sat down on Cotti's bed and fluffed up the pillow before putting it back behind Cotti's head.

Just as Napolie lifted Cotti's head to place the pillow behind it, Cotti woke up like he had been zapped with two thousand volts of electricity.

The machines hooked up to the President went off. Flashing red lights and loud sharp beeps echoed throughout the room.

Doctors and nurses flew into the room, thinking Cotti had gone into cardiac arrest. They were surprised to see their patient sitting up and awake, though in a daze.

"What the fuck happened?" Cotti whispered as Doctor White checked his vitals.

Napolie stood back, somewhat shocked at what he had just witnessed. President Cotti was alive and well.

Napolie now wondered if Cotti had heard the words that spewed out of his mouth. It put him in a very precarious position. He didn't know if his old pal would seek revenge or not. He would have to find out and find out quickly. But he had to do it discreetly. Did Cotti even know who had shot him? What would he say when he learned it was his most trusted bodyguard? These questions and more were running rampant through Napolie's mind.

Cotti looked around the room and saw his wife and then Napolie.

"Johnny. How ya doing?" Cotti whispered.

"I'm doing fine, Jack. How you doing?"

"Please, Mr. President," said Dr. White. "Don't speak. Save your energy."

The story leaked through Secret Service to the reporters that President Cotti was awake.

***

The media went into a frenzy in its rush to break the incredible story. The headline of the ***New York Times*** read: "PRESIDENT COTTI AWAKE!" The ***LA Times*** read: "PRESIDENT COTTI—1 COMA—0." Nearly every newspaper in the country had a similar headline. But the media wanted more. They had a thousand and one questions to ask both Cotti and Napolie. Unfortunately, neither was talking.

However, the McLaughlin Group's political pundits were talking about the "miracle."

John McLaughlin held up the front page of the ***New York Times*** to the camera.

"An unnamed source," said McLaughlin, "told a ***New York Times*** investigative reporter that President Cotti was awake, alive, and doing better than expected. I ask you, Pat

Buchanan: when will President Cotti take the reins from Acting President Napolie and run the country?"

"I don't know, John. The doctors will decide that."

"Will he be of sound mind, John?" interjected Mort Zuckerman. "That's what I worry about."

"You want to expand on that, Mort?" McLaughlin asked.

Zuckerman nodded. "Well, he was shot in the back of the head. That's got to affect the brain."

"And how much rehab will be needed?" asked Eleanor Clift.

"Well," interjected Tom Rogan, "we can say one thing about the Cotti and Napolie leadership: there'll be plenty to talk about in the days and weeks to come."

"Not to get off the subject," said McLaughlin, "but what do you think about the new Press Secretary, Bobby Legend? He looks like he just graduated high school."

"I don't know, John," said Buchanan. "He held his own at the hospital the other day. Those reporters were out for blood. They wanted their questions answered and were willing to kill to get them. But Mr. Legend fought them off. I kind of like the kid, John. I think Napolie made a good choice."

"He's going to get a lot of practice answering questions from the peanut gallery," said Clift.

They all laughed at that little joke.

"Yeah, I think the kid will do all right," quipped Rogan.

"But will President Cotti keep the kid?" McLaughlin

asked his pundits.

"Sure, John," retorted Zuckerman. "Bobby Legend was invited to Cotti's inauguration as Cotti's Press-Secretary-to-be."

"And let's not forget," interjected Clift, "It was Bobby Legend who first called Cotti 'the Godfather President.' That's the reason the President will keep him on."

McLaughlin had the last word. "That's all the time we have for today. Bye, Bye."

***

The Feds back in New York City were talking about the Cotti miracle too, but in a somewhat different manner.

"***Fuck***," griped FBI Agent Meadows. "I thought Cotti was going to die—again."

Agent Lundy jumped into the conversation. "And I thought we had one down and one to go," he joked. "But I guess I was wrong!"

"Will Arms be ***Cotti's*** pick for Attorney General?" wondered Agent Brunson.

Agent Meadows spoke the feelings of all the agents in the room. "For ten days, the bastard was in a coma. Why couldn't it have been ten thousand?"

Everyone in the room nodded at the thought.

Cotti's personal Secret Service agents were wondering what would happen to them if Cotti finally began his term as President.

Working for Acting President Napolie was bad enough.

But this was the second time that their client had been shot under Secret Service protection.

"Has anyone told Cotti who shot him?" wondered Agent Ray Stewart.

"I don't think so," replied Owen. "Nobody had the chance. He was taken away for X-rays and a CAT scan."

"What the hell are we going to do," Secret Service Agent Mark McIntosh asked Supervisor Owen, "when Cotti takes over as President? He's going to fire all of us."

"Not to worry, Mark," replied Owen. "I'll take care of it." He let out a nervous laugh.

But Owen knew how Cotti felt about the Secret Service's competence. And it wasn't good. He did have one thing going for him, however. It was Cotti's most trusted bodyguard who had shot him—a person whom the agent had wanted disarmed and had tried to ban, along with DeNato, from the inauguration. It was Cotti himself who refused the Secret Service's actions and allowed Partelli to stick to him throughout the festivities. That was Agent Owen's "out."

Now it was in Cotti's hands to decide Secret Service's fate. But at that moment, Cotti was in the hands of his doctors. Minutes after he had awakened, the doctors entered the room. They had ordered everyone out, including Napolie and Maria, and wheeled Cotti down the hall for X-rays and a CAT scan.

Nearly six hours later, after putting Cotti, "through the ringer," the doctors returned him to his room. They allowed him visitors, but only for a few minutes at a time.

The first to see him was his wife, Maria. She came into the room happy as can be, seeing her husband alive, awake, and apparently doing as well as could be expected under the circumstances.

Cotti was sitting up in bed when she entered. She went over, stood at his bedside, and explained her feelings to him.

"Honey, I've had enough of this life," she said.

"What do you mean, baby?" Cotti whispered, his voice still weak and scratchy.

"I'm talking about this life we've been living for the past year and a half. When are you going to realize that somebody doesn't want you in the White House? I can't stand it no more! I want you to resign your Presidency, Jack. Come home… and take care of the Family… and your family. I am not staying in Washington any longer. I am going back to Queens. This kind of life I don't need."

"But, honey, things will be back to normal soon. I'm getting stronger by the hour. You'll change your mind. You're just tired. You've been through a lot this past week."

"Politics is not normal, Jack. Those politicians are sleezebags. They are the dog shit I scrape from my shoes. And now you are becoming one of them. I am going home!" She kissed her husband on the forehead. "Goodbye, Jack. I hope you come to your senses and come back home with me."

With that, she left her husband alone to ponder his future. And she was true to her word. She returned home that very evening, taking the shuttle from the White House.

Just after his wife had left the room, Cotti thought back to the day of his inauguration. Nobody had told him who had shot him. So, he ordered Secret Service to bring Napolie to his bedside. Pronto!

Secret Service whisked Napolie from the White House to Cotti's room within fifteen minutes of Cotti's order.

Napolie was standing nervously at Cotti's bedside, still hoping his boss wouldn't remember what he had whispered into his ear.

But Cotti sensed his nervousness. "What's wrong, Johnny?" he asked his Vice President in his scratchy whisper. "What ya so nervous about?"

Napolie froze. He didn't know what to say. They kept playing over and over in his head, those words he had uttered when he thought Cotti would never recover. Now Napolie was worried about ***his*** future.

"How ya feelin, Jack?" Napolie asked. "I passed by Maria on my way into the hospital. She said she was going back to Queens. What gives?"

"She wants me to resign my Presidency. I can't do it. Not after all I've—we've—been through. I gotta give it a shot! ***Forget about it!***"

"Good for you, Jack. Now you can bring your girlfriend to stay with you. Then we'll have a Jew in the White House."

Cotti reached out, grabbed Napolie's arm, and asked, "Who in the fuck tried to kill me? Was it Talluchi?"

"You mean nobody has told you?"

Cotti shook his head. "No. Why in the fuck do you think I'm asking ***you***?"

Just then Doctor White came into the room with a hypodermic needle and ordered Napolie away for the night.

As Napolie was leaving the room, Cotti strained and, in a scratchy voice, shouted, "So who in the fuck shot me, Johnny?"

Just as Napolie passed through the open doorway, he turned, looked to the floor and replied in a soft tone, "Tommy Partelli shot you, Jack."

"What?" Cotti whispered.

Napolie left it at that and hurried back to the White House.

"Johnny, get back here. We're not done!"

Cotti wanted answers and was clearly upset, so the doctor injected her patient with the sedative she had brought with her. Within a few minutes, Cotti was resting quietly.

"Damn, he's had a long day," Dr. White said to herself as she left the room.

The following morning, Cotti was up early, ready for a new day. Hour by hour, he was getting stronger and more alert; his voice was also getting stronger and louder.

As soon as the doctor left his room, Cotti was on the

phone, making calls to his mentor, Karl Rove, and his Vice President.

Cotti believed he would be in the White House working within a week at most. So, he wanted to coordinate schedules with Rove and go over work that needed to be done.

Rove, meanwhile, had been going to meetings with donors and politicians and scheduled meetings with them for Cotti as soon as his "boy" was up and out of the hospital.

Cotti wanted to speak with Napolie about the hit on his person. He thought so much about it and who had done it that his blood pressure went through the roof. He was given a Valium to relax.

***

Napolie was the first to visit later that morning; he was still apprehensive about Cotti's knowledge of the hit. He wondered if this was the day that Cotti would let ***him*** have it.

"Hey, Jack," said Napolie, "you're looking better."

"Quit kissing my ass, Johnny. I got things that need to be done and done ***now***! I want you to get in touch with Tommy Valoppi and have him snoop around for answers concerning my hit. And at my inauguration, for Christ sake. That's a day for celebration, not my extermination!"

"But, Jack. If you watch the video, it looks like Partelli's gun went off accidently."

"***Bullshit!*** It took two ounces of pressure to pull the trigger on his gun. I know 'cause I gave it to him a year ago on his birthday. Accidently! Johnny, I think you're losing it."

"You look at the video for yourself, Jack. And then you tell me."

At that moment, Cotti called in Agent Owen to retrieve for him the video of his assassination attempt.

Within fifteen minutes, Cotti was watching his day of celebration turn into a day of destruction. He watched the video over and over and came to a different conclusion than Napolie. He believed the assassination attempt was a hit sanctioned by someone in Cosa Nostra, and he told his Vice President in very explicit terms how he felt.

"I don't know what the fuck you were watching, Johnny, but I didn't see no fucking accident. Partelli tried to kill me!"

"That's why I wanted you to watch it," answered Napolie. As he looked down at the floor, he added, "I'll find out for you, Jack. Whoever ordered the hit, we'll find them and take care of them. ***Forget about it!***"

Napolie already knew who had ordered the hit; he believed that he had gotten away with it, so far.

Cotti, meanwhile, believed Napolie wasn't telling all that he knew. He had noticed how Napolie looked down at the floor when he told Cotti he'd take care of it.

"Johnny, how long we known each other?"

"Long time, Jack."

"So, what aren't you telling me?" Cotti barked. "You know something, and you're not telling me. I know you. When you look down while you're telling me something, I know you're lying or leaving something out. Now which is it?"

Before Napolie could answer the question, Doctor White came into the room and ordered Napolie to leave so Cotti could get his rest.

"We'll talk about this again, Johnny," said Cotti as Napolie left the room.

***

The following morning, Karl Rove was brought to the hospital to visit his boss.

Cotti told Rove he would be leaving the hospital within the next few days. "I'm getting the fuck out of here before the week is out. Get everyone together at the White House, so I can meet them and thank them for sticking with me."

"I got you the best professionals in the business, Mr. President. Most of them have served in previous administrations, and seventy-five percent of them have worked inside the White House, directly serving the President."

"Are they Republicans?" Cotti asked him.

Rove nodded. "Yes, sir."

"Get rid of them! I'll bring in my own people!"

Rove nodded and didn't say a word. The boss had spoken.

Minutes later, the room was empty, and the President was resting again.

Chapter 7

Karl Rove had been working behind the scenes, getting everything in order for Cotti's return to the White House. This time, he would come as President, not as President-elect.

Cotti was true to his word. Four days after the Rove visit, Cotti returned to his new home.

Waiting in the foyer were the Acting President, Rove, and approximately twenty-five professional White House employees that Rove had hired to work under the President, such as White House Counsel, the Staff Secretary, and all of the other positions that didn't need Senate approval.

President Cotti shook each and every person's hand and thanked them for being loyal to their President. He then explained what he expected of them.

"While you're working for me, you see no evil, hear no evil, and speak no evil. Get me? What happens here, stays here, within these sacred walls."

He also ordered them to take the Presidential Pledge.

"What's that?" asked one.

"You must pledge your loyalty to me—that you will back me in all my endeavors and decisions. You will ***plead the fifth*** when applicable. And you won't be afraid to do time, if needed. Your families will be well taken care of and rewarded while you're away. So, I want you to repeat after me—,"

Before he could begin, an elderly man in the crowd made known how he felt about this so-called ***pledge***.

"I'm sorry, Mr. President. I cannot take your pledge. You have our loyalty and confidence. We don't need to take a pledge to prove it."

Cotti shot back. "If you don't take the pledge, you don't work for me!"

"I'm sorry, Mr. President," the man replied. "You'll have my resignation on your desk within the hour."

"Me, too," said another, who then walked away.

One by one, they rejected Cotti's demand, sulking as they walked away to pack their things.

Cotti yelled, "You're all fired! Get the fuck out of my house!"

Cotti walked with Napolie and Rove to the Oval Office. Napolie and Rove had to show him the way.

"Nice room!" quipped Cotti.

"It's all yours now, Jack," Napolie told him, as Cotti took the seat behind the throne.

"It feels good," Cotti said, as he bounced in his chair.

Within a few minutes, coffee and cannolis were brought in and handed to each of them.

After a few sips of coffee and a few bites of a cannoli, Cotti lit one of his expensive Gurkha cigars, then handed one to each of his guests.

After lighting his cigar, Rove was bursting at the seams

to get something off his chest.

Cotti noticed how uncomfortable Rove had become and that something seemed to be bothering him. "What's the problem, Karl?" he asked.

Rove gave it to him with both barrels. "Mr. President, those people you just fired were the best people in their field. You have to get them back. Please!" he begged.

"Fuck 'em!" Cotti answered.

"But how can we run the country without their expertise and input?" Rove retorted.

"***Forget about it!***" Cotti responded. "I'll bring in my own people. We got some smart ones, too. Some even graduated from high school. A couple even went to community college."

"But Mr. President," whined Rove.

Cotti would have none of it and raised his hand to shut Rove up.

He looked at Napolie and ordered him to call Capo Family members. "Get them here, ***pronto***!" he demanded.

Napolie just shook his head, not believing Cotti's command. "But, Jack," he answered, "they're our biggest earners. You'll leave the Valoppi Family cupboard bare."

"Well, then, we'll have to call up some of our associates to help man the helm for Valoppi. It's time we bring in some new blood. And while you're at it, I want a dozen of our top hitters here to take over as my bodyguards. I'll make Nino Canotelli my new Pit Bull. Capiche?"

"Mr. President," interjected Rove, "it's mandated by Congress that the Secret Service protects the President. How can you override that?"

"I'll have you write up the executor order that makes them Secret Service agents, and I'll sign it."

"That's 'executive order' and you don't need one," replied Rove. "Just have the Director of the Secret Service hire them on."

"Done!" Cotti retorted. "We'll call them the Special Secret Service Brigade. ***Forget about it***!"

Napolie jumped into the conversation because he didn't want to drain the Family of its manpower.

"Jack, we can't be taking all our top ***Goombas*** out of circulation. The other Families will take advantage because they'll think we're weak."

"Well, they'll think wrong. Me and you, Johnny, are the most powerful men in the world. Karl's number three."

"Here, here!" Rove answered.

Cotti continued: "Johnny, right now I gotta do what's right for the country. I have to think about everyone, not just our Borgata."

"And Karl," he added, "I want you to vet each wiseguy for the position their most suited for. You can clue me on what positions need to be filled, and I'll give you a list of the Goombas who I think are most qualified for those particular positions. You can fine tune them for me. You'll be my Chief of Staff and my Political Advisor."

Rove nodded. "That's fine, Mr. President. I'm glad to

be of service to your administration and to the country."

"All right, Karl. That's enough ass kissing. Your lips are swollen as it is."

They all laughed at that one.

"Oh, sir," said Rove.

"Karl, that's enough of that 'sir' shit! When we're together like this, you can call me Jack. Out in public, you can call me 'sir' or 'Mr. President.' But behind closed doors, for you and Johnny, it's Jack. ***Forget about it!***"

"Okay, ***Jack***. I just wanted to tell you that I've set it up so you can take the oath of office, which you never got to finish, and give your inauguration speech on TV. I contacted all the major television stations, and they agreed to have their equipment here and ready to go in two days, for a seven-pm time slot."

"Great! I'm ready. I've got some things to tell the public. This is a ***new day***, motherfuckers!"

Cotti smiled. He was a "happy camper." His ego was bigger than it had ever been before. He was actually sitting in the Oval Office, smoking a Gurkha cigar, and stretched out in his swivel chair with his feet up on the desk that John F. Kennedy had once used during his tenure.

"Hey, Karl," said Cotti. "You want to leave the room. Me and Johnny's gotta talk."

"Sure, Jack. I'll be downstairs in my office. Call me if you need me."

Cotti nodded, and Rove left the room.

Napolie walked over to the bar that he had installed and

used during his tenure. He poured each of them a glass of Marquis de Montesquiou brandy made in the year nineteen hundred and four. He had brought the nearly seven-thousand-dollar bottle of brandy with him from Queens after it fell off a truck.

The two wiseguys sat on the leather couch, smoking their cigars and drinking their brandy while reminiscing about the old days.

"Can you believe it, Jack?" asked Napolie gleefully. "Where we came from to where we are now! Unbelievable!"

"Yeah," Cotti replied, "that's exactly what we said when we got made. And then again when I made Don and you made Underboss. No difference! ***Forget about it!***"

"Except now, Jack, we're running a multi-trillion-dollar enterprise instead of a multi-billion-dollar enterprise."

"That's for sure! We're gonna come out of this, very rich men."

"To the future," they said in unison as they clinked their glasses together.

Then their conversation switched from the old days to the present.

"You know, Johnny, I got some great ideas to get Congress to play together. I figure we take a few of the top dogs and make then an offer they can't refuse!"

"I don't know, Jack. I had a couple of them in here already, and they ain't too fond of us. I don't think they'll help us at all."

"Oh, they'll cooperate. I'd bet my life on that," said a confident Cotti as he puffed on his cigar.

"I figure we'll get Ryan and McConnell in here, and they'll either leave here as our partners or they'll simply disappear."

"Ryan's a real hard ass though, Jack!" Napolie quipped. "He thinks nobody can touch him. He thinks his shit don't stink!"

"Well he's got another thing coming, Johnny. Remember those trunks I told you to buy. Well, now we need at least one. In fact, buy a couple, just in case. As soon as our soldiers are here we'll act on my plan. We need to shake things up right away, and tell these punk politicians ***how it is*** and the ***way it will be!*** I'm not gonna fuck around. ***Forget about it***! It's a new day, ***motherfuckers***!"

A ring of the phone broke up the celebration between the two Goombas. It was Rove. He wanted to take Cotti around the White House and show him the fun spots, like the swimming pool and Jacuzzi, bowling alley, movie room, and the conference room where the planning of wars took place. Basically, the same amenities as he had at home in Queens, except for the bowling alley.

Cotti loved what he saw, and acted like a little kid in a candy store. He was proud of what he had accomplished. "It's all mine," he thought to himself.

***

During the next two days, Cotti was on cloud nine and

floating on air. He was feeling giddy seconds before taking the oath of office. But then, came to his senses.

As the television cameras purred, Chief Justice Roberts gave Cotti the oath, which Cotti had no trouble finishing this time. It went fine as wine. Then there was a half-hour of media commentary while Cotti prepared for his inauguration speech.

"You got your speech ready, Mr. President?" Rove asked him.

"Don't need it. Got it right here." Cotti pointed to his head.

Rove asked him again. "Sir, do you think that's a good idea?"

Cotti nodded and then took his seat behind his desk. The makeup girl powdered his face and brushed his hair just before the cameras rolled.

"Good evening, ladies and gentlemen. As President, I intend to make big changes in government; I'm giving fair warning to any politician here in Washington that puts politics and their Party ahead of the country and the needs of the people that I represent. In no way will I stand for any fu—screwing around!"

The President caught himself nearly cussing on live TV and remembered what had happened during a previous Republican debate, when he had let out a few choice words before walking off the stage, long before the debate was supposed to end.

After a few seconds, he continued: "I expect the

politicians in the House and Senate to pass the bills I present to them. In their entirety. If not, I'll see to it that heads will roll. I do mean that literally. I intend to get this country back to its glory days! I also intend to have my budget passed within days of presenting it to Congress, as well as my nominations for my administration. I have lots of work to do, as do my colleagues in Congress."

"I also give warning to the Pentagon and our military. Until they can give an exact accounting of where monies have gone, there will be a budget cut like no other. We will have to get along on what we have for the time being."

"I also give fair warning to the CEOs of all those financial institutions that raped the people. The institutions that defrauded people out of their homes with their real estate and foreclosure scams, just like they did during the eighties with the Savings and Loan Debacle. Other administrations might have looked the other way. I will not. I tell them this: if they do not return the bonus money that they made over those eight or so years, I will have no choice but to have the Department of Justice file fraud charges against them; and other charges may be forthcoming. If those Wall Street con artists want to gamble with the People's money, then my government will gamble with their lives and put their behinds behind bars. I am not fooling around! Had the scams been done by mobsters, then I could understand. That's the kind of thing mobsters do! The CEOs, in this instance, acted no differently. And then to reap seven hundred and fifty billion dollars of taxpayer money. I ***want*** and ***demand*** that the money be returned. One financial institution built a new high rise with the money and moved into it, lock, stock, and barrel. The gambling on Wall Street with investor's money will end. I will have Congress pass a law that bans betting on derivatives. I will not stand for this! So, I give fair warning to all those involved.

"We will pass more bills in my administration than the previous two administrations combined. I promise you that! Congress will no longer waste time with trying to rid the country of the Affordable Care Act. The Supreme Court has already ruled that it is good for everyone in this great country of ours. European countries have had great healthcare for all their citizens for decades, and we are a much greater and richer country than any in Europe."

"We will pass a competent, compassionate, and intelligent immigration bill."

"Our politicians are getting paid and paid well to do the People's work, and I will see that they do it... and, as Frank Sinatra once said, '***They'll do it my way***!' Or heads will roll. And I mean that literally!"

"I have many plans on my agenda, and they will come to fruition. There will be no filibusters or government shutdowns on my watch."

"I will also order the CEOs of all the major manufacturing companies to stop sending jobs overseas and to put millions of people back to work with good paying jobs. They will do this, or they might never work as

CEOs again. I will see to it personally!"

"The Republicans in Congress want to shut down government in order to defund Planned Parenthood. I will not let them! If it weren't for women, most men in Congress wouldn't be here. The others, who in the hell knows where they came from! Probably from some type of bacteria that grew out of some dog crap and formed into a callous human being. I don't know, but those men know who they are."

"So, you see, there is much work to be done. I could go on and on talking about Global Warming, the interference in government by lobbyists who I want to run out of the city. For good! I'm tired of them bribing our politicians, who only think of the companies they represent and not the whole Borgata. This will change. I'll see to that."

"I say again: I will have no corruption in Congress on my watch—whether it be politicians or Wall Street CEOs. Lobbyists will no longer be buying Congressmen or Senators. That day is over. It's a ***new day, People.***"

"So now, I think I've talked enough. It's time we here in Washington roll up our sleeves and get things done for the People of this great country. And I promise you, change is coming. Good night, and God bless!"

With that, the speech was over. Rove was bewildered at how Cotti would go about getting the politicians on his side. He kind of knew how Cotti would get things done; he just hoped the President wouldn't revert to a "street thug." But that's how Cotti had gotten himself elected, and that was how he would probably go about his business with anyone that went against his policies. Only time would tell if it would work or not.

As soon as Cotti finished his speech, the media commentators began to give their opinions ***for*** and ***against***.

Fox News Sunday with Chris Wallace and Company were basically laughing at the President's speech. They said Cotti was acting more like a dictator than a President.

But Cotti felt he had to be a dictating President to get things done "his way," without all the bullshit and shenanigans pulled off by certain politicians. Those who gave Cotti trouble wouldn't be doing it for long. The President had his "street" ways to deal with hard-ass politicians that didn't want to make alliances with him.

NBC News' Lester Holt, along with Chuck Todd, gave their opinions on the new President's inauguration speech. They believed that if President Cotti could get done what he had promised, then he might have a chance in getting this country moving again and headed in the right direction.

George Stephanopoulos of ABC News was a bit more apprehensive. He took a "wait and see" approach.

The McLaughlin Group pundits also gave their opinions on the President's speech.

John McLaughlin held up the ***New York Times*** front page, which read: "PRESIDENT COTTI—FINALLY IN WHITE HOUSE!"

"I didn't think he'd ever get there," said McLaughlin.

"I almost got it right. But I ask you, Pat Buchanan, what did you think of the President's speech?"

"It was a good speech, John," replied Buchanan. "Especially the part about bringing those CEOs of financial institutions up on charges. He's doing something, quite frankly, that the last two Presidents were afraid of doing. I liked his speech. If he can get done what he promised, then he will have done something that no other President since FDR has done in the history of the United States."

"Pat's right, John," interjected Eleanor Clift. "The President has outlined some important subjects that should have been dealt with years ago. I hope he can get over the obstacles without doing damage to his new administration."

"What administration, Eleanor?" asked Mort Zuckerman, sarcastically. "The Attorney General was fired, along with the Deputy Attorney General under Acting President Napolie. And now President Cotti has fired his White House staff, whom Karl Rove had put together for him while he was recuperating at the hospital. He has no administration to speak of."

"You're right, Mort," interjected Tom Rogan. "But with Karl Rove at the President's side, it won't be long before the President has the people that he feels he can work with."

McLaughlin jumped back into the conversation. "I'd like to know how the President is going to stop politicians like Ted Cruz from shutting down the government."

Zuckerman was quick to answer. "I think I have the answer to that one, John. The President will call Cruz to the White House. There, he will take Cruz into a back room and tell him '***the way it is,***' and '***how it will be.***' If Cruz doesn't listen, then maybe he'll be '***food for the fishes***' and never be heard from again."

"Yeah," added Rogan, "and the Potomac river is only a short distance from the White House."

They all laughed at that thought. Then they all realized that, with this President, it could very well happen!

"Predictions!" barked McLaughlin. "Pat."

"John, I believe the President will use some very unorthodox ways to get his bills passed in Congress."

"I predict, John," added Eleanor, "that the drought in California will end this fall, and El Nino will come back with a vengeance."

"Mort, prediction."

"John, I predict the President will have hard days ahead. The Republicans in Congress will not cooperate with him after the convention debacle."

"I predict, John," said Rogan, "that the President will not finish his term in office."

The others looked a little shocked at that comment.

"What will happen to him, Tom?" asked McLaughlin curiously.

Before Rogan could answer, however, the McLaughlin Group ran out of time. All John McLaughlin could say was:

"Bye, Bye!"

Both the House and Senate Republican leaders gave their replies to the Cotti speech. Each wanted to work with the President in a bi-partisan manner, if his bills were slanted to their party's way of thinking. They were not, however, going to pass any of the President's bills simply on his say so.

But Cotti saw it differently. He wasn't going to let anyone interfere or stall his plans for the future of the country. "If the Republicans or Democrats, for that matter, filibuster or add crazy amendments to my bills, it will be the last time," President Cotti promised Rove.

After a small celebration at the White House with his Vice President and Political advisor, the three finally crashed in their bedrooms, looking forward to a ***new day***!

Chapter 8

The following morning, President Cotti began his day in high gear. The phone calls to his Capos and soldiers had been taken care of and, within just a few hours, they were standing in front of their boss in the Oval Office, waiting to take his pledge.

Cotti ordered them to raise their right hands and said, "Repeat after me."

They repeated the words to his pledge, and this time they pledged their loyalty to their President, not their Don.

Suddenly, out of the crowd of twenty-eight members of the Valoppi Family, stepped six-foot-six, two-hundred-and-sixty-pound Nino Cantelli, Cotti's new number one bodyguard.

He walked up to the President and told him, nearly in tears, "I die witch you, Mr. President." Then he returned to his place in line.

A few minutes later, they all went downstairs to the party room and its open bar. There they had drinks and eats, which of course included cannolis.

After a few hours, they were taken by bus to an expensive, refined hotel, where they would live until other accommodations could be found.

Cotti had made a list of recommendations for the open positions in his administration, and all the people that he recommended were Capos. But Rove would make the final decision. The soldiers would take the place of Secret Service and become the President's personal bodyguards—that is, if everything worked out as planned.

The next morning, the Director of Secret Service was called into the Oval Office, where he was ordered to resign. He did so without question.

Now the President could appoint his own man as Secret Service Director. He named longtime Capo Joey "the nut" Feterro, who was sixty years old and three hundred and fifty pounds on a six-foot frame. When told, Feterro happily accepted the position. He was ordered to swear in the Valoppi soldiers and give each a security clearance and a license to carry firearms. That was all that was needed, and Karl Rove made sure that all went well.

The next to fall was the National Security Director, who also resigned when asked. Taking his place was Valoppi Capo Donny "four eyes" Domino. He was also a big man, nearly six feet four and close to three hundred pounds, who wore thick lensed bifocals.

Secret Service Director Feterro would now have to answer not only to the President but also to National Security Director Domino.

Cotti placed Capo Carlo "the shooter" Marnetti as DEA Director; Marnetti had been in charge of all narcotic sales for the Family. Cotti appointed Capo Freddy "friendly" Sartano, who owned a number of gun stores and ranges, as ATF Director. Then Cotti made FBI Agent Dennis Arms his FBI Director. They were all perfect for the job at hand.

Even many of the Congressmen and Senators were somewhat satisfied with the President's choices and hoped they would work out for the best.

Cotti also selected Capos for the rest of the open White House positions. His Consiglieri was now the assistant to the President and Karl Rove. He had his girlfriend, Toni Ryeburg, as Staff Secretary so he could have sex with her whenever the urge came up—and the urge came up quite often. Cotti's choice for White House Council was Louie Lamatto, the law partner of his Attorney General appointee, Salvatore DomAchelli, who had been Cotti's attorney in three separate cases brought by the Federal government. Cotti had been acquitted in all three. The only office without a Director was the Office of the First Lady. She was nowhere to be found because she was living happily at home in Queens and wanted nothing more to do with politics.

***

Everything was set. Cotti's Capos were in place, and his soldiers were now protecting him twenty-four/seven. The next step was to get his appointees confirmed without any problems.

So, he had the leaders in both the House and Senate brought to the White House. He invited them into the Oval Office one at a time to tell them the "***way it is***" and "***how it will be***! ***Forget about it***!"

The first politician to visit was a hard ass: Paul Ryan.

Cotti complimented the man, though he didn't like him. He didn't know him but knew of him, and he respected him. Ryan was also a man of power.

Napolie, Bartolo, and four mammoth-sized bodyguards were also in the room. Sitting against the wall was a three-by-three-by-four-foot open trunk. Big enough to hold a dead body if need be.

Ryan was offered drinks from the bar, coffee, and cannolis. He accepted these and had one of each. He lit a cigar that Cotti offered to him. Then he was put to the test.

"Mr. Ryan, I know you don't like me... but you must respect me and the Office that I hold."

Ryan just smiled and shook his head. "I'm sorry, sir, but I don't respect you. You are a mobster, Mr. President, along with your room full of friends."

"You're right, Mr. Ryan," Cotti retorted. "But remember, it was the People who voted this mobster into this Office."

Ryan's face remained stoic, and his voice was quiet as he puffed on his cigar.

Cotti continued: "Now I'll get right to the point, Mr. Ryan. I know you rejected Vice President Napolie's offer to take his place as Vice President in case of my death. You see, that wasn't very smart. You're putting your political party and career ahead of the needs of the country. We need to change that view you have of yourself. And we'll start today."

"Mr. President," Ryan said, smirking, "I think I'm wasting time here. I believe we have nothing left to say."

Ryan began to get out of his seat, but two of Cotti's bodyguards grabbed his shoulders and sat him down with emphasis. They made sure that Ryan would listen to what their boss had to say.

Cotti continued: "As I was saying, the reason I brought you here is that I want your cooperation to help me get my appointees confirmed without any problems. I want you to speak with your peers in the Senate and make sure they give my appointees a 'free pass.' And when they are confirmed, I want you and your friends to help them, and not hinder their decisions, however they turn out. ***Get me***?"

Ryan let out a nervous laugh and, looking down at the floor, suddenly became soft spoken. He said, "I'm sorry, Mr. President. I will not be threatened."

Cotti continued sizing Ryan up. "Then let me ask you this, Mr. Ryan. How much money does it take for me to buy your loyalty? One mil? Two? Ten? What's your number? I'll tell you what. By the end of the day, I'll have ten million dollars wired to the bank of your choice in the country of your choice—if you pledge your allegiance and loyalty to me and to the country, not to your political party. Do we got a deal?" Cotti asked him, holding out his hand for Ryan's.

Ryan shook his head and barked, "I've heard enough! I'm leaving." He tried standing again, but the two bodyguards pressed their hands down on his shoulders.

Cotti told him, “Either you’re with me… or against me. Either you’re my friend… or my enemy. And I warn you now, you don’t want to be my enemy.”

“Mr. President, am I being held hostage?” Ryan looked around the room and, then, at the bodyguards. “I want to leave, but your thugs won’t allow it.” He pointed to the two mammoth-sized hoods standing behind and on each side of him.

“Let’s try it one more time, Mr. Ryan. I don’t like being a hard ass to my friends but, as you know, this country is in dire straits. We need to work together, as a team… for the good of the country.”

“I’m sorry, sir. I can’t jump into bed with a bunch of mobsters and thugs.”

“Is that your last word?” Cotti asked him.

Ryan nodded.

“Well, you can’t say I didn’t try,” Cotti said to no one in particular, adding, “Mr. Ryan, you see that trunk sitting over there next to the wall?” Cotti pointed to it.

Ryan turned his neck to look and then nodded, “Yes, I see it. So?”

You can either walk out of here alive… or be carried out in that box and buried in it,” threatened Cotti. “Your choice!”

“I’d rather you just throw my body into the Potomac River,” Ryan whined sarcastically.

“Oh, that can be arranged,” interjected Napolie.

“Okay, boys,” said Cotti. “Let’s take him down to the

swimming pool and see if he can swim."

"I know how to swim," Ryan yelled as the two Goombas lifted him out of his chair and literally carried him down the stairs to the swimming pool, where they unclothed him and threw him into the deep end of the pool. As they tossed him in, Ryan's feet slipped out from under him, and his knees hit the edge of the concrete pool as he fell in.

"Ooh, that hurt," joked Nino Cantelli.

Ryan began moaning.

The two bodyguards then stripped down to their shorts and jumped in too, each swimming on either side of Ryan, while Cotti stood by and watched.

Ryan was trying to keep his head above water as he shivered in pain.

"Okay, boys. Baptize him!" Cotti ordered.

The two Goombas pushed Ryan's head underwater for a good minute and then let him come to the surface to breathe.

As Ryan was gasping for air, Cotti yelled the question to him again. "Will you pledge your loyalty and allegiance to me and this country?"

"No!" he yelled between coughs.

Cotti motioned for his boys to continue with the swimming lesson.

They obliged and held Ryan's head underwater for a good ninety seconds. Then they pulled him up so he could once again catch his breath, hoping he would make the correct decision when asked to take the Cotti pledge.

But Ryan, being the Republican hard ass that he was, again refused. Cotti's shadows dunked Ryan's head underwater for an even longer period of time, until Ryan fought to get his head above the surface. The two Goombas pulled him up as he was about to drown.

"This is the last time I'm gonna ask you," Cotti promised. "If you refuse, you won't walk out of here alive. You'll take that long ride in the trunk."

"You won't get away with it," Ryan yelled, still spitting up water. "The Secret Service will see you and arrest you."

"We are the Secret Service," Nino told him, adding, "All Secret Service in and around the White House are all Valoppi Family soldiers."

"Shut up, Nino!" Cotti yelled. "You got a big mouth!"

"I can't take any more of this," Ryan whined while treading water. "You win. I'll take your damned pledge."

The Goombas helped Ryan out of the pool and, true to his word, he pledged his allegiance and loyalty to the President. He was then allowed to dress and leave, but he walked out on crutches due to his knee damage. A limo was waiting to drive him back to the Capitol Building.

Ryan limped into the congressional hall and was met by news reporters, who wanted to know how he had hurt himself.

Ryan was in pain and in no mood to talk to the media. So, he ignored them and went directly to his office, aided by his subordinates.

***

The next politician to be called upon and invited to the Oval Office to face the new President was the Senate Majority leader, mean Mitch McConnell, the man with the face of a snapping turtle.

He was nearly the same age as the President, but Cotti looked forty years younger.

McConnell happily accepted the President's invitation. But his happy demeanor changed when he learned the reason for the visit.

He was greeted at the door of the Oval Office by the President himself, who escorted the Senator to his seat, where he happily accepted coffee and cannolis.

Shortly afterwards, McConnell listened to the President's vision for the future of the country. When he heard the President's plans to rid Congress of anyone who interfered with his aims, McConnell actually liked the idea and wanted to help bring the young and radical Senators in line—to tame them into following the President's and Senator's advice. McConnell was happy to accept the President's deal and made the same exact pledge as the Speaker, Paul Ryan. But he did it without any repercussions or intimidation from Cotti's Bulldogs.

"I already took my swim this morning," McConnell joked to the President, having heard the rumor floating around the Halls of Congress about Ryan's swimming lesson given by the President.

McConnell didn't know for sure if the rumor was true, but he decided it would be better to agree than to disagree to the President's suggestions.

Ryan had learned the hard way before relenting to the President's orders; McConnell did not need to.

Once McConnell had taken the pledge, Cantelli made drinks for the two powerful politicians. For nearly an hour, they drank and smoked cigars, reminiscing about the past and hoping for a better future.

Before McConnell left, the President had one more thing to say to him.

"If any of those Senators gives you a hard time or disagrees with you, just let one of my boys know who it is, and we'll take care of it. I guarantee they won't challenge you again," Cotti promised him.

McConnell smiled, happy that he could count on the President to help him with any problems that came up with disrespectful Senators.

However, McConnell didn't like the fact that Cotti's soldiers would be roaming the Halls of Congress, watching over them as if they were kids. When he returned to the Capital, McConnell went directly to the Speaker to talk about it.

"What's wrong, Mitch?" Ryan asked him. "You seem a little down."

He nodded. "I just got back from the White House. I had to take the President's pledge."

"I, too, took his pledge," Ryan answered.

"I see he had to talk you into it." McConnell pointed to Ryan's crutches lying next to his desk.

Ryan nodded. "You could say that! At first, I rejected his advances. But I finally relented."

"I had no choice," McConnell acknowledged, "or I would have ended up like you… or worse!"

"I know what you mean," Ryan retorted. "This President doesn't fuck around!"

"Tell me about it! He's got the fucking Mafia running the government."

"And there isn't much any of us can do about it," Ryan acknowledged, "unless we want to end up as ***food for the fishes***!"

"Hell, any fish that tried to eat my carcass would spit me out," joked McConnell.

"So, what do you want to do, Mitch? The President's got the FBI, Secret Service, DEA, ATF, and National Security Directors in his pocket. And now he wants the Senate to hurry his appointments through for AG and his Deputy, along with the Chairs for Economic Advisor and Environmental Quality."

"Don't forget the US Trade Representative and Director of the Office of Management and Budget, plus another thirteen hundred positions that Rove sent over for him," McConnell reminded Ryan.

"The only thing we can do now," Ryan answered, "is hope that his picks are confirmed with no problems. If not, we got the problems."

The two most powerful men in Congress were very disgruntled over the way things were getting done by their new President. But decided they couldn't do much about it at the present time.

Their conversation ended, and the two went their separate ways. But wherever they turned, they were always running into Cotti's bulldogs in the hallways.

***

Over the next few weeks, Cotti called up additional Family soldiers from New York and had them flown to Washington D.C. Within a few days, he had thirty of them vetted for security clearances and hired on as Secret Service agents. All of them were ordered by the President to roam the Halls of Congress and make sure everything ran smoothly.

The President not only had the Secret Service in his pocket but also the Congressional and DC police, who took commands from his underlings: namely Nicky Barnatti, who oversaw the special detachment of Secret Service agents mandated by the President to watch over Congress.

***

The President also called into the Oval Office approximately fifty other Congressional politicians (more than enough to sway the vote the President's way), mostly Republicans, many of whom were troublemakers within their own Parties.

President Cotti used the same strategy on them as he had on Ryan. Each politician was invited to the Oval Office one at a time and were praised by the President for their work for the country. Then they were given liquor to drink, food to eat, and expensive cigars to smoke before getting down to the business at hand.

When the President believed that they were most vulnerable, he showed them the trunk and told each one a story of survival, like the assassination attempts that the President himself had to deal with, which they understood completely. His threats weren't taken lightly, and only a few out of the fifty needed additional coaxing. Those few were given a long swimming lesson, ordered by the President, before finally pledging their loyalty and allegiance to him.

Those who were not invited were sure to get the message from their colleagues concerning the President's way of handling certain situations. ***Forget about it!***

***

Less than a week after the appointees had been vetted by the Senate, they were confirmed without hesitation.

Now the President had his own man, Salvatore DomAchelli, as Attorney General and DomAchelli's other law partner, Angelo Danassi, as Deputy Attorney General.

Cotti's other appointees were vetted and confirmed by the Senate within a few weeks.

It seemed that Cotti's Special Secret Service Brigade,

by parading up and down the Halls of both the House and Senate, were keeping everything running smoothly for Cotti and his administration.

When one of the President's bills was brought to the floor of the House or Senate, Cotti's Secret Service Brigade sent each and every Representative and Senator a memo ordering them to pass it without hesitation and without amendments. If any of them refused to go along with the President, they were dealt with swiftly. They were typically stalked, assaulted, and robbed, and they usually didn't make it to the floor the following day to cast their vote.

The formula that Cotti was using to run the country and, especially, to control Washington D.C.'s politicians was working rather well.

No longer were there threats of shutting down the government, quashing a bill, or adding amendments; everyone knew full well that no bill would pass with added amendments, and that if they get out of line they would be punished severely.

***

Everyone from the citizens of this great country to the media were talking about how well the politicians were working together. One headline in the ***New York Times*** read, "COTTI RUNS DC WITH IRON FIST!" A headline in the ***LA Times*** read, "COTTI WAS MADE FOR PRESIDENCY!" A ***Detroit News*** headline read, "COTTI:

BEST PRESIDENT EVER!" These were just a few of the front-page stories running throughout the country's largest newspaper chains. They glorified Cotti for having such a great start as President.

The reporters were all over the Cotti story—again! They saw how effectively things were getting done in Congress. Bills were being passed quickly, with very few politicians going against them. There was also an upward surge in the economy; the financial institutions and stock market had confidence in the Cotti Presidency even though he had threatened the CEOs of those corporations.

But others, like the FBI agents in New York City who had once run surveillance on the sitting President, were not happy about the reaction from the media to the Cotti Presidency.

The agents were questioning Cotti's motives and the way in which—or so they had heard—he had threatened politicians. Some FBI agents from the New York City Office had tried to investigate the allegations, but the investigation was quashed by both Attorney General DomAchelli and FBI Director Arms. These leaders also let it be known, in a classified memo sent to agents across the country, that President Cotti and his people were not to be "harassed or questioned for any reason without the written consent" of either Director Arms or Attorney General DomAchelli.

The Agents let it be known that they were very pissed about this directive.

"Can you believe this shit?" barked Agent Meadows. "Cotti can't be touched. He's running the country like he ran his mob, but nobody cares because he's getting things done in Washington. Who wooda thunk?"

"I never thought Cotti would make it to the White House alive," opined Agent Lundy. "Now look at him. The media is calling him the 'best President ever!'"

"Fuck that!" interjected Brunson. "Reagan was the best President ever!"

"I don't know about that, Brunson," said Meadows. "I think FDR was our best President."

"FDR, Reagan, now Cotti," retorted Lundy. "The fucker's been in power for six short months, and everybody's acting like he's some type of Svengali or something. I just don't get it!"

"He must be!" acknowledged Meadows. "The People voted him into Office!"

"Hey, not to get off the subject, but did anybody here congratulate Arms on his promotion?" Brunson asked his peers.

"No," replied Meadows.

"Not me," answered Lundy.

"Me neither," added Brunson.

The others all shook their heads. They were angry at Arms for joining the Cotti crew when it had been Arms' job to arrest and jail him. They felt that, in working for the Cotti administration, Arms had become a partner in crime with Cotti. They wanted nothing more to do with him or, for that matter, President Cotti, unless they were to arrest him.

The Secret Service crew that had briefly protected Cotti before being transferred to another department (one that protected dignitaries from other countries) also had a low opinion of the "great" President Cotti. And weren't afraid to say it.

"That motherfucker in the White House," snapped Special Agent Owen, "shouldn't be there. He's escaped death once too often."

"The cocksucker must have been a cat in a previous life," quipped Agent Mark McIntosh, "because he seems to have nine lives... and he has probably used up eight of them."

"I just don't understand why the President is so popular," said Agent Ray Stewart. "He's a fucking mobster."

They were all miffed at the sudden rise in President Cotti's approval rating, which had reached an unimaginable seventy-six percent. In fact, ***Time Magazine*** had nominated him for "Man of the Year."

"It was bad enough," said Owen, "that they once voted him Gangster of the Year, but now this? Give me a break!"

Even the political pundits from the McLaughlin Group were flabbergasted at how President Cotti had gotten the country into gear in such a short time and in a rather unorthodox fashion.

John McLaughlin started his program like he had

started many others over the last two years, talking about mobster-turned-President Jack Cotti.

"I'm sure you've all seen the recent headlines of many of the country's newspapers, like this ***Detroit News*** headline." He held it up for all his viewers to see: "COTTI: BEST PRESIDENT EVER!"

McLaughlin continued: "President Cotti's administration is doing better than anticipated. But is he the best President ever? What do you think? I ask you, Pat Buchanan."

Buchanan laughed. "John, it's just too early to tell. Yes, he's got Congress finally, after years, working together and getting things done. But to say he's the best—it's way too early to tell."

"That's right, John," interjected Eleanor Clift. "He has only been in Office for a little over six months. How can anyone call him the 'best President?' That's a little premature, to say the least."

"So far, so good, John," added Mort Zuckerman. "The President's doing something right. You have to give him credit. I mean, he's done something that the last two Presidents were unable to do: that is, getting both sides of the aisle working together."

"Mort's right, John," added Rogan. "The economy's robust and moving again. We've already added over three million manufacturing jobs in just the last six months. The employment rate has fallen to four-point one percent, and President Cotti has promised to get twenty million people employed before his first term is up. I believe he'll get to those numbers and do so without bankrupting our country."

"I think he just might get there too, John," interjected Buchanan. "I think the President has got the CEOs of these companies afraid of disappointing him."

"Yeah," interrupted Mort. "They don't want to end up missing, never to be heard from again."

"Or ***food for the fishes***," quipped Rogan.

They all laughed, but they knew it could happen.

"Not to get off the subject, John," said Rogan, "but is it true that the President and Ryan were talking politics while swimming in the White House pool?"

"Some say it is, Tom," Buchanan answered. "That's how Ryan hurt his legs, slipping on the pool floor."

"That's not what I heard, Pat," said McLaughlin. "I heard that the President's goons nearly broke Ryan's legs and drowned him before he relented to the President's wishes. What those wishes were, I have no idea. What do you make of that? I ask you, Mort."

"Has anyone asked Ryan about it?" Buchanan asked.

"Ryan's not talking, Pat," answered McLaughlin. "What's your answer to my question, Mort?"

"What? About Ryan's swimming lesson? I don't know if that story is true or not."

"Will the People allow the President to continue bullying Congressional politicians to get his way?" McLaughlin asked his pundits.

"John," answered Zuckerman, "whatever the President is doing, let him keep doing it because things are finally getting done for the American People. And, I might add, getting done quickly. Not one of the President's bills that has been brought to the floor in the House of Representatives or the Senate has failed. In fact, they've passed without a hitch."

"If that's what it takes, John," answered Clift. "It seems those politicians need a big brother looking over their shoulders. The President has gotten bills passed that's been sitting on the stove for years."

"Then the President doesn't need to change his ways?" McLaughlin asked them.

"If it ain't broke," replied Zuckerman, "don't fix it! That's what I say, John."

"And we have to leave it there for now. Bye, Bye," said McLaughlin to his viewers.

Chapter 9

After nearly a year of running the country, President Cotti was satisfied with the way things were going. The economy was growing expeditiously, employment had fallen to three-point eight percent, a constructive and comprehensive immigration bill was being worked on, and a new budget from the President was in the works.

But, just as the future of the country was looking bright, the financial wizards on Wall Street again tried to bring down the country with their greed and stupidity.

The stock market fell more than four thousand points in one week when it was learned a number of CEOs from the largest banks and financial institutions had colluded to fix the market by betting on derivatives: betting that the DOW stock market would continue its upward climb continuously for five straight days by purchasing hundreds of millions of shares over that period of time. The scheme didn't work—they lost on the last day, and as a result they lost the pension money of more than six million retirees. Many of those retirees were police officers, firemen, and blue-collar workers who had been hard-working Americans all their lives. Now they had nothing and were bankrupt.

The President was livid over this and believed the SEC

was at fault for their ignorance of the situation. Cotti was only allowed to replace one member of the Commission. The others were appointed by the last administration and had many years left to their appointments.

Cotti could do nothing to the remaining Commissioners, but he could do something to the people who lost the money of their investors. He also had to somehow stop the selling off of shares. So, the President had Rove contact the television stations, arranging time with their networks so that he could speak to the People concerning the problem at hand and its solution.

The following night at eight pm, the President, sitting at his desk in the Oval Office, began speaking to the American people.

"Good evening," he said to the camera. "I have a brief announcement to make. As you may or may not know, the stock market has taken quite a hit in the last ten days, dropping more than four thousand points. If the DOW continues to fall, I will order the New York Stock Exchange closed and the selling and buying of stocks suspended until the market calms down. The reason for this sell off was the lack of confidence in our financial institutions: a situation similar to the one in 2007 and brought on by greedy CEOs wanting to pad their bank accounts. Like they're not making enough money! ***Forget about it!*** They scammed the People then, and now they've scammed them again by betting on derivatives like a bunch of addicted gamblers. They lost their bet, a big bet that cost more than six million hard-working Americans their life savings. I blame the SEC for keeping their heads in the sand and allowing this to happen, for not having enough oversight, and for allowing these financial institutions and big banks to overstep their bounds. Had my administration been able to replace all the Commissioners in the SEC instead of just one, I guarantee that this would not have happened."

"I have ordered Attorney General DomAchelli to investigate and to leave no stone unturned in bringing these people to justice. I will make good on a promise that I made during my inauguration speech concerning those same individuals. Attorney General DomAchelli has been ordered, by me, to bring charges against all of the CEOs involved in the real estate/foreclosure scam that they pulled on the American people starting in 2002 and that came to fruition in 2007. If these guys wanted to be in organized crime, they should have joined the Mafia. Or maybe they think they ***are*** the Mafia. I don't know, but I'm sure they'll end up like many ***in*** the Mafia, and that's in prison. Which is exactly where these CEOs need to be. This will send a loud message to the Wall Street hierarchy that the American people won't stand for having their pensions and life savings siphoned off by these crooks. I promise to put an end to corruption and greed on Wall Street and in government. And with that, I say goodnight!"

While the President was giving his speech, the CEOs involved in this matter were at one of their weekly parties in the main ballroom at Trump Towers. They had been talking about their next scam to reap the wealth of their investors, who they called idiots and fools. Their attitudes suddenly changed after listening to the President's speech. They now needed a new approach, and they began making calls to their lawyers, hoping to stay out of jail. However, the lawyers weren't much help.

***

A few days later, President Cotti made good on his promise. FBI agents arrested Richard S. Fuld Jr., the first name on the President's list. He had been the CEO of the bankrupted financial institution Lehman Brothers, which had committed a fifty-billion-dollar fraud and was never charged by the two previous administrations. This lack of charges was probably because Fuld had been a big donor to both administrations. Now, however, he was charged with fraud and held without bail as a possible flight risk.

The President didn't care who he was. He was going to take down every one of the CEOs who he believed had committed fraud at the expense of the American People.

Even though Fuld was charged with fraud and held without bail, the arrest didn't faze his peers, who carried on with "business as usual." It wasn't until James (Jamie) Dimon, CEO of JPMorgan Chase, was also arrested, charged with fraud, and held without bail that they began to worry.

The others weren't waiting around. They fled the

country to their homes in other parts of the world. They met up with their attorneys in Amsterdam to plan their next move—which was to meet with Oleg Brakinov, the head of the Russian mob in Amsterdam, and explain to him their problem.

"What can I do for you gentlemen?" Brakinov asked the nearly dozen CEOs. He spoke in broken English and with a strong Russian accent.

"Our President," explained John Stumpf, CEO of Wells Fargo, "is coming down on all of us in this room. He's having us arrested one by one and thrown in jail… And without bail, for Christ's sake!"

"So… what do you want me to do?" Brakinov asked him.

"We figure," interjected Brian Moynihan, CEO for Bank of America Corporation, "if Cotti doesn't quash our subpoenas and warrants, then we'll have no other option but to have Cotti hit. We figure that, if we cut off the head of the snake, the rest will die."

"And how do I do this?" Brakinov asked them. "It won't be easy to get close to a President to kill him."

"I beg to differ," replied Michael L. Corbat, CEO of Citigroup Inc. "Cotti has been shot a few times already—even while he was taking the oath of office, for Christ sakes. So, it is possible to get close enough to whack the cocksucker. He could really fuck things up for all of us. ***Big time***!"

"Listen," Brakinov demanded, "whacking the boss of

America's largest crime Family would be suicide. But whacking the President of the United States is ***insanity***!"

"Yeah, but can you do it?" John J. Mack, CEO of Morgan Stanley, asked Brakinov.

Brakinov remained silent for a long while, smoking his cigar, drinking his glass of vodka, and thinking. Finally, coming out of his stupor, he gave his answer. "Yes, for a large sum of Euros, I can do it. But it will cost you, ah, ah, fifty million Euros." A big smile crossed his weather-beaten face.

"When?" asked Stumpf. "When? The hit needs to be carried out as soon as possible."

Brakinov nodded, let out a cloud of cigar smoke, and said, "I will wire you my bank account number. Then, within a month, he will be dead! I guarantee it!"

"Good!" retorted Lloyd Blankfein, CEO of Goldman Sachs Group Inc., who had remained silent until now. "Now, Mr. Brakinov, if you'll excuse us, we need to talk among ourselves."

Brakinov nodded and left the room.

The men of finance all agreed to Brakinov's demands and left Moynihan to take care of the transaction.

After a few more drinks, the ten CEOs decided to leave Amsterdam and return to their vacation homes in all parts of the world. They would continue doing business and running their companies from their homes, away from the long arm of the United States of America. They would meet up again in Amsterdam once a month, on the same day and in the same time and place, until the task at hand was over.

***

While others were conspiring against Cotti, he was at Bethesda Naval Hospital getting his yearly checkup. Of course, the media made a big deal of President Cotti's hospital visit and, especially, of the doctor's opinion concerning the President's health. This was one of the topics raised by John McLaughlin to his group of political pundits.

"You heard the opinion of the President's doctor. He said, 'the seventy-five-year-old President has the body and health of a forty-five-year-old.'"

"Of course, he did, John," replied Mort Zuckerman. "Had he said anything differently, the President might have had him whacked!"

They all laughed at Zuckerman's little quip.

"But seriously, people," continued McLaughlin. "It seems the President is in great shape, which is great news because he gives his first State of the Union address to Congress in two days. What's he going to talk about? I ask you, Pat Buchanan."

"He'll speak about the things that he's gotten done in the first year of his administration, about how he has gotten the two parties to finally work together."

"Yes, John," added Eleanor Clift. "And he'll definitely talk about his accomplishments with the economy. The stock market has taken a nosedive lately, but that will settle down soon."

"It's already settled down, Eleanor," said Zuckerman. "It's been closed down for the last week."

"John," interjected Tom Rogan, "the President's Press Secretary, Bobby Legend, told me that President Cotti was going to say something about the future of pot."

"Do you think," said McLaughlin to his pundits, "he'll say anything about the CEOs fleeing to countries that don't have extradition treaties with the United States?"

"I'm sure he will," Zuckerman responded.

"Yes, John, I'm sure he will," added Buchanan. "He wants to make an example of them and show the American People that you can have all the money in the world, but if you break the law it won't save you."

"Predictions!" McLaughlin demanded. "I ask you, Pat."

"John, I predict the President will see even better days ahead. He's creating jobs, and I believe he will raise taxes on the rich."

"Eleanor!" McLaughlin barked.

"Soon the stock market will bounce back, and it will explode even higher once those CEOs are caught and jailed."

"John," said Zuckerman, "I predict the President will have the highest rating ***ever*** once ***Time Magazine*** makes him Man of the Year."

"He'll have to get to about an eighty percent favorable

approval rating to get that record, John," Buchanan acknowledged.

"John," interjected Rogan, "I predict that the President will have an even better second year than his first and that the employment rate will fall below three-point three percent."

McLaughlin gave his prediction. "I predict President Cotti will run for a second term in 2020! Bye, Bye!"

***

The day before the President's first State of the Union Address before Congress, Rove tried to have Cotti go over a speech that had been written for him by a political speech writer—with most subjects dictated by Rove. But Cotti would have none of it.

"I don't need no fucking speech, Karl," Cotti declared. "I will speak from the heart. ***Forget about it!***"

Rove relinquished without a fight. No whining, no argument. He just declined a battle he knew he could not win.

***

That big night finally came when President Cotti, followed by Vice President Napolie and Chief of Staff Karl Rove, walked into Congress surrounded by a dozen bodyguards while thirty others roamed the aisles, keeping an eye out for any troublemakers.

While walking to the podium, the President was

greeted by both Republican and Democratic Senate leaders, along with both leaders of the House. He shook hands with and said hello to the Supreme Court Judges and a few of the top generals before heading up to the podium.

As the President walked quickly up the stairs, his bodyguards stood in front of the stage, facing the audience, watching for any strange reactions. To some in the crowd, they seemed like the Hell's Angels guarding the Rolling Stones at Altamont. To say the least, fear was in the air.

Once in front of the microphone, Cotti thanked his Vice President, the leaders of both House and Senate, and many other top officials in the audience. Then he made mention of his wife and children, who weren't here for this special night. He used the excuse that his kids were back home taking care of their sick mother. This was a lie; she just didn't want anything to do with politics, especially after the profession had nearly killed her husband—twice! After all his adulations were completed, President Cotti began his speech.

"One year ago, I was shot down by a dear friend before I could begin my Presidency. Thanks to the 'man above,' my doctors, and all the hospital staff, I was able to get back to the job I was elected to… and that is as President of this great country."

The audience went wild, giving him a standing ovation for nearly a minute before sitting and allowing the President to speak again.

"I just want to say how proud I am to be an American,"

he shouted. "***Forget about it!***"

The crowd again leapt to their feet and gave their President another rousing ovation. After thirty seconds of that, he continued his speech, using no cheat sheet or teleprompter. It was all from the heart. ***Forget about it!***

"The first year of my Presidency, Congress and I couldn't have worked together any better," he acknowledged.

Again, a rousing applause.

Cotti said, "Look what we've done for the economy. More than six million jobs have been created; eighty percent of them are manufacturing jobs. The unemployment rate is nearing three-point three percent, and there is plenty of room to grow. We are bringing back the number one mainstay of this country, and that's manufacturing. We are going to bring back the textile and apparel mills that we cherished and that helped grow this country. We will do it again, and crush China and anyone else with cheap labor, because we will put out a finer product for a better price. We can do it," he yelled, pumping his fist into the air. The crowd leapt to their feet once again, giving their President his due.

He continued: "We no longer have obstructionists who want to shut down the government when they don't get their own way. We are ***now*** one party. And that's the ***Party of the People***. We now have to think of everyone, the whole Borgata!"

The crowd again gave the President a standing ovation,

but he scolded them for it.

"Please, I know you're excited about the way things are going, but I have so much more to talk about. If you guys keep interrupting me with applause every other sentence, I'll be up here all night. And I don't want that. I have more subjects to speak about and would like to get through it without the applause. But I do thank you for it."

The crowd finally settled down and allowed the President to continue.

"As I was saying: We now have to think of the whole Borgata, not just one particular state or another. I will not stand for anything else. Just remember," he reminded them, "there are consequences for your actions when they are contrary to my wishes. ***Forget about it***!"

The whole House was in complete silence. The President's bodyguards' eyes peered through the crowd looking for any dissenters, ready to pounce on anyone who got out of line.

The President went on. "I now want to talk about a fundamental right that all of us share; one that our Forefathers wrote in the Bill of Rights. We have the right to ***life***, ***liberty***, and the ***pursuit of happiness***. And the ***war on drugs*** is not anyone's ***pursuit of happiness***! Except maybe for the authorities, and those people will even throw their own children in jail. You know what I call that?" he asked the audience. "Very stupid! That is not being patriotic. Instead, let the person doing the drugs be responsible for their own behavior. If they act out and jail is warranted, then by all means, throw their behind in jail; just like we do with people who abuse alcohol. But to say one can't do drugs in their own homes responsibly is to have no confidence in the American way of life. People are using drugs. Up to now, over these past forty-plus years, the war on drugs has been an utter and complete failure. All because a few politicians were bought by the pharmaceutical companies to keep the competition away from their sales and profits. That's what started the ***war on drugs***. And as you know, there are more drugs coming into this country than ever before. The war on drugs has added many departments within government, with large budgets to fight that ridiculous war. Instead of the police being seen as the People's friends, they now are seen as enemies, murderers, and jailers. But I'm about to change that. So… starting in my second year as your President, we will try it another way. ***My way***! We will no longer incarcerate nonviolent drug offenders. We will offer them help and hope they seek rehabilitation. But definitely, no jail time."

"My administration will no longer go after medical marijuana co-ops or stores, and I'll ask Congress to pass a bill decriminalizing pot to a schedule two narcotic."

"The Israeli government allows its hospitals to prescribe marijuana for their patients. Whether it be through smoking, eating, vaporizing, or using oil made from the drug, Israeli hospital doctors know that the use of marijuana is helping their patients."

"I have the DEA, ATF, FBI, and the Justice

Department under my complete and strict control. They do as I say. If anyone steps out of bounds and goes against my orders, they will be dealt with severely. Jail time or worse will be their downfall. I will not tolerate insubordination. It seems our draconian laws on the war on drugs have been useless and asinine. As of today, that war will come to a halt. I will ask Congress to pass a comprehensive and compassionate bill for medical marijuana and to drop it down to a schedule two controlled drug. This will be a major priority for my administration this year. I will not stop until the bill has passed, and I sign it into law."

The crowd reacted with a rousing standing ovation. The President's words hit home with his peers. He allowed them to react for nearly a minute before speaking more about the different things that still needed to get done to help the People of this great country.

"There's only a few more things I want to touch base on before ending this special night," President Cotti told his peers. "But before going, I want to give special thanks to those of you who stayed on from the last administration to help my administration. And I think I've worked you long enough. So, after speaking with each one of the following people and telling them my plans for the future of the country, I've decided that later this year I will replace Secretary of State John Kerry, Secretary of Defense Ashton Carter, Secretary of the Treasury Jack Lew, Secretary of Labor Thomas Perez, and many others who are, nonetheless, true patriots. Oh, and let's not forget

CIA Director John Brenner. How about a round of applause for these great Americans that have given many years to helping this nation? We, the People, thank them wholeheartedly."

The audience erupted in great applause.

"Please stand and show yourselves," barked the President.

Twelve members of the audience stood up and took their bows, acknowledging the praise from their peers.

"And I'll want my appointees passed as quickly as possible," President Cotti reminded the politicians.

A minute or so later, the President made a historic announcement never before seen at a State of the Union Address.

"I won't keep you much longer," the President promised. "But we need to show the American People that we are here for them! And we will do that tonight. I'll let Chief Justice Roberts explain."

The Chief Justice walked from his seat and up the stairs to the podium. He tapped the microphone to make sure it was on before speaking.

"Yes, ladies and gentlemen. The President has asked me to ask those of you who haven't taken the President's pledge, as of yet, to take it now. For those who have taken it at the White House, please take it again to show your loyalty and allegiance not only to your President but also to the citizens of this great country. Now if you'll all stand, hold up your right hands, and repeat after me."

Nearly all the politicians in attendance stood and raised their right hands. The few who remained seated were seen by the President's bodyguards, given the evil eye, and their names written down into their little black books to be dealt with at a later time.

Roberts continued: "I pledge my loyalty and allegiance to President Cotti and the citizens of the United States. And I pledge to back President Cotti in all his endeavors, whether for or against, to the best of my abilities."

Once Chief Roberts had finished giving the pledge, he returned to his seat, as did the politicians who had taken the pledge, to listen to the President finish his speech.

"Thank you, Chief Roberts, for your help," Cotti remarked, giving him a wink.

Roberts nodded.

"Now, I have one last important subject to discuss. It might upset some of you, but that's not important now. What is important is getting this country back in the shape that it needs to be for the future of our kids and grandkids. So, I am sending a bill to Congress that will raise taxes on the wealthiest five percent. These people have not been paying their fair share for decades. Now, all that is about to change."

"As we've seen, trickle-down economics does not and has not worked. We've seen our cities, our roads and bridges crumble because there is not enough tax money coming in to repair them. We've seen our schools close because the cities can't afford to pay the utility bills that continue to gouge the average customer. One day, we might have to nationalize all energy industries in this country just so we can keep prices reasonable for all. But for now, we will concentrate on raising the taxes for those precious few that make thirty to a hundred million a year in bonuses. Not only were they getting tax benefits that I, personally, do not believe they deserve, but also many companies have not been paying their fair share. So, I give explicit warning to all involved. You will be paying your fair share, and you will be happy to do it." Cotti looked directly into the camera. "And you know who you are. If you run and hide like those financial wizards have done, I will send my ***boys*** to find you. And I don't think you will like that," Cotti promised. "And neither will the politicians in this room who go against my proposals for tax increases. I know many of you took Grover Norquist's tax pledge, but now you've taken mine, which overrides his. Now you belong to me! I'm the one who will now tell you ***how it is*** and ***how it will be***! ***Forget about it***!"

There were some ooh's and ah's, but most in the crowd remained silent, not wanting to get on the President's bad side. Machiavelli was right. It's better to be ***feared*** than ***loved***. And all the politicians feared the "***Godfather President***."

The President continued to tell his audience his expectations for the future of a comprehensive tax bill in the budget.

any reason why a person making thirty to one hundred million dollars a year in bonuses can't give back half of it to the country in which he made it. And fifty percent, in my opinion, is low. If that person returned eighty percent of a hundred million, he'd still have twenty million clear and free. So, I find a fifty percent tax base reasonable, and that's without tax loopholes or exemptions. If a person makes thirty million a year, he can expect to give back fifteen million to his country to help those less fortunate. These people will then be called ***patriots*** instead of ***greedy crooks***. So, mark my words, change is coming! You're either ***with me***... or ***against me***. You're either ***my friend*** or ***my enemy***. And believe me... you don't want to be my enemy. ***Forget about it***!"

"And on that note," the President added, "I say: let's do it again next year!"

President Cotti stepped away from the podium, shook hands with the leaders standing above and behind him while saying a few words of appreciation to them. He then went down the stairs and shook hands with many in the first couple of rows before walking toward the exit with his train of bodyguards all around and behind him. The guards trusted no one. Not after the close call at his inauguration.

***

A few minutes later, the President and Nino Cantelli hopped into the President's limo while the others, were driven back to the White House. There they went directly to the President's living room to rest and relax after a rather long and hectic day, and to have coffee, cannolis, brandy, and Gurka cigars.

Chapter 10

Nino Cantelli stood inside the room next to the doorway, facing the President, while the ***four horsemen*** plopped their behinds into plush, leather couches. The butler came into the room and offered each a glass of brandy and cannolis, while the President handed out his favorite Gurkha cigars, which were ten times more expensive than a good Cuban cigar.

As the boys ate their cannolis, puffed away on their cigars, and sipped their hundred-year-old brandy, the room remained silent. It seemed they were too tired to talk.

Rove, however, had something to say. "You gave a great speech tonight, Mr. President," he remarked, commending his boss.

Before Rove could say another word, Cotti asked him to leave the room.

"Hey, Karl. I need to talk to Johnny and Benny, privately. ***Not for nuthin'***, but we'll talk about the speech in the morning. I have important matters to discuss with these guys." He pointed to his boyhood friends.

"Sure," Rove answered, putting his cigar out before finishing his drink. He stood up and left the room.

Cotti then ordered his Consiglieri to make examples of the Wall Street CEO's so other CEOs would get the point.

"Benny," said Cotti, "I want you to contact our people

in Europe, Asia, and South America. I want those financial ***fucks*** found and dealt with. When they're found, tell them it will cost each of them two hundred and fifty million dollars to have their warrants quashed and their cases dropped. If they don't pay up, ***kill 'em***! Just do what you have to and make sure their bodies don't float back to the surface. Get me?"

"Sure, Boss," answered Bartolo.

"I will have Arms search for these animals. We'll see if we can pinpoint their whereabouts and make it a little easier for our hitters to find them."

Bartolo nodded.

Cotti continued: "And get a couple of our best shooters to hit that fuckin' Grover Norquist. Him and his fuckin' tax pledge has gotten this country all ***fucked up***! I want him taken for a ride out to the country. Drive him to Charlie's place. I want him tortured and then whacked. Then have Charlie cut up his body and dump it in the ocean. ***Food for the Fishes***!" We'll get rid of this fuck, ***once*** and ***for all. Forget about it***!"

The three snickered at that thought. It was just like old times.

"Oh, and one more thing, Benny," Cotti added. "You're my appointee for the next Secretary of State."

"What about my job as assistant to Rove?"

"Don't worry about that," Cotti told him. "I want you as my Secretary of State. But make sure you're always near a phone. I might need your opinion. Remember, you're still my Consiglieri."

Bartolo nodded. "Got it, Boss!"

The three wiseguys continued drinking and smoking their cigars for the next few hours before Napolie and Bartolo left the White House and returned to their residences.

***

The President went to his bedroom and was met there by his girlfriend, Toni. After a few hours of some heavy and passionate sex, they fell asleep. But it wasn't a peaceful sleep for Cotti. Something strange was happening to him. He tossed and turned, punched his fists into the air, and talked in his sleep. He was so loud that he awakened Toni. It seemed Cotti was having a nightmare, so she shook him awake.

"Jack, you're having a nightmare," Toni told him. "You were punching the air and talking in your sleep."

"What the fuck was I saying?"

She told him she didn't know, adding, "Whatever it was, it scared the hell out of me! What were you dreaming about?"

Cotti wiped the sweat off his forehead and took a deep breath before trying to explain his dream.

"I was in the hospital, I think. Johnny was standing over me whispering something in my ear. But I can't remember what he was telling me. I wish I could remember." He seemed stressed out.

Toni saw Cotti's frustration and began rubbing his temples and head with her fingertips to ease the tension that seemed to have enveloped his entire body. After a few minutes of this, the President was able to fall back to sleep, resting peacefully throughout the rest of the night.

***

The next morning, while Cotti and Rove were talking about the President's speech, so were many of the television commentators, particularly Fox News and Chris Wallace and Friends. Wallace was the first commentator to give his opinion.

"After listening to President Cotti's speech last night, I've come to the conclusion that our President is nothing more than a dictator. Pure and simple," Wallace told his viewers.

Chris Wallace wasn't the only Fox News commentator to call the President a dictator. So, did Megan Kelly, Bill O'Reilly, Sean Hannity, and others on the Fox News network. They all must have received the same memo telling them to call the President a dictator.

Ted Nugent even commented on the subject, saying, "President Cotti is a joke and a dictator in a woman's dress," referring to the story about the President wearing a dress.

Nugent's and the political commentators' comments didn't sit too well with President Cotti when he heard about them. He released his fury on Rove.

"Semantics!" Cotti yelled. "Who in the ***fuck*** cares what word they use to describe ***me***? If they want to describe me as a ***dictator***, so what? The government is finally running smoothly. Crime's down. The economy is purring. And the People are satisfied. That's what counts!"

Rove calmed the President down by telling him how quickly the People forget.

"Mr. President, in forty-eight hours the People will forget all about the dictator comments."

Later that afternoon, at the daily press briefing, Bobby Legend told the Press Corps: "To get things done in this town, we sometimes need our President to act like a dictator. If you haven't already noticed, the President has Congress working together in a bi-partisan way, which hasn't happened in more than a decade. Before that, all we had was obstructionism." He took a swig of water and continued: "Look, the President hasn't gotten things done in this town by using his beautiful smile and handsome face."

The crowd laughed.

"I mean, that might have helped," Legend acknowledged, "but it's his dynamic personality that has won over the politicians in Congress. He knows exactly what to say to them to get them on his side. If that's being a dictator, then so be it."

Before Legend could choose a reporter to ask the first question, they all began speaking at once, all trying to get their questions answered; it was so frustrating to Legend that he walked away from the podium and exited the room, leaving the reporters in limbo.

***

The term ***dictator*** was still going strong on the Political shows more than forty-eight hours after the word was first heard on a network.

Karl Rove's prediction to President Cotti was incorrect. The topic would not go away.

One show that was still talking about the new word that had been used to describe the President was John McLaughlin and his political pundits of the McLaughlin Group.

"Lately, we've heard the word ***dictator*** used to describe President Cotti," McLaughlin told his viewers and political pundits. "Pat Buchanan, I ask you: do you think the President is a dictator?"

"John," Buchanan answered, "I don't think he is a dictator, ***per se***. He does, however, wield his power at times like a dictator."

"Yes, John," said Eleanor Clift. "Pat is right. President Cotti does act like a dictator at times, such as in the way he reacts to Congress when he thinks they are giving him a hard time."

"Hey, whatever the President is doing, it's working," argued Mort Zuckerman. "Call him what you will, but leave the guy alone. I've said it before: if it ain't broke, don't fix it. And President Cotti doesn't need fixing."

"Mort's right, John," added Tom Rogan. "Who cares if they call the President a dictator? I mean, he was called a mobster during his run for President, and that had no effect on the voters. If some Republican-leaning commentators call President Cotti a ***dictator***, well, it comes with the territory. But it will not have any effect on his Presidency."

McLaughlin asked them, "What do you think about the President saying during his speech that he may try and nationalize all energy companies in the country? Do you think he will do it? I ask you, Pat Buchanan."

"Not in this term, John. Maybe if he runs for a second term and wins. Then he might."

"You have to admit, John," interjected Zuckerman. "Utility bills are getting outrageous. Soon the poor and middleclass won't be able to afford to pay them. I can see, one day, this happening. Whether it will be under a Cotti administration or not, it's hard to say."

"If anyone can get it done, John," said Clift, "I do believe President Cotti could do it, especially if he gets a second term. He wields a lot of power now, but in a couple of years, who knows? He'll be stronger than ever."

"I agree with Mort, John," added Rogan. "One day, I do believe, the energy sector will be nationalized. Either that, or Congress will have to pass a bill to put a limit on utility prices for those in need."

"Yes, I agree," replied McLaughlin. "Whether energy companies will be combined into one conglomerate or be nationalized, I too believe it will happen. Whether it is done by President Cotti or a future President, I truly believe that, one day, this will happen. And that's all the time we have for today. Bye, Bye."

Watching the McLaughlin Group, Cotti was overjoyed by the fact that the pundits on the show had actually stood up for his Presidency. In fact, he went to bed in a very good mood—something that didn't happen very often. But, according to his girlfriend, his mood suddenly changed in the middle of the night. Cotti again talked in his sleep.

Toni was suddenly awakened when she heard the President yelling the words, "***Johnny, not you***! ***No***! ***Not you***!"

The President's hands were in the air and looked as though they were strangling someone.

Toni shook him awake. "Jack, Jack," she whispered. "Wake up. You're having a bad dream again."

He pulled her close and hugged her. "Oh, baby. I had a nightmare. It was Napolie, and he was telling me something in my ear. He looked like he was ready to kill me, so I grabbed him by the neck and choked him. You woke me up before I killed him. What a fucking dream." He exhaled a lung full of air and laid back down. Then he wiped his brow and went back to sleep.

***

The following morning, after having a light breakfast of bacon, eggs, toast, coffee, and cannolis, President Cotti dictated a few orders to Rove.

"I want you to invite Ted Nugent to the White House. I want to mend the fences. Maybe I can get him on my side for a change."

"Are you sure, Mr. President? You two don't get along too well. You won't do anything crazy, will you, sir?"

Cotti smiled and shook his head. "No, Karl. I just want to find out why he hates me!"

"Well, you did beat the shit out of him—twice! That could be a reason."

"Yeah," Cotti barked, "and if he doesn't keep his mouth shut, I might just kick the shit out of him again! But get him here, Karl, so we can talk."

"What do I say to him?"

"Tell him whatever! Just get him here!"

"What if he refuses?"

"Use your charm, Karl." Cotti smiled, adding, "And get Director Arms over here. I need to speak with him."

"Will do, sir."

Rove did as ordered. Nugent reluctantly accepted the invitation to the White House.

"Why?" His associates and friends asked him.

He told them he had a few things to say to the guy.

"Will they let you carry your gun into the White House?" they asked him.

"They will, or I won't go," Nugent answered, adding, "Wherever I go, my gun goes with me. It's as simple as that."

When Nino Cantelli, the leader of the Special Secret

Service Brigade, first heard about Nugent's statements to his friends about his gun, he contacted Nugent and told him, "***Go fuck yourself!*** Nobody carries a gun into a meeting with the President. ***Nobody!***"

When President Cotti heard about the problem, he relented, allowing Nugent to bring his gun. Cotti figured he had more than enough guns protecting him to keep Nugent from trying anything. Cotti had a surprise in store for Nugent, anyway.

***

Later that afternoon, FBI Director Dennis Arms showed up at the White House and was escorted to the Oval Office for a meeting with the President.

Arms didn't know what the President wanted to speak with him about, but he had some very important business to discuss with Cotti.

But just a few minutes before the meeting was to start, Cotti, while in deep thought, had a flashback of his dream. He kept seeing his childhood friend, Johnny Napolie, standing over his body while he was in a coma at the hospital. He thought he had heard Napolie taking the credit for his assassination attempt.

Just then, the President was awakened from his daydream as Director Arms walked into the room.

Cotti stood up and shook his hand. "Take a seat!"

Arms did as ordered.

Cotti handed Arms a cigar, which he accepted, and then

lit it for him.

After a few quick puffs, Arms spoke up. "Thank you for this meeting, Mr. President. I have never really thanked you for my appointment. I owe you a lot. I appreciate the fact that you trust me."

"Trust you?" Cotti replied as he lit his cigar. "You haven't done anything yet to earn my trust. But I'm giving you the benefit of doubt."

"Thank you, sir. I appreciate that. Now what did you want to see me about?"

"I want you to find those fuckin' CEOs that took their money and ran without facing the music. I've got my soldiers tracking them down now, but they could use some help. Check in with your boys overseas and find out where they're hiding. Then, I'll send my boys to take them out—I mean, to pick them up for extradition."

"Yes, sir. We have Interpol helping us in the search for these felons. We'll find them and arrest them, if we can."

"I don't want you to arrest them. My boys will take care of that. I just want the locations of their hideouts. I'm sure they're in countries that don't have extradition treaties with the United States. That's why my boys are needed to bring these guys home."

"How will you get them here if they refuse?" Arms asked.

"Leave that to me! I'll make them an offer they can't refuse. ***Forget about it!***"

Arms snickered and nodded, exhaled a big cloud of

cigar smoke, and then told the President that the FBI had gleaned some noteworthy information from wiretaps and bugs.

"What do you got?" Cotti asked him.

"Mr. President, we got some information about the CEOs' meeting in Amsterdam a few days after they fled the country."

"Like what?"

"We've pieced together recordings that prove that the CEOs have hired the Russian Mob in Amsterdam to have you assassinated. It's costing them some big bucks."

"Which ones?" Cotti asked.

"All of them. It is definitely a conspiracy. They're all involved."

"How much do they have to pay?"

Arms swallowed hard. "Fifty million Euros," he replied between puffs on his cigar. "About sixty-five million bucks. I guess that's the going price these days to whack the President of the United States."

"Well, I guess we can forget about extraditing them," Cotti quipped. "I've gotta whack them before they whack me. ***Forget about it!***"

"Sir, please don't do anything that could get you in trouble. I'll have ***my*** boys take care of them."

"No, Dennis. You find them for me. ***My*** boys will take care of them! In fact, I might have to make a call to Putin and tell him to call off his dogs."

"His dogs, sir?"

"Putin runs the KGB," Cotti replied. "And the KGB runs the Russian mob. Putin would definitely know about the hit. So… when I see him, I'll ask him about it. Now is there anything else?"

"I do have one other thing to say. It's about a tape that I destroyed. It was delivered to me by an agent from the New York City surveillance team. The last tape that I should have destroyed and didn't came back and bit me on my ass. I wasn't going to let that happen twice."

"So, what was on this tape that you destroyed?" Cotti asked.

"I don't really know how to tell you this, but it concerns your very good friend, the Vice President."

"Johnny?"

"Yes, Mr. President," Arms answered, nervously puffing on his cigar.

"Yeah? So?"

"Well, it's… it's about the assassination attempt on the day of your inauguration. The tape was a recording of the Underboss of the Genovese Family telling a Capo that the Commission ordered your hit that day. They didn't want you in the White House. We believe they gave the order to Napolie, who gave the order to Tommy Partelli."

"Fuck! That's what my dream was telling me," Cotti whispered to himself.

"What? I'm sorry," said Arms, struggling to hear what his boss said.

"Nothing! I was just talking to myself," Cotti admitted.

"Yes, sir. So, what do you want me to do?"

"Do? Nothing for the moment. I want to verify this information you gave me. I just hope you're wrong. For Johnny's sake. Who else knows about the tape?"

"Just me. There was one other agent, but I transferred into my office so I could keep my eye on him. Which turned out to be a good thing because, a week after his transfer, he was hit head on by a drunk driver and killed while driving home. I'm now the only person who knows what was on that tape, and with the tape destroyed, no one will ever know unless you want it known, Mr. President."

"Good! Let's keep it that way. I don't want one word said about the subject. Capiche?"

"Got it. Not a word. Now, if there's nothing else, I'll be on my way."

Arms stood up and shook the President's hand. As he was leaving the room, Cotti called out to him.

Arms stopped and turned to hear what his boss had to say.

"Don't forget," Cotti reminded him, "Keep me informed of any info on the financial wizards. I got a debt to settle with them."

Cotti then contacted Bartolo and ordered him to the Oval Office.

Within ten minutes, Benny Bartolo was in the Office.

"What's up, Boss?" Benny asked, lighting a cigar.

"***Shut up*** and ***sit down***, Benny!" ordered Cotti.

"What's up, Jack?"

Cotti put out his cigar stub, picked another from his humidor, and lit it. As he did, he looked deeply into his Consiglieri's eyes, trying to read his soul, to feel him out, to see if he had been involved with the hit.

Cotti finally spoke up. "I got some fuckin' news that's hard to believe. So, until I can verify the information, what I'm about to tell you is confidential. Strictly between us. Capiche?"

Bartolo nodded, puffing on his cigar and waiting to hear what his boss had to say.

"I just found out from a good source that the Commission ordered the hit on inauguration day. They ordered Napolie to carry it out, and he ordered my good friend, Partelli, to do the hit. ***On me***! On ***my inauguration day***!"

"Johnny?" Bartolo couldn't believe what he had just heard.

"What the fuck was Johnny thinking?" Cotti asked himself. "He wanted to be President. That ***greedy fuck***!"

Bartolo leaned forward in his seat and asked, "Are you serious, Jack? I… I don't believe it. I just don't believe it." The more he thought about it, the angrier he became, until he lashed out at Cotti and barked, "***Who told you***?"

Cotti shook his head.

"Come on, Jack. Who told you this ***bullshit***?"

"Let's just say that I heard it from a reliable source. ***Forget about it***!"

"Jack," yelled Bartolo, frustrated with his boss's

answers. "I'm your Consiglieri, for Christ sake. I'm supposed to give you my opinions on things like this. So, if you want my opinion, tell me who you heard this ***bullshit*** from?"

Cotti smiled and remained silent. After a few big puffs on his cigar, he gave Bartolo his answer.

"Arms told me. His ***boys*** recorded a conversation between Genovese Underboss Pete Tolato and a Capo. I don't know which one though."

"I find this hard to believe, Jack."

"Did ***you*** know about the hit, Benny?" Cotti barked at his childhood friend, giving him a cold stare. "Don't you lie to me! And I know when you're lying, Benny!"

Bartolo shook his head and replied: "Fuck no, Jack. How could you even ask me that? I knew nothing about it."

Cotti leaned back into his seat after reading Bartolo's body language and nodded. Then he said, "I believe you, Benny."

Cotti stared at the ceiling as he puffed away on his cigar, thinking about his next step. But before he took out his childhood friend and Vice President, he wanted Bartolo to return to Queens and find out if Arms was telling the truth.

"Benny, I want you to get back to the neighborhood and do whatever you gotta do to get this ***shit proved*** or ***disproved***. If we gotta hit Johnny and the bosses, I want a definitive answer to this ***fuckin'*** nightmare."

"Got it, Boss. I'll see what Tommy Valoppi knows

about it. I hope he wasn't involved in this thing too."

"I gotta know who my enemies are," Cotti reminded him. "I've given them a pass too many times. Not no fuckin' more. Now it's my turn to get even!"

The meeting ended on that note. Bartolo returned to Queens to ply information out of some ***wiseguys*** and see if he could get to the truth about the President's assassination attempt. He knew it wasn't going to be easy.

***

As the months passed, President Cotti was getting anxious. He had heard nothing concerning the Commission's sanctioned assassination attempt or the whereabouts of the CEOs.

***

While the President was worrying about his personal being, he was also worrying about his son, who was running as a United States Congressional Representative for the People of New York and leading in the polls by a wide margin.

During this time, there was also a rash of missing and hospitalized Congressmen, nearly twelve in the past two months. And just by coincidence, all had disrespected the President during his State of the Union Address by refusing to take the Cotti pledge.

Most DC politicians, though, seemed to have gotten the message: "You don't fuck with the President, or else the

President may ***fuck*** with you, and in a very different way."

***

Nearly five months after the President's State of the Union Address, Rove had the new appointees' applications delivered and submitted to the Senate Confirmation Committee for confirmation. Every appointee was a Valoppi member; they included Benny Bartolo, who was Cotti's pick for Secretary of State, and Valoppi Capo Charlie "Carlo" DeMarco, appointed for Secretary of Defense. DeMarco's crew killed and then dismembered the bodies of their enemies, who were never seen again. Cotti thought that he and all the others were great choices for their positions. For CIA Director, he had picked Capo Vinnie "College Boy" Giancana, whose father had once worked for the CIA.

***

It wasn't until the mid-term elections were over that the President got confirmation of all his choices. While celebrating the win, President Cotti also celebrated his son's victory in the run for United States Representative from New York. The President was a proud papa, telling anyone and everyone about his son's victory.

During the celebration party at the White House, Cotti and son were the main attractions of the night. They were having a great time and getting very drunk. ***Forget about it!***

Cotti told Rove, "Junior won by running on the

American Family Freedom Party platform. He's a chip off the old block."

Rove nodded.

"That's two in a row for our party, Karl," Cotti added while puffing on his cigar. "You know, I might have to run for a second term. I think the voters have had their fill with the two draconian parties. I should be a shoo-in for another term."

"Here, here!" Rove shouted over the crowd noise, adding, "I second the motion." He raised his glass of scotch high into the air.

The party lasted long into the night but ended just like it had begun: peacefully, with many going home very tipsy. As did Rove and the President.

Toni had to practically carry him back to their bedroom. And as soon as his head hit the pillow, he was out like a light.

The next morning, everyone working at the White House came in hung over, including Rove and President Cotti. Neither were in a very good mood and wanted nothing more than peace and quiet. Both had massive headaches. That was more than enough to ruin their day. So, they thought, that is, until none other than Ted Nugent came strolling through the front doors of the White House and let it be known by shouting, "The Wildman is here!"

The Special Secret Service Brigade met him in the foyer and treated him with respect, even though they loathed him and wished him dead—preferably by their own hands, after torturing him for hours at a time over a period of weeks. But now, they were on their best behavior. Nino Cantelli and a few others escorted the "Wildman" into the Oval Office to meet his nemesis, President Jack Cotti.

The President wasn't interested in conversing with the Rock and Roller. He had a big surprise in store for Mr. Nugent.

As Nugent came through the doors of the Oval Office, he was all smiles. Just as he was about to greet the President, his smile suddenly turned to fear as Nino and another bodyguard each grabbed him under an armpit, lifting him into the air. A third bodyguard unbuckled the holstered gun that Nugent carried under his left armpit. He pulled it away from Nugent's body and handed it to Cotti. The President slammed the gun onto the top of his desk in a fit of anger, but then quickly returned to a calmer state.

Cotti had a big grin on his face, and he let out an evil laugh as he asked Nugent a very important question.

"Hey, Teddy boy, do you know how to swim?"

The bodyguards laughed.

Nugent thought for a long second and then answered meekly, "Yes, I know how to swim. Why?" he whined.

"Good," Cotti replied, puffing on his cigar. "Boys, take Mr. Nugent down to the pool and teach him that new stroke! And Nino will take your gun so it can watch you swim. I've heard you say you were so close to your gun that, if the holes were bigger, you'd fuck it. Well, I don't think you'll ever get the chance now." Cotti threw the holstered gun to Nino as they turned to leave.

"No! No!" Nugent shouted as he tried fighting his bodyguards. But it was of no use. They were much bigger and stronger than the weak and whining "Wildman."

Just as the boys started down the stairs, Rove saw what was happening. He opened his mouth to say something but then thought better of it. He figured it would do no good to say anything—he knew how Cotti felt about Nugent and vice versa. So, he acted as though he hadn't seen a thing and continued up the stairs.

The boys continued their trek into the bowels of the White House, where they ordered Nugent to undress. Nugent did as ordered, wondering what they had in store for him.

Two of the bodyguards took turns hitting Nugent in the gut and kneeing him in the balls. They did this a number of times before throwing him into the deep end of the pool. Nugent was then ordered to tread water while the boys shot bullet after bullet all around him. They kept him treading water until he tired to the point of no return.

After he nearly drowned, the boys allowed him to climb out of the pool and dry himself off before dressing. Then he was led back upstairs, being pushed and shoved by his handlers, all the way to the Oval Office to face the President once again. With a hard shove from one of the boys, Nugent flew across the room before landing hard on the President's desk.

Nugent straightened up and stood nervously at attention, not knowing what was going to happen next. He was no longer his old, arrogant self, but a docile and womanlike figure waiting to be scolded. And the President didn't let him down.

"Did you enjoy your swim, Teddy boy?" Cotti asked him.

Nugent remained silent, too afraid to speak, not wanting to fall any deeper into this ***den of inequity***. He only hoped to get out of there alive.

Cotti looked at Nugent in an evil way and continued his diatribe. "If you continue to mouth off and say bad things about me, ***Wildman,*** next time I won't be so nice! Had I wanted, I coulda had my boys break your fingers and hands. That would have definitely ruined your career. So, think wisely from now on. I know you're a racist and bigot. You're one of the worst. But kids follow your ways. And your ways and opinions are bad for the kids and the country. Capiche?"

Nugent remained silent, not knowing what to say.

"Capiche, Teddy boy?" Cotti barked, puffing away on his cigar.

Nugent could only nod. Evidently, he had swallowed too much water and was unable to speak.

"Now, you are free to go," Cotti told him, brushing him away with his hand.

Nugent didn't say a word. He just turned, looked at the President's bodyguards, and slowly walked away, a broken man. He was escorted out of the building. Just as he was about to head out the front door, Nino Cantelli threw Nugent his holstered gun, less the bullets of course.

That was the last time President Cotti had a run in with Ted Nugent. And Nugent never said another disparaging remark about the President.

After seeing the results of the meeting between the President and Nugent, Rove entered the Oval Office to speak his mind. He did some scolding of his own.

Standing in front of a seated President, Rove cut into Cotti without remorse.

"Mr. President," Rove barked, "Ted Nugent was your invited guest. And you kick the shit out of him—again! You can't do that! What if he goes to the FBI and complains?"

Cotti had a simple answer for him. "You mean the FBI that I have full control of? If anything, I'll have Director Arms quash the investigation. ***Forget about it!***"

It was useless to argue with the President. Rove knew better. He just threw up his hands in despair and left the room without saying another word.

Chapter 11

Rove didn't have anything else really important to speak with the President about... until a week before Cotti's second State of the Union Address. During a debriefing session, Rove had a few things to tell the President that would be of importance to him and make his day. He gave Cotti the ***low-down*** on a memo addressed to the President from FBI Director Arms concerning three bodies believed to be those of CEOs wanted on fraud and other charges.

"Mr. President, the memo from Director Arms," Rove explained, "states that the first CEO to be found was Bank of America's CEO, Brian Moynihan. He was found in Dubai with his arms and feet bound with rope, but his hands and head were gone—hacked off." Rove stopped for a second to catch his breath and then continued: "The head was later found sitting on the steps of the local branch office of Bank of America. Then there was a body found in Brazil, believed to be that of Wells Fargo CEO John Stumpf. He was found tied to a chair in a basement. He had been tortured before someone slit his throat; then, just to make sure he was dead, they placed a plastic bag over his head—I assume that was to suffocate him, just in case he didn't bleed to death first."

As Rove talked about the deaths, Cotti had a big smile

on his face. He sat back in his chair, puffing on his cigar while staring at the ceiling.

Rove took another deep breath and a sip of water before telling Cotti about the third body. "The last body, Mr. President, was found on a Greek island and is believed to be that of John J. Mack of Morgan Stanley. His body was cut into pieces and placed in seven different trash bags. They were found at the island's dump and, believe it or not, Mack's identification was found in one of the bags. The others' identifications, however, have yet to be found, and those bodies will need DNA testing to be positively identified. No suspects have been rounded up or arrested. The memo states that any future information will be forthcoming. It's signed by FBI Director Dennis Arms. There you have it, Mr. President." Rove added, "Three down, and many more to go."

Cotti smiled and nodded.

"Do you have any idea who killed them?" Rove asked the President as he placed the memo on his desk.

"Oh, I might have an idea, but I ***plead the fifth***!" Cotti answered, eating a cannolis.

Rove shook his head in disbelief. "I don't want to hear any more," he said.

As he was about to leave the room, he remembered an important issue that he had forgotten to mention. "Oh, Mr. President, I forgot to tell you that the heliport at your house has finally been completed. Now you'll be able to fly from here to there in about forty minutes instead of landing at the airport and having a train of cars following you. Now, the Secret Service and military will be there waiting for you."

"That sounds great, Karl. It's about time they finished that damn thing. Hell, my guys could have completed it in a month. The only bad thing about it is, my wife will expect me to come home every weekend now. ***Forget about it!***"

Rove remembered one more thing. "Oh, yeah, I should mention: Bobby Legend wrote you a short speech for your State of the Union Address. I know you don't like using speeches others have written for you, but just look it over. You might like it. I know Legend put his heart and soul into it."

"Just leave it on my desk. I'll read it, if nothing else. But I told you before, Karl, I like to speak off the top of my head without any dummy cards or teleprompter. I speak from my heart. Then the People know I'm not lying to them or just telling them what they want to hear."

"Well, it's up to you!" Rove pulled the one-page speech from the inside of his jacket pocket and placed it on the President's desk before leaving the room.

Later that day, the President did read it. It was a heartfelt speech; but it was Legend's heartfelt words, not Cotti's. Even though Legend said things the President would have said, they were still Legend's words. So Cotti rejected the speech and decided to wing it!

***

Nothing remarkable or surprising came out of the President's mouth on that special night of his second State of the Union Address. He mentioned how the government was running smoothly and efficiently and how more jobs (eleven million) had been created more quickly during his first two years in office than during any other administration's first two years. He believed that another eleven to fifteen million would be created before his first term expired.

He also gave special thanks to the government officials that were new to his administration, though he did not mention their names. He talked about his upcoming meetings with Russian President Vladimir Putin and Chinese President Xi Jinping, and he promised major concessions from both Russia and China that would help pay down the country's debt expeditiously. He didn't mention how this would be done, but nobody was brave enough to question him about it.

The biggest surprise of the night came when the President told the audience that he was running for a second term.

"Though things are going great within our government, I think we can do better. That's why I'm running for a second term," he announced.

When the crowd heard those last words come out of the President's mouth, there was complete silence. You could have heard a pin drop. They didn't react; it was as though they were all mesmerized by his words. But then one member of the audience looked over at Cotti's bodyguards, who were walking up and down the aisle, taking notes. That audience member decided that, to stay in good health, he should stand and clap. Once he began clapping, the entire audience quickly joined in, giving the President, a rousing standing ovation.

With that, the President thanked the crowd, the television viewers, and the hard workers of the country. Then he left the podium. Just as he had done the year before, he shook hands and gave thanks to the leaders behind him and the people among the first and second rows before shuffling out of the room.

The speech had been short and sweet: a total of twelve minutes. The President was eager to get back to the White House "super quick" and have a smoke and a few martinis before the party started. Everything was set up and ready to go as soon as all the guests arrived.

***

While the President was relaxing and having a few drinks, the majority and minority leaders of both the House and Senate were giving their opinions on the President's speech.

But others were also voicing their opinions—about the President's speech and about the three dead bodies that had finally been identified as the CEOs wanted for fraud.

Not only was the media commenting on both subjects, but so were the FBI agents in the New York City Office.

"So, what's the deal with Director Arms?" Agent Brunson asked his peers. "He knows Cotti had something to do with those deaths. He sent his soldiers to hunt them down, for Christ's sake."

"What do you want him to do, Keith?" interjected Lundy. "A mobster lawyer is his boss. And a mobster is DomAchelli's boss. If he went against them, they'd probably whack him too."

"I'm wondering why Arms hasn't busted Cotti's whole damn administration." remarked Meadows. "I mean, all the motherfuckers that Cotti's got running the government are mobsters; it's practically the entire Valoppi Family."

"Yeah, and remember what Cotti said in his speech: he's running for a second term!" Brunson acknowledged. "The cocksucker will be nearly eighty years old in 2020."

"If his enemies don't kill him first!" Lundy added.

All the agents in the room were partial to that line of thinking.

***

Many of the television commentators were also talking about the surprising declaration that the President was running for a second term. One of those, as usual, was John McLaughlin and his pundits of the McLaughlin Group.

"You've all seen the headlines in the ***Washington Post***," said McLaughlin.

He held up the front page of the newspaper and showed it to his pundits and viewers; it read: "COTTI RUNNING

AGAIN!!!"

"You were right, John," acknowledged Pat Buchanan. "You predicted that the President would run for a second term. And it looks like he is."

"And why not?" interjected Mort Zuckerman. "He's got the country running like a well-oiled machine. He deserves a second term."

"I agree, John," said Eleanor Clift. "I mean, who would be foolish enough to run against him? They're sure to lose: Republican ***or*** Democrat. After his speech, the polls showed a seventy-eight percent favorable rating. Not even Ronald Reagan had that kind of rating."

"Eleanor's right, John," replied Tom Rogan. "President Jack Cotti's got the Presidency sewed up for a second term. His American Family Freedom Party has more members than either the Republican or Democratic Parties. And it took him only four years to get to that point. I don't think he can be beat."

"He'll win by a landslide," McLaughlin predicted.

"Yes, he will, John," added Zuckerman.

"The President and Vice President will be eighty years old when they start their second term," McLaughlin acknowledged. "Will President Cotti pick a younger Vice President or stay with Vice President Napolie? I ask you, Pat Buchanan."

"I think he'll stick with Vice President Napolie, John."

"Why break up a good thing?" quipped Zuckerman. "They came in together. They'll go out together."

"Yes, John," said Clift. "I'm in agreement with Mort and Pat. They make a good pair. Why break them up now?"

"You're talking about President Cotti and Vice President Napolie, aren't you, Eleanor?" asked McLaughlin, who seemed confused by Eleanor's answer.

"I thought you meant Pat and Mort made a good pair, Eleanor," joked Rogan.

The pundits laughed at the confusion.

"I meant the President, John," Clift replied.

"Okay, let's change the subject," McLaughlin told his pundits. "We've heard about those Wall Street CEOs that were found murdered. Each body was found in a different country, none of which had extradition treaties with the United States. The rumor circulating is that the President had a hand in the murders. Some are saying that President Cotti ordered his henchmen to hunt these guys down and kill them. What do you make of the rumor? I ask you, Mort Zuckerman: a fan of the President."

"I'm a fan to a point, John," Zuckerman retorted. "I mean, look what he's gotten done in government. You can't help but be a fan."

McLaughlin then asked Zuckerman about the rumor that had been circulating in Washington. "Do you think, Mort, that the President ordered the deaths of those CEOs?"

Zuckerman shook his head. "Complete nonsense, John. That's what the President's opponents want you to believe."

Rogan jumped into the conversation. "I believe he may have had a hand in the deaths. But can it be proved? It's one thing to slander someone, especially the President, but is what the naysayers are claiming actually true?"

"That's right, John," said Clift. "Let those who cast the first stone show proof and not just spew conjecture."

"I think we have another President Cotti fan," joked Buchanan.

"I'm not a fan, ***per se***, Pat," Clift retorted. "I just want those people that are circulating that rumor to show proof! It's that simple."

"Well, we have just enough time for predictions!" McLaughlin told his pundits. "Pat. Prediction!"

"John, I predict those other CEOs that fled the country will give themselves up to the authorities. If they don't, they could end up like their friends."

"Eleanor, prediction!" McLaughlin barked.

"I predict the President will win every state in his reelection bid."

"That's hard to do, Eleanor," argued McLaughlin. "Even for President Cotti."

"John," said Rogan, "I predict that the President will have created more than twenty-two million new jobs before his term ends."

"Mort Zuckerman. Prediction!"

"John, I predict the President will ask Jinping for concessions on the debt owed to China. I believe he will ask for a two- to four-trillion-dollar reduction in our debt in return for our backing their expansion of the China Sea."

Now it was McLaughlin's turn. "I predict," he said, "that the President will choose a new Vice President before his reelection campaign begins. Bye, Bye."

***

While the media commentators were busy critiquing the Cotti administration, the President decided to try out his new heliport, flying home to Queens to visit his wife and family.

But after a long, four-day vacation with his wife, Cotti was eager to visit with his Consiglieri and Secretary of State, Benny "the brain" Bartolo, to hear what Bartolo had learned about his last assassination attempt. And Bartolo had plenty to tell him.

Once contacted, Bartolo arrived at Cotti's house in less than an hour. To his dismay, he was followed by his own entourage of Secret Service agents.

Cotti and his wife greeted Bartolo in the foyer.

"How ya doin, Benny?" Cotti asked as they shook hands.

Bartolo then hugged Maria. "Hey, Maria. You're looking well," he told her.

She smiled and nodded.

"Where's Johnny, Jack?" Bartolo asked.

He shrugged. "I don't know. Probably back in D.C. Why?"

"Just wondering."

"Let's go into the den, Benny," Cotti told him.

The two walked into the den while Maria walked to the kitchen and packed a tray with coffee and cannolis. She took it to the two wiseguys, setting it on the table in front of them before leaving the room.

After lighting cigars and adding brandy to their coffee, they talked seriously about the problem at hand.

"So, what did you hear, Benny?" Cotti asked.

"Jack, I got some bad news to lay on you."

"Let's hear it!" Cotti demanded, nervously puffing away on his cigar.

Bartolo took a deep breath. "It's true, Jack. The Commission ordered the hit. They gave it to Johnny to carry out. He was ordered to get it done before you took Office."

"Are you sure, Benny?" Cotti gave Benny the evil eye.

"I heard it from a good source. It seems like Johnny gave them the idea. I guess he wanted your job."

"I don't fuckin' believe it! Johnny wouldn't do that."

"Jack, Johnny went to Talluchi and told him he would have to get the Commission's approval before he would do the hit."

"Fuck me!" Cotti shouted. "I don't fuckin' believe it!"

"It's true, Jack! I know you don't like to hear that a dear old friend would do this to you… to the Family. But what's done… is done!"

"I want to fuckin' know who the fuck told you," Cotti demanded.

Bartolo told Cotti that he had gotten the information from Bobby Valli, the Consiglieri for the Colombo Family.

"He said he was at the meeting when the Commission sanctioned the hit, Jack. Talluchi told the other members about his meeting with Johnny. Johnny made a deal with them that if they backed his play, he'd be responsible for the hit. They agreed. And Johnny ordered Partelli to do it. Partelli agreed to do the hit for a million dollars in cash, paid in advance. DeNato was just collateral damage. ***Forget about it!***"

"I still can't believe that Johnny would do that to me. I mean, we knew each other as kids. Hell, my mom gave us baths together. And he tries to kill me? FUCK!"

"I'm sorry, Jack. I know you didn't want to hear it. But that's it. I was also told that they tried three other times to take you out. Tommy Valoppi was at that meeting, and he voted with the others. It was unanimous."

"I need to have confirmation from more than just one source."

"I know," Bartolo exclaimed. "That's why I went to three Capos in three different Families to confirm Valli's story. They all told me the same thing. It's confirmed, Jack. ***Forget about it!***"

Jack leaned back into his chair, thinking and puffing on his cigar, pondering his next move.

"So, what do you want me to do, Jack?"

Suddenly, Cotti had the answer. "We'll take the helicopter back to D.C. tomorrow. We gotta make plans."

"Plans? Plans for what?"

"I'm gonna take down the whole fuckin' Mafia, Benny. Except I'll do it in a way that the Valoppi Family will end up being the biggest and strongest Family in the world. ***Forget about it***! The Yakuza has thirty-seven thousand members. By the time I'm through, the Valoppi Family will have nearly fifty thousand."

Soon after the two wiseguys ended their conversation, Benny left Cotti's abode. He returned the following morning.

Cotti was beyond angry at learning who had been responsible for his last assassination attempt and possibly others. He went berserk, shoving everything on top of his desk to the floor. His psychotic side suddenly came out. He wanted revenge on those who had schemed to take him out, and he had a pretty good idea of how he would achieve that goal. However, the more he thought about "this thing of ours," the more he ranted and raved. Finally, his wife came into the room and calmed him down.

"Jack, have you gone crazy?" she yelled. "Calma, calma!"

She quickly made him a double dry martini and handed it to him. He drank nearly all of it in one gulp. She made him another, and he downed it as fast as the first. That one seemed to calm her husband down.

"What has gotten into you, Jack?" she asked as she sat down next to him.

"Nuthin', baby. Benny told me something that upset

me. That's all. ***Forget about it!***"

She didn't argue the point. She remained silent, worried but not knowing what to say. When he lit a cigar, and laid his head back on the top of the couch to rest, she knew his psychotic outburst was over and left the room.

The rest of the day and night, Cotti thought of different ways to get even with his so-called friends. Finally, he settled on a specific plan to rid his life of the ones who had tried to destroy him.

***

The following morning, after Cotti said goodbye to his wife and family, he, Bartolo, Cantelli, and a few other bodyguards boarded the helicopter to return to D.C.

Not a word was said during the ride. But once they were sitting in the den at the White House, all bets were off.

Before Cotti could vent his frustration, however, Rove came into the room and handed the President a memo from Director Arms. Cotti quickly read it and smiled, then lit a cigar. It seemed that another CEO had been found murdered, in Kazakhstan of all places. His head was nearly severed, and his hands were missing. The memo stated that this was believed to be the body of Lloyd Blankfein of Goldman Sachs. No identification was found on the body.

The other subject mentioned in the memo was Grover Norquist. He had been missing for more than three weeks.

Cotti knew better. Norquist would be missing for eternity. The last one to see him was the ***Great White Shark*** that had him for lunch. The shark evidently hadn't liked his tax pledge, either, and finally put a stop to the madness.

The President, to say the least, was happy with the good news. But now, he wanted to concentrate on the problem at hand. He asked Rove to leave the room.

"I'm sorry, Karl," said President Cotti. "But Benny and me have to talk over some important business. It's better you don't get involved in our talk. It might not be healthy for you. ***Forget about it!***"

"No problem, Mr. President," said Rove before he left the room.

Besides Cantelli, Cotti and Bartolo had the room to themselves.

"Benny," said Cotti, "I got a plan to rid the world of the Commission and Johnny in ***one fell swoop***. But first, I have to get DomAchelli and Arms to start busting wiseguys from all four Families across the country. I'll have them go after the Underbosses and Capos. The Dons and Johnny, I'll leave for last."

"But Jack, Johnny's your Vice President. It ain't gonna look too good, your Vice President gets whacked."

"Who says he gets murdered? He just might leave the country and never return. ***Forget about it!***"

"Whatever you say, Jack."

"But right now, Benny, I have something more important that I want you to do. I want you to go to Europe, Russia, and China and set up meetings for me with their leaders… say, three or four months from now. I'll have

Rove set up the final dates."

"Who do you want me to see in Europe?"

"Fuck! I don't know! Whoever the leader is in that country. You're the fuckin' Secretary of State. Act like it!"

"But Jack, Europe's not a country. Europe's made up of many countries. Which one do you want me to visit?"

Cotti thought for a minute, then said, "The one Hitler came from."

"Germany?"

"Yeah! They've got a nice-lookin' broad as President."

"Okay, Boss. I'll leave in a few days."

"Good! After the meetings, I gotta get my campaign for reelection started."

"You're really gonna run again, huh?" Bartolo asked his boss.

"***Forget about it!*** I can't lose."

"I'm beat, Jack. I gotta get home and rest for the trip."

The two shook hands, and then Bartolo left for his home in DC. Rove entered the room seconds later.

"Do you need me for anything, sir?" Rove asked.

"Yeah! I was just gonna call you," Cotti replied after taking a sip from his glass of brandy.

"What do you need, Mr. President?"

"I want you to get DomAchelli and Arms in here on the double. We got work to do!"

"Okay."

Cotti took a few puffs from his cigar and added, "And I need you to get together with Bartolo before he leaves for

Europe."

"What for?" Rove asked.

"Give him some dates for meetings with Putin, Ping, and that German broad in Germany. I want meetings set up within the next three or four months, and when I return, you'll need to get our volunteers up and running for my reelection."

"I'm way ahead of you, sir," Rove replied. "I've already got the ball rolling. The American Family Freedom Party volunteers and donors are ready when you are. All I have to do is say the word and the doors will be open within forty-eight hours. I've had people on the phones contacting past donors and volunteers since the day after your State of the Union Address."

Just then, the phone rang. Cotti got up and answered it.

"Yeah?"

"Mr. President, Arms here. I need to see you."

"I was just gonna have Rove contact you. But now that I got you on the phone, I need you and Dom to visit with me tomorrow, here in my office. Say, two o'clock. So, call Dom and let him know."

"See you tomorrow, Mr. President."

As Cotti hung up the phone and returned to the couch, Rove's curiosity got the better of him.

"What's up, Mr. President?" Rove asked. "What's the meeting about with DomAchelli and Arms?"

"Well, I'll tell you, Karl. Some people think that, just because I was a mobster, I'm soft on organized crime. I'm not! And the People will soon see just how fanatical I can be when I set my mind to it."

"What are you going to do?"

"Come to the meeting tomorrow and find out."

"Will do, Mr. President."

Rove noticed a bright shine in his boss's eyes when he talked about being a mobster, evidently remembering the ***good old days***. But Rove still wondered what the President had in mind about fighting organized crime. He would just have to wait.

The wait wasn't long. Just eighteen hours later, Rove was in the Oval Office, sitting with the President and waiting for DomAchelli and Arms to arrive. At precisely two o'clock, the two Feds entered the room and took their seats.

The first words out of Arms' mouth after sitting down were directed towards Rove. He looked in Rove's eyes and said, "Let me be blunt, Mr. Rove. What I have to speak with the President about is something you don't want to be part of. It's a highly classified matter."

The President looked at Rove and nodded.

Rove stood up. "Call me if you need me, Mr. President," he said, and then he left the room.

"Okay, Dennis, what's up?" Cotti asked him.

"Can I speak freely, Mr. President? Maybe the Attorney General shouldn't hear this either."

"Dom and I go way back. ***Forget about it!*** You don't have to worry. Dom is loyal, one hundred percent. So, go ahead, Dennis. Spit it out."

Arms explained the situation. "Just to let you know, sir. We got a hit on a wiretap of one of your Capos speaking on the phone. He was talking with someone whom we believe to be a Valoppi soldier calling from Amsterdam. The call was concerning the Russian mob boss who controls the crime in Amsterdam and Western Europe, Oleg Brakinov."

"What about him?" Cotti asked.

"He was found in a whore house, beaten and supposedly tortured. Witnesses told of two American thugs that tricked the Russian mobster into a meeting but then turned the tables on him and a couple of his henchmen. They shot and killed Oleg's bodyguards before beating the shit out of Oleg. Evidently, they tried getting information out of him. The witnesses said they heard the word "shooter" mentioned more than once. So, we believe the thugs were trying to find out the name of the shooter who had been hired to assassinate you. We think they wanted to kill him before he kills you."

Cotti was confused and asked Arms about it. "You said the mobster died. Was he shot? Stabbed? What?"

"No," Arms replied. "The authorities in Amsterdam believe he died from a heart attack. His heart couldn't take the stress of being tortured, I guess."

"Well I'll see what I can find out," Cotti replied. "I'll see if Benny heard anything. I don't think he has, or he'd have told me. ***Forget about it***!"

DomAchelli finally spoke up. "Now, why did you call

us to the White House?" he asked Cotti.

"I want to take care of a small problem that I seem to have."

"What problem?" asked Arms.

Cotti took a few puffs from his cigar and answered, "The People think that I'm weak on organized crime because I'm a mobster. Well, I want to disprove that thought from their minds."

"How?" Dom asked.

"I don't care how!" Cotti barked. "I want you to roust the businesses of every Family in New York and across the country. Hit 'em, and hit 'em hard! Except for one: the Valoppi Family. Keep your mitts off!"

"Jack," Dom said, forgetting who he was talking to.

Cotti gave him a dirty look.

"I'm sorry," Dom told Cotti apologetically. "Mr. President, why are you doing this now? And please don't tell me it's because the People think you are weak on organized crime. There's got to be another reason."

Cotti thought for a long moment before giving Dom his answer. "There is, Dom. But it's one I'm not willing to share at this time. Just put those Families out of business."

Cotti looked at Arms. "And Dennis, I especially want your guys to hit them hard in New York. Take the gloves off!"

"You got it, Mr. President," Arms replied happily. "I know the guys I used to supervise will love to hear this."

"Good! I'll help you guys out as much as I can. But

don't touch the Dons. Leave them for me! ***Forget about it!***"

As the two left Cotti alone, each of them had opposite feelings about their desire to crack down on the mob. DomAchelli left the White House confused and disgruntled, not wanting to take action against the Families.

Director Arms, on the other hand, was happy to get Cotti's order to roust the Families' businesses and members. And he would do as Cotti asked, however, and not roust or arrest the Dons. He would let the President take command of that situation, leaving them to his whims.

***

When Director Arms gave the order to his crews across the country to "Hit the Families, and hit them hard," many of the agents were caught off guard and in disbelief—especially the New York City surveillance crew. They had lots to say about this recent command from their boss, and they expressed their views while sitting around the table during a lunch break.

"How are we going to do it?" FBI Agent Greg Delahant asked his peers. "Most of our agents have been transferred to Homeland Security."

"We'll just have to do the best we can," replied their new Supervisor Agent, Mark Law.

Ken Lundy entered the discussion. "I'm just wondering, why now? Why is Director Arms clamping down all of a sudden? Was it an order from above?"

Agent Brunson also had a few things to say about this rush to bust up the mob. "Why were we ordered to crush every Family but the Valoppi Family?" Brunson asked anyone that would listen. "I'm telling you now! Cotti's got something up his fucking sleeve."

"Yeah," Agent Meadows agreed, "that'll leave the Valoppi Family with all the marbles. They'll have control of everything. Which means that Cotti, when he leaves Office, will be in control of all organized crime in the country."

Chapter 12

As the months passed, and while the President was traveling the world, Director Arms and his federal agents took it upon themselves to close down each and every business that the mobsters owned. They took no prisoners. By the time the President was meeting with President Putin in Russia, the Feds had arrested more than twelve hundred wiseguys throughout the country. The majority of those mobsters were now sitting behind bars.

***

While the Feds were having fun busting wiseguys, President Cotti was having fun busting moves on Putin. The two leaders seemed to be getting along quite well, although most of the time they were out of sight of the Paparazzi. They wanted to be alone together to talk about "some things!"

At first, the two were having a jovial time. They spoke to each other matter-of-factly and honestly. But when their conversation turned to the Russian mob, it got a bit more heated.

"I know you control the Russian mob, Vladimir!" Cotti barked, puffing away on his cigar. "And I want you to call off your dogs and the shooter who was given the job of assassinating me. Oleg Brakinov took the contract for fifty million Euros from the CEOs my government has been hunting down. We took care of most of them, and we'll get the rest soon. And Oleg, we found him, too. But my boys weren't able to get the shooter's name out of him before he died. Now I need ***you*** to stop him!"

Putin looked quite stunned. Cotti was accusing him, the President of Russia, of conspiracy to assassinate a United States President. He didn't mince words in his rebuttal.

"Why do you think I control the Russian mob? Who told you that?" Putin barked.

"Listen, Vladimir, I've negotiated with your boys in New York. They told me they were all ex-KGB and that you controlled them… and their brothers like them."

Putin really didn't know what to say. He thought for a few seconds, looking for an answer, and then exclaimed, "So what if I do control the Russian mob? Do you think I control every one of their operatives? But for you, Cotti, I will look into it and see who Oleg outsourced it to!"

"Well, do it quick!" Cotti told Putin, adding, "I've ducked enough bullets from ***my*** mob. I don't need yours trying to kill me too."

"Don't tell me what to do," Putin snapped. "I don't take orders from you."

Putin then smiled and spoke to Cotti in a mocking tone. "You're nothing but a thug!"

"Hey, get off your high horse, Mister! I am the most powerful man in the world," Cotti told him.

"Fuck you!" Putin stood nose to nose with Cotti,

wanting him to throw the first punch. "I am a black belt in Ju-jitsu and will fuck—"

Before he could finish his sentence, Cotti sucker-punched him with a right uppercut. The blow caught Putin squarely under his chin and sent him flying backwards to the floor.

Putin stayed motionless for a good minute before sitting up and shaking his head to get the cobwebs out.

"I'm sorry I had to do that, Vladimir," Cotti said as he put out his hand to help Putin to his feet.

"Me, too," Putin replied, still a little shaken.

As the two sat down in chairs across from each other, Cotti explained to Putin how the two leaders could control the world if they worked together—not only the ***real*** world but also the ***criminal*** world.

"What rules the world?" Cotti asked Putin.

"You?" Putin replied, not sure what answer Cotti was looking for.

"No. Well, yes! But also, power and money. That's what rules! ***Forget about it!*** That's what really counts in this world. If you got the power, then you got money. If you got money, then you got power. It's as simple as that."

"I'm already rich and powerful."

"What happens when your term ends, Vladimir? Hook up with me and I promise you, once you leave Office, you'll have more money than you could ever dream of. ***Forget about it!***"

Putin, at first, had wanted nothing to do with Cotti and

his crazy promises. But after thinking it over, he figured, 'Why not listen to what the man has to say?' "What did you have in mind?" he asked the Godfather President.

"I figure, the three most powerful leaders in this world are me, you, and Hu Zing Ping. If we work this thing out right, we could tell the rest of the world ***how it is*** and ***how it will be***!"

"Who is Hu Zing Ping?" Putin asked.

"Who is Hu Zing Ping? That Chinese guy. I'm gonna see him next. Isn't he the President of China?"

"No. Hu Jintao used to be the Chinese President but was ousted in 2012. Xi Jinping is the President. Which one are you to see?"

"I thought it was Hu, but I guess it's Zing Ping. Who in the fuck knows? Karl Rove takes care of that shit for me."

"Well, both men are very powerful. One can't run the country without the other. And Xi's first name is pronounced Chee."

"Well, ***fuck*** that shit! Let's get back to what I was saying—about how we can get much more done if we work together. If you back my play, I'll back yours. So, if you want to invade another country, I won't criticize or condemn you or your country for the invasion. And vice versa."

"I don't know."

Cotti continued: "If we integrate our criminal organizations, we'll be bigger than the Triads and Yakuza. And if we can get the Triads to join us, we'll be able to control and tax illegal contraband everywhere. You don't have to give me your answer today, Vladimir. Just think it over. But don't take too long. In fact, I'm in the process of incorporating the Five Mafia Families into one as we speak. And I'll control it all. See! There's still life after the Presidency. And a rich one at that! ***Forget about it!***"

"You may be right. It sounds good. But let me think it over, and I'll give you an answer before you leave Office."

"Well, that may be a while. I'm running for reelection and will start that process when I return to America. So, I intend to be in the White House for another term."

"Are you sure you can win, Mr. President?"

"***Forget about it!*** I'm the most idolized mobster in the country. I just may win all the states this time."

"I wish you good luck!"

It seemed the two had become very good friends by the time President Cotti left Russia. He had gotten a cold reception when he first visited the country. But the Russian people changed their perception of America's President when their President took a liking to Cotti.

Before leaving and flying to China to meet with Zing Ping or whomever, President Cotti invited President Putin to the United States for a red-carpet visit before his term ended. Putin happily accepted and promised to give Cotti his answer to his business deal at that time.

Cotti saluted Putin and the Russian people as he boarded Air Force One.

***

Nearly ten hours later, President Cotti was being warmly greeted by President Xi Jinping (or, as Cotti called him, Zing Ping) and not Hu Jintao. But unfortunately, President Cotti's visit wasn't the biggest story or event happening at that time. It seemed everyone in the country was talking about recent UFO sightings, which had been going on for nearly a week before President Cotti arrived in Beijing.

***

After a few days of sightseeing, Cotti returned to Beijing to meet with Xi Jinping once again. Once Cotti had greeted many of the important leaders within the Chinese government, he and Xi walked alone among the cherry trees and lotus flowers behind the President's residence before holding a closed-door meeting in Xi's office. Xi sat in the chair behind his desk while Cotti took a seat directly in front of his host.

President Cotti was curious about all the talk about UFOs and asked his host if he believed in them.

"Well, I saw them with my very own eyes," Xi answered in broken English. "Saucer shape, moving in all different directions at incredible speeds. We're just not sure if they're extraterrestrial or yours."

Cotti was shocked to hear that the Chinese Hierarchy believed the United States had built flying saucers. "What are you saying, Mr. President? Do you think we have flying saucers?"

He nodded. "Yes, we think that."

Cotti still found it hard to believe and replied, "Well, I guess that's one thing I'll have to look into when I get back home."

Cotti was eager to get down to business and, after lighting a cigar, he asked if Xi wanted to control the flow of drugs in China.

"Of course," he replied. "What do you have in mind?"

Cotti told Xi that he believed people within Xi's government controlled the Triad criminal organization.

Xi became angry. "Not true!" he exclaimed.

Cotti tried to calm the situation, saying, "Hey, look, Xi. Just think about this. Me and Putin are hooking up together, integrating our criminal organizations so we can control supply and demand. We can make billions in a very short time. Wouldn't you like to live like you deserve to after you leave the Presidency?"

Xi thought about it for a second, smiled, and then came to his senses. "I don't need or want big money. I am satisfied with my life now."

"Look, Ping. Listen to me. While your pals are getting rich and living the high life, you're taking all the shit… and when a problem arises, you get the blame. You don't owe those blood suckers a thing, Xi. Just think about what I said. Talk it over with your Commission and, when you come to visit me in the near future, you can give your answer then."

Xi smiled and told Cotti that he could have his answer now. "No! We don't control the Triad. These are thugs. Just like you… and like Putin, if what you say is true."

"Okay, that's your prerogative. Now, let's talk ***important*** business."

"About what?"

Cotti stood up and walked over to Xi. Standing by Xi's side, he pulled, from his inside jacket pocket, a trade agreement that he wanted the Chinese President to sign. He quickly opened it up and handed it to his host.

Xi smiled, bowed his head, and looked at the document. Once he began reading it, his smile turned to a scowl. He looked up at Cotti and barked, "You must be crazy. I can't sign this."

Cotti stepped directly behind the President's chair, placed his hands around Xi's neck, and gave him an ultimatum.

"Either you sign the agreement, or I'll snap your neck," Cotti promised him. "You pencil-neck geek!"

"But my men will kill you," Xi retorted, trying to pull Cotti's hands away.

"Yeah, but you'll still be dead." Cotti continued. As he spoke, he increased the pressure around Xi's neck. "Look it's a good deal. I agree with your expansion of the China Seas and you absolve twelve trillion of our debt. And for every other trillion that's written off, I'll promise you future technologies. It's a win-win for both of us."

Xi's face turned red, the pressure cutting off his blood

flow.

"Sign it quick, before you pass out," Cotti whispered in his ear.

Xi slowly picked up his pen and signed the document. Cotti quickly grabbed it and placed it back into his jacket pocket. Then he returned to his seat with a big smile on his face and kept puffing away on his cigar.

As Xi was trying to catch his breath, he thought about President Cotti's words. Xi figured that if Cotti was brazen enough to assault the leader of the Chinese government, he could be just as tough. So, a partnership seemed convenient. The two Presidents would rule the world together. Even though President Cotti had threatened him with death, he came to the conclusion that a Trade Agreement made with the American President was truly a great deal for both countries. Now China could expand their military might in the China Sea with America's blessing.

Afterwards, the Chinese and American Presidents called the paparazzi into Xi's office and allowed pictures to be taken. When reporters asked what the meeting was about, Xi answered for both of them.

"We signed a very good trade deal," Xi told the reporters. "I don't want to say anything more until President Cotti has a chance to explain to the American people this once-in-a-lifetime deal."

President Cotti refused to answer the reporters' questions, including those of the American Press Corp. He simply said that his Press Secretary would explain the trade deal to them on the flight home.

"Bobby Legend will be able to brief you on our meeting today. I'm just too tired… and right now, I have to get ready for tonight's dinner with President Xi." He added, "It's been a long three weeks of traveling for a man who rarely left New York City… and I still have to visit that broad in Germany."

***

During dinner with President Xi and guests, President Cotti hadn't tasted anything quite like the dishes served, and he asked his host about them.

"Mr. President," said Cotti, "what are the names of these dishes? I've never tasted anything like them, especially that first course we had."

"Yes, President Cotti. They're exotic dishes. The first dish served to you was raw monkey brains mixed with thyme, salt, and onion. The second dish was fried lizard intestine. It tastes similar to chicken but just a little heartier. Wouldn't you say, Mr. President?"

Cotti felt a bit queasy after learning what he had just eaten. He wiped his sweating forehead and asked Xi, "What was the third dish I ate?"

"The third dish was crushed black scorpion without the poison sacks. Tasty, wasn't it?"

"Oh, shit. I think I'm gonna be sick," Cotti whispered to himself. "Yes! Very tasty," he said to Xi, smiling.

After a few big glasses of wine, President Cotti said his goodbyes to his host and hostess. Soon after, he and his staff returned to their hotel for a few stiff drinks to wash the ***exotic*** out of their bodies; then turned in early in preparation for the long flight to Europe.

***

The following afternoon, President Cotti and his entourage were off and flying to see that ***broad*** in Germany. He was anxious to meet her and to see what she was made of. He thought she looked too hot and sexy to be the leader of a European country, let alone an economic powerhouse. Cotti was hoping his manly charisma and charm would overpower her female senses.

But President Cotti would never get that chance. When Air Force One landed at Frankfort Airport, Cotti received a message from Federal Chancellor Merkel's staff that the Chancellor was indisposed and resting in bed from a bad bout of German measles. She would have to postpone the meeting between her and President Cotti for another time in the near future.

Cotti was livid when he heard the excuse used to postpone the meeting, and he let Rove know his disgust.

"This is bullshit!" Cotti exclaimed to Rove. "German measles my ass. Does she think she has the patent on measles? Are her measles special? Just because she's from Germany doesn't mean that she can call her measles 'German measles.' That's fuckin' bullshit!"

"But, sir, German measles really are a strain of measles."

"Oh! I didn't know that. So, you really think she's sick, Karl?"

"I don't know. Maybe she heard about your interview in China, when you called her a ***broad***, and thought you disrespected her. That could be why she isn't seeing you. Or… maybe she really does have the German measles."

"German measles. Fuck! Sounds like a dish they would serve in China. Here you go, sir, a nice steamy bowl of German measles." Cotti was disgusted by the fact he couldn't meet with that ***broad***.

"We'll set up another meeting for next year, Mr. President."

Cotti didn't want to hear it. He was pissed, and he decided that he wanted to leave the country, ***now***! "Fuck that broad! Let's get the plane started and get the fuck out of here, Karl. I've done enough traveling for a while."

"I know what you mean, Mr. President."

"Anyway, we got lots of work to do, especially for my reelection campaign."

Rove nodded. All he had to do was make one phone call, and the campaign would be in play. Rove was an expert in politics and in raising money for his candidate. Everything was already set in motion and ready to go.

***

Once Air Force One had been topped off with fuel,

Cotti and company left Frankfort, flying into the wild blue yonder. Cotti was biting at the bit, anxious to get back home.

The Press Corp was anxious to find out why he had suddenly departed from Germany before meeting with the Chancellor. Cotti refused to answer their questions and summoned Bobby Legend to handle it. Legend did, telling the reporters that German measles had been the reason for their quick exit from Frankfort. He left it at that.

***

As Cotti and Rove relaxed over a glass of brandy and a good cigar, Cotti brought up a subject that had clearly been on his mind since he left China.

"Karl, when we get back home, I want you to find me a general in the Pentagon who's knowledgeable about UFOs. I want to prove or disprove the UFO question. Are they real or not? If so, are they extraterrestrial or ours? And I want the truth!"

"That'll be the second thing on my list."

"What's the first?" Cotti asked him, puffing away on his cigar.

"Getting your campaign going one hundred percent. We're at about thirty percent right now. But in a week, we'll be running full blast."

"I like that," Cotti happily exclaimed.

Just then, their conversation ended as Toni suddenly interrupted them. She led the President to his bedroom.

The two spent the rest of the trip there and weren't seen again until the aircraft landed.

The President and his entourage didn't arrive at the White House until three in the morning. The President and Toni went directly to the bedroom while the Special Secret Service Brigade went directly to their stations within the White House. Rove went to the guest bedroom.

***

After resting up for three days, the President went in front of television cameras in the Oval Office to finally answer the Press Corps' questions. He explained to the audience his recent travels and meetings with the leaders of the world, and the trade agreement with China.

"You people watching may be wondering what I accomplished during my trip overseas. I must tell you, I accomplished quite a bit. President Putin and I have developed a close working relationship as a result of my visit with him. We've built a kind of trust and partnership for bettering the world, which I'm sure will last into the year 2020 and beyond. I also had that type of relationship with President Xi of China. In fact, we had such a good time in China with President Xi and his wife that we became very good friends. President Xi and I were left alone in a closed-door meeting to negotiate a trade agreement that would benefit both of our countries equally. And we found one. The United States will, as soon as the agreement is ratified by Congress, receive from the

Chinese government a twelve-trillion-dollar debt reduction. Which leaves only a four-trillion-dollar deficit. And President Xi and I have worked out a way for the complete debt to be wiped out. I have promised President Xi that, for every trillion dollars of debt written off after the twelve trillion, the United States will share one important new technology with China. The only ***quid pro quo*** for the twelve trillion in debt reduction is my word that America won't interfere in their expansion of the China Seas. Before some of you become upset over this agreement concerning the China Seas, let me say this: China would have expanded their hold on the China Seas anyway, even without this agreement. And let me reiterate: The United States just dissolved twelve trillion dollars of debt instantly, and I hope to have the final four trillion wiped out before my term ends. If possible, I intend to leave a surplus. I'll speak more about that during my upcoming and last State of the Union Address. But before I say goodnight, I just want to remind the voters that I hope you will allow me and my administration another four years. The American Family Freedom Party is now in full swing for another Cotti/Napolie administration. And with that, I say goodnight and God bless."

But Cotti knew that Napolie would never make it back for another term—that is, if he won. But of course, he would win another four years in the White House. The President was confident of that.

***

Shortly after the President's speech nearly all the news networks were covering the story. It seemed President Cotti was the toast of the town. The People were ecstatic with his negotiating skills. Not only were the citizens of the country giving the President their accolades, but the television commentators and political pundits were also thrilled. Chuck Todd of NBC's Meet the Press called President Cotti a "miracle worker." Lester Holt of NBC Sunday Night News called the President a "wizard." Chris Wallace of Fox News Sunday called him a "genius." Affectionate names were given to the President on a variety of news shows. One called him "the Negotiator." Another called him, of all things, "the Peacemaker."

The shows were saying only good things about the Godfather President, including the McLaughlin Group.

"Okay," said John McLaughlin, "you all heard the President's speech and the debt that China has written off. How did President Cotti do it? I ask you, Pat Buchanan!"

Before Buchanan could answer, Mort Zuckerman jumped in and answered for him. "He made President Xi an offer he couldn't refuse. Either his signature would be on the trade agreement or his brains. Evidently, Xi signed it."

All the pundits laughed at that little bit of humor.

"Well, I'll tell you what I think, John," said Buchanan. "I think the President made the deal of a lifetime. Twelve trillion of debt owed to the Chinese government is wiped out in a heartbeat. And what did we have to do for that? Just go along with China in their expansion of the China Sea, something they would have done anyway. The President is one heck of a negotiator. That's all I have to say, John."

"Yes, John," said Clift. "The President got an extraordinary deal from President Xi Jinping. How he did it, I'll leave it to others to figure out."

"He did it, Eleanor," said Tom Rogan, "by using his great negotiating skills. Remember when he first ran as President and gave that interview where he said how, as a Mafia Don, he had negotiated with the toughest of people? He mentioned the Russians, Chinese, Columbians, and many other nationalities. And these were killers. I remember the President saying, 'If I can negotiate with these guys, dealing with the heads of state will be a cinch.' And evidently, he has proved it!"

"You have to admit," McLaughlin exclaimed, "since the President's speech, his approval rating has gone through the roof. It's over seventy-eight percent. Why? Pat Buchanan!"

"Easy, John. Twelve trillion dollars in debt has magically disappeared, which, to some, has made President Cotti a ***god***."

"I agree with Pat," interjected Eleanor Clift. "Even Time magazine has recently placed President Cotti at the top of their list for Man of the Year. One of their reasons for this is the fact that never has such a large debt been dissolved in one swipe of the pen."

"The pen is mightier than the sword, John," said Zuckerman facetiously. "And the President proved it."

"I don't know about that, Mort," retorted McLaughlin. "There's a rumor going around that President Cotti threatened President Xi with death if he didn't sign the agreement."

"I don't believe that, John," said Clift. "I've heard that rumor too. Was the threat in jest? Did he hold a gun to his head? I just find it hard to believe."

Rogan jumped into the fray, saying, "I'm sure, John, that if our President truly threatened President Jinping with bodily injury, someone within Jinping's government would have arrested President Cotti or killed him."

"Not true, Tom," Zuckerman exclaimed. "The Chinese people have great respect for a man of power. One who doesn't back down, who takes the initiative. And that's President Cotti. If the rumor is true, Xi didn't take revenge because he saw someone who he wanted to emulate. And instead of becoming the enemy of the President of the United States, he has become President Cotti's partner. That was a smart move on both Presidents' parts."

"I'm just wondering who started the rumor," Clift asked McLaughlin. "Do we know the answer to that, John?"

McLaughlin shook his head. "I heard it from a guy, who heard it from a guy, who heard it from a guy," he said. "No, I believe I heard this from Karl Rove. But I couldn't say positively. At my age, who can remember anymore?"

The pundits snickered.

Just then, Buchanan remembered something that Zuckerman had predicted on a previous show. "Mort, I just remembered that ***you*** predicted, weeks ago, that the President would get a debt reduction from China. You are a true psychic. Incredible!"

"Yeah, but not a debt reduction of twelve trillion dollars, Pat," replied Zuckerman. "Who would have ever predicted that?"

"No one, Mort," answered Clift.

Time was up and McLaughlin let his viewers know it. "That's all the time we have for today," he acknowledged. "Bye, Bye."

***

For months afterward, the President's negotiating tactics were echoing throughout the Fortune Five Hundred Companies' hierarchies and the Halls of Congress. They too, wondered how President Cotti had negotiated such a great deal for the country, and they wanted to use similar tactics in their wheeling and dealing. They were a little dumbfounded, however, by the fact that they didn't know exactly what those tactics were.

***

Going into the winter months, the President was busy flying from one state to another, wooing voters for his reelection bid. His approval rating was still in the high seventies. His administration couldn't have been doing any better. The country was in great shape, the economy was purring like a kitten, and the unemployment rate was at its lowest point in over twenty years. And Cotti couldn't have been happier. But three days before his third and last State of the Union Address, FBI Director Dennis Arms came to the White House unannounced for what he deemed to be a very necessary house call.

Arms was let in to see the President immediately.

As soon as Arms took a seat in the Oval Office, the President asked him, "What the fuck is so important that you interrupt my free time?"

"I'm sorry to tell you this, Mr. President," Arms answered. "I hate to be the bearer of bad news, but I'm afraid I have some embarrassing information for you and your administration."

Cotti gave him a look of surprise, shock, and then anger. 'How could this be?' Cotti thought to himself. "What's up?" he asked Arms.

"It's about DEA Director Don Domino. The top cops around the country have branded him the biggest dope dealer in America."

"What? That can't be." Cotti couldn't believe what he was hearing.

Arms continued: "The police in many different states have been investigating drug distribution centers all across the country that are under Domino's control."

"So! How is Domino involved?" Cotti asked, lighting a cigar.

Arms thought for a minute. He decided that he would tell it like it was and not sugarcoat it. "They say, Mr. President that he's been diverting large shipments of confiscated drugs from police stations around the country and taking them to various warehouses. The police departments are told that the drugs will be incinerated—not in the warehouses' incinerator, but at a different site that's classified. But instead of burning the drugs, Domino has his people distributing them all throughout the country, and is making tons of money from it. He's been doing this for three years."

As Arms explained the situation, the President seemed to get very upset, clenching his fists as his face turned red. He was very angry and did not hide his feelings.

"That stupid motherfucker!" hollered Cotti.

"I'm sure, Mr. President, that he didn't mean to hurt your administration," Arms opined.

"I'm not worried about that! I'm just pissed because he got his ***tit caught in the wringer***. Donny was the Family's ***go-to*** guy for all narcotic transactions. He ***knows*** to be discreet. This should have never come back to him. He ***fucked up***!"

"But that's only the first problem you have, Mr. President."

"Oh, ***fuck***! What else?"

"It seems some of your judges that you appointed to the

bench have been abusing their power by abusing the accused."

"Like what? Give me an example," Cotti asked, leaning back in his chair and puffing away on his cigar.

"Well, some judges have come down from their bench and either hit, punched, or slapped defendants… and some have even tased defendants for disrespecting them and their courts."

"The hell with them punks. I'll bet you that those pukes that opened their mouths and disrespected the court won't do it again, knowing that they may get punched out by the judge. Good for them. And I'll tell anyone who wants to give me a hard time on the subject the same thing."

Arms didn't know what to say to that answer, although he agreed with the President. If more judges acted in the same fashion, the accused might just have a little more respect for higher authority and follow a straight and narrow path and not a criminal one. But enough psychology.

Arms still had one other problem for his boss to hear. That was the case of Richie "***Roundtop***" Rinaldo, Secretary of Housing and Urban Development. (They called him ***Roundtop*** because of a bald, four-inch circle on the top of his head. It looked like he had been scalped.) Rinaldo had been one of the Valoppi Capos that dealt with window replacement and construction contracts for the City of New York and New Jersey. He seemed to be very good at his job, getting many multimillion dollar contracts annually.

But now he was in a little bit of trouble. It had been discovered that Rinaldo had been giving preferential treatment to Family members, handing out billion-dollar government contracts to many of them. But the President might not have to worry about this particular problem.

Even though Secretary Rinaldo gave big money contracts to many of his friends, the construction projects involved all came in under budget and were finished in record time—which never happened with government contracts. Usually, the companies went over budget and soaked up as much money as the government allowed before abandoning the project and leaving the taxpayers to foot the bill.

The President did, however, have to figure out a way out of this mess before it ruined his reelection campaign and administration. He would have to make some drastic changes; a crack had just appeared for the first time in his Liberty Bell, and he had to fix it before it grew. And fast!

The President was thinking that very same thought as he smoked his cigar and looked up at the ceiling. Suddenly, he seemed to have an epiphany, and he ordered his FBI Director to keep the investigations "under his hat."

"Whatever you gotta do, Dennis, to keep this shit outta the newspapers, do it—at least until I can get a handle on it and decide what needs to be done. Capiche?"

Arms nodded. "Yes, sir, Mr. President. I'll do my best. I think I can keep this under wraps for a week, maybe ten days. But after that, I can't promise you anything."

Two days later, Bobby Legend told the Press Corp that DEA Director Don Domino had resigned his post that very morning and that Deputy Director Gitano Banduchi would replace him until a new DEA Director could be found. The only reason given for the resignation was that the President had lost confidence in the job Domino was doing. The drug investigation was never mentioned.

The following morning, the President also accepted the resignation of the Secretary of Housing and Urban Development… before anyone could "throw stones." Renaldo was replaced by his brother-in-law, Deputy Secretary Joseph Ambello. The reason given for the resignation was health issues. The President did thank both for their service to the country. Off the record, though, he told them that, if they were "convicted of any charges," he would pardon them.

As far as the judges were concerned, the President had a different view on things. He refused to get involved with their judgement calls and would let the ethics' committee handle any reprimands or sanctions.

The decisions made by the President over the resignations seemed to quell the reporters' questions for now, and they didn't rock the administration in the least.

Many in the media were still amazed with the President's negotiating skills and wanted to say nothing derogatory of him or his administration. With his campaign going so well, and with no competitors worth speaking about, most reporters and commentators predicted the President would win another term.

President Cotti was in good spirits. But he still had many things to worry about. He hadn't found out yet who the Russian hired to assassinate him. There were still fugitive CEOs that hadn't been brought to justice. And the President still had to deal with Napolie and the Heads of the Five Families. Other than that, President Cotti had "piece of mind".

Chapter 13

The President's last State of the Union Address was at hand. Everyone of importance was sitting in the audience—that is, everyone that was still healthy. Twenty-three Congressmen were absent due to being in the hospital or at home recuperating from injuries—injuries resulting from so-called robberies and assaults. Seven, including two Senators, had been listed by the Justice Department as ***missing***. Coincidently, all of these politicians had, at one time or another, disrespected the President. It was possible that they had paid the price for their indiscretions.

As the President entered the room, he received a hearty and roaring standing ovation that lasted at least five minutes. He was once again accompanied by his entourage of at least thirty agents of the Special Secret Service Brigade. Others had been stationed earlier, patrolling the halls and aisles of Congress.

The President's speech was, again, short and sweet. He told the audience many things that were on his mind. He also told them about the projects he wanted to complete in the last year of his Presidency.

"I thank you all for coming," Cotti told the crowd. "I won't keep you here too long tonight. I only have a few things to talk about—things that are very important to me and that should be important to everyone in this great country of ours. The first thing I want to talk about is ***fracking***! This particular way of getting gas and oil out of rock is ruining the country's water supply and creating earthquakes where there were none before fracking began. The people that run these gas and oil companies are greedy bastards… and if they want to ruin the People's ground water for profit, our government just might have to nationalize all energy companies and take the profit out of the equation. I will treat the CEOs of these energy companies, who rape the land, contaminate our water, and pollute our air without disregard for health concerns, just like I did the CEOs of Wall Street. I will have the Justice Department deal with them in the harshest of ways, which means longer jail terms or worse. We can live without oil, but the human body cannot survive without clean and drinkable water to quench one's thirst. Try and quench it with a swig of oil. ***Forget about it!***"

The crowd snickered at the President's comment, and some even clapped.

The President continued: "When confronted with this knowledge of the damage that these companies have created, they deny all responsibility and then hire PR firms that use psychological warfare to deal with it. Instead of fixing the problems they have caused and created, they brainwash the people hurt by their evil deeds or bribe public officials. This will not continue. I give forewarning to those people involved that these are treasonous actions. If they did this in the Middle East, they all would be beheaded. If they continue with their destructive behavior and disregard for health concerns, they will not continue for very much longer if I have my way. And I usually get what I want. Oh, they can deny it all they please, but their words and excuses will fall on deaf ears. I have already found them guilty of domestic terrorism. And I promise you, they will answer for it! And the same goes for those in the pharmaceutical industry. I will not allow them to set exorbitant prices for drugs that are used to control ravaging diseases. If they want to make enormous profits, it better be without causing detrimental health concerns for patients. Otherwise, the government will come in and price these drugs reasonably. I give fair warning now. Don't do it, or else! ***Forget about it!***"

The crowd roared with approval and gave their President a standing ovation.

Cotti added, "And if you CEOs run and leave the country, taking your money with you, you'll most likely end up like your Wall Street buddies. So, I give you warning now. If you want to ***frack,*** make sure you have your neighbors' backs or suffer the consequences. You can either heed my warning or take it with a grain of salt. It's entirely up to you! ***Forget about it!***"

The audience again gave the President a rousing standing ovation for nearly five minutes before the President quieted them.

"Let me talk to you about another subject that I've been thinking about for quite some time… and that's ***prison***

profiteers. I plan on making prisons non-profit organizations and will begin by returning those two-million-plus jobs to honest, hardworking citizens. I won't let some thug work those same jobs, making slave wages and allowing all the profit to go to the prison profiteers and their multi-billion-dollar companies. Slave labor will no longer be tolerated in the prison system. The prisoners will do their time behind bars. They weren't sentenced to do work while in prison, they were sentenced to do time. Many of these prisons are nothing but vacation homes for some. Hell, the ones from the streets are living far better in prison than they were where they came from. So, let them serve their time without working for multi-billion-dollar companies. The companies that profit from this form of slave labor will have to find new workers from the legitimate work force and pay them decent wages. And I'm not just talking about the prison profiteers. I'm also talking about the defense industry, the electronics industry, and many other big manufacturing companies. If their CEOs fight me on this and refuse my order, then they will have to pay the consequences. And believe me, it won't be some little fine. They'll be vacationing with the other criminals in the toughest of prisons. That, I can guarantee! ***Forget about it!"***

The President looked down to the top military chiefs sitting in the front row and reminded them of his expectations from the Pentagon leaders. "And let me just say a word to my military friends who are here tonight. I just want to remind them that I have yet to get a proper accounting of the two-trillion-plus dollars that are still unaccounted for. If you and your people skimmed the money for your own personal riches, tell me. I can maybe overlook that. But before I allow Congress to raise the necessary amount of money in this year's budget for the military, I need to find out where that money went. And I would like to know before my term ends. Because if I don't get it, and I happen to win another term as your President, you won't like it. So, think about it and take it to heart. And remember, for the time being, it's my military, not yours! ***Forget about it!***"

After hearing that, the military leaders stood up and stormed out of the room.

"Go to hell," shouted a three-star army general as he walked out of the room with his pals. A half-dozen of Cotti's bodyguards, disliking this rude behavior toward their President, followed the military men into the hall… to make sure they left the building without incident. The audience didn't know how to react to all that had happened. They just sat on their hands while murmuring to their neighbors.

The President noticed the unrest in the audience and continued with his speech. "Evidently, our military leaders didn't like what I had to say. But they're big boys. They can take it. And now that I've gotten that off my chest, I can tell you what I expect from Congress before my first term ends. We have yet to get a compassionate and comprehensive immigration bill passed. And I'd like to get it passed before the end of the year." He took a swig of his bottled water and then continued: "The last thing I want to talk about is employment. We need a little more than six million new jobs created before the end of the year to reach the level that I promised the American People. That would put the number of newly employed at nearly twenty-four million, all created during my four-year term. But I say, we can do better in the future! There's still more that needs to be done, but right now I can't think of anything. I mean, the rich are paying their fair share—finally! The economy is strong and getting stronger now that we've paid down twelve trillion dollars of debt. We again have close ties with the major countries of the world. And we have the new trade agreement with China. Oh, and let me just say a few words on that for those of you who disagreed with me. The technologies that will be offered to and shared with China will be technologies that they would get eventually by reverse engineering the technology and then building it themselves. So, we're really not giving up anything. And let me say that Presidents Putin and Xi will be my guests at the White House in the near future, hopefully before the political conventions begin. If the voters are smart, and I know that they are…" The President looked deeply into the television cameras and said, "I hope you elect me to another term as your President, so I can finish the job that we've started. I want to leave this Office with a multi-trillion-dollar budget surplus and let the voters reap the rewards. Thank you for watching and, to those of you still in the audience, thank you for coming tonight. God bless you and God bless this country. Thank you and goodnight."

The audience gave the President a standing ovation.

The President smiled, then turned and thanked the leaders above and behind him. As he was shaking Vice President Napolie's hand, Napolie leaned down and whispered into his buddy's ears.

"Jack, I gotta talk with ya. It's important."

"Come over later. We'll talk."

He then turned and walked down the steps to the crowd, shaking hands and making small talk to many of the important guests as he made his way out of the room and to the limos.

***

The President and Bartolo went directly to the White House. Napolie didn't arrive until two hours later. He was taken directly to the living room, where the two wiseguys were sitting and relaxing, each with a glass of brandy and smoking a fine cigar. The door opened, and they turned to see who had just entered the room.

"Hey, Johnny. How ya been?" Benny asked him as they shook hands.

"Can't complain," Napolie answered. "It wouldn't do a damn bit of good if I did."

He walked over to the bar, grabbed a cigar from a box

on top of the counter, lit it, and then helped himself to a glass of brandy before sitting down in a reclining chair directly across from his two childhood friends.

"What's up, Johnny?" Cotti asked him. "What's so important that you need to speak with me now?"

Napolie rubbed his hands together nervously, trying to explain the situation without upsetting his boss.

"Jack, I'm worried," he replied. "You've got all the Families angry at you for allowing the Feds to destroy their businesses and arresting their Capos and soldiers. What the ***fuck*** is going on? Why did you allow DomAchelli and Arms to crack down on our friends?"

Cotti took a few puffs off his cigar, then answered Napolie's questions with a short and caustic answer. "It had to be done, Johnny!"

"But Jack," Napolie replied, "the Dons are very pissed off, including Tommy Valoppi. They want a sit-down to straighten things out."

"Tell them to be patient and that it's only business. The crackdown was necessary to show the voters and reporters, who thought I was soft on crime, that I'm not. That I'll even have my friends arrested if they break the law. I had to do something to ensure our reelection win."

Napolie shook his head. "Jack, I'm not sure if I want to run again."

Cotti gave him a cold stare and said, "You will, and you will like it! If we get elected to another term, we'll leave D.C. with more riches than the sheiks in Saudi Arabia. I made side deals with both Putin and Xi for our future. I made some great connections. So, you tell the Commission that we'll have a sit-down after the election. If we win, we'll have it at our reelection party. That's less than ten months from now. But until then, just tell them to be patient."

"But Jack," Napolie protested, "I don't think the Commission will want to wait that long. They may get itchy fingers."

Cotti shot back, "We can't worry about that. My boys will protect me. I'm not worried about the Commission. I'm more worried about the assassin that the Russian in Amsterdam hired. We need to find ***that*** guy and take care of him before he takes care of me."

Napolie was angry. Talking to Cotti was like talking to a brick wall. He gave up trying to talk sense to his childhood friend and stood up to leave.

"Jack, I'm going to leave," Napolie said. "Have Karl send me my schedule for campaigning."

"Okay," Cotti replied.

As Napolie took a few steps toward the door, he added, "I think we should talk to the Commission as soon as possible. It's not healthy to wait." He looked to Bartolo. "Tell him, Benny!"

Benny shook his head and replied, "He's the boss. He knows what he's doing. The Commission will have to wait!"

Those words made Napolie even angrier. "I'm outta

here," he snapped. He left the room, heading for God-only-knows-where.

"Take care, Johnny," yelled Bartolo.

Then Nino Cantelli entered the room and looked at the President. "Everything okay, Boss?" he asked.

"Yeah, but stick around. We got things to talk about with Benny."

Nino took a seat next to Benny and waited for his next order. Benny offered him a drink, but Nino declined. He was still on the clock.

Benny looked to Cotti and remarked, "Jack, it's a sorry thing to say, but I don't trust Johnny anymore. You better watch your back."

"That son of a bitch is worried about the Commission," Cotti replied. "I wonder what they promised him."

"Probably his own Family," Benny surmised.

Cotti nodded. "I hear you. But me and Nino came up with a plan to see just how tight Johnny is with the Commission. I don't wanna say too much about it for the time being. But when the time comes, and it will, I will order Johnny to make the hit. I will order Nino to go along with him for muscle and an extra gun. If Johnny takes out the Commission, then we'll know he's still loyal and one of us. If not, Nino knows what to do. That's all I can say for now, Benny. I'll fill you in totally when the time comes. But until then, I can't take the chance that this information will leak out. If that happens, the media will be all over it, and it will ruin my plans for a second term. And I can't have that! ***Forget about it***!"

***

Cotti was right about the media. They were all talking about the President's demanding State of the Union Address and the military leaders who had stormed out of it.

Many television commentators agreed with the President; they especially wanted an accurate accounting of the military's spending. These particular commentators were calling President Cotti one of the top ten best Presidents ever. Fox News network commentators, however, were again calling the President a dictator. Some went a step farther and called him an ***unstable*** dictator.

Chris Wallace and his political pundits were calling the President not only an ***unstable dictator*** but also a ***communist dictator***—this was because he wanted to nationalize the oil and gas industry and possibly the pharmaceutical industry.

"President Cotti has gone too far," griped Chris Wallace. "He's overstepped his bounds if he thinks he can threaten these important business professionals and get away with it."

"He has gotten away with it so far with the Wall Street CEOs, Chris," replied Juan Williams, columnist from ***The Hill***. "Half of them are dead, and the others just haven't been found yet."

"The President is nothing but a thug," exclaimed Brett

Hume. “As I stated before he was elected. And he’s proven that with his speech.”

“I agree with Bret, Chris,” remarked Fred Barnes of the ***Weekly Standard***. “The President is acting more like the mobster that he is than like the President who got Xi to forgive twelve trillion in debt.”

“Not just that,” said columnist Charles Krauthammer, “but he also disrespected our military leaders. It was Major General Borske,” Krauthammer added, “that told the President to ‘go to hell!’”

“That he did,” agreed Barnes.

Wallace jumped into the fray, saying, “I’m sure we’ll be talking about the President’s State of the Union Address for weeks to come. Let’s just see if it will cost him votes in the long run. This may just cost him his reelection bid for a second term.”

The political show Fox News Sunday, headed by Chris Wallace, had much harsher words to say about the President than others, like John McLaughlin and the McLaughlin Group, who also gave their opinions on the President’s speech.

“You all heard the President’s speech,” McLaughlin stated to his viewers and pundits. “Did President Cotti step over the line when he warned the CEOs of the top Fortune five hundred companies that they could get jail time or worse if they continued on the path of water and land destruction? I ask you, Pat Buchanan!”

Buchanan gave a rational answer. “What I think the

President was angry with is that, just like many of the crooks in prison, these multi-billion-dollar companies don't take responsibility for their actions. But yet those crooks are right where they need to be. Maybe some of those CEOs need to be there as well."

"I agree with Pat, John," interjected Eleanor Clift. "I think those CEOs need to be warned. They will drill over a thousand fracking wells this year, and they need to do it in a responsible way. They say they are not responsible for the horrendous damage that is done by fracking. Now they know that if it continues, they will end up in jail… or worse!"

"John," said Mort Zuckerman, "these companies don't care if they pollute our ground water. Congress has given them ***carte blanche*** to pollute. They don't have to live with the EPA regulations like other companies do. The Republicans have given the oil and gas companies a get-out-of-jail-free card for fracking. It's utterly ridiculous."

Tom Rogan gave a similar opinion concerning the oil and gas companies' destruction of ground water and land. But another subject was on his mind that crept into the conversation.

"As far as I'm concerned, those CEOs reap what they sow. But I'm wondering when President Cotti will get serious about ISIS. He mentioned nothing on the subject. This man knows what war is. He fought them in the streets. We need to destroy this festering wound."

McLaughlin responded. "Tom, he's following the same

strategy as the last administration; bombing but no troops on the ground. But I predict that, if President Cotti wins a second term, he will get more involved in the Middle East."

"I don't know, John," replied Zuckerman. "It seems the military leaders aren't too fond of our President right now."

"That's true," McLaughlin admitted. "I believe it was Major General Borske that told the President to 'go to hell.' And during the President's State of the Union Address, no less."

"Not just that, John," said Buchanan, "but all the top military leaders stormed out of the building during his speech right on live TV. I don't think either the President or the military leaders are very fond of one another," he added.

Zuckerman opined that the President had every right to belittle the Pentagon and its leaders over the accounting debacle. "I mean, there are over two trillion dollars from the Pentagon's budget that have never been accounted for. President Cotti at least had the courage to bring up the subject. Many administrations just swept it under the rug. The taxpayers deserve to know how that money was spent. So, I give credit to the President for standing up to those military leaders."

"And the Pentagon is still fudging the numbers," stated Clift.

McLaughlin interrupted the conversation, diverting the subject. "Predictions! Pat," he demanded.

"John," Buchanan replied, "I predict the President will find a way to have a few of those fracking CEOs jailed before his term ends."

Clift predicted that the President would get more concessions from the Chinese government when President Xi came to Washington.

"John," said Zuckerman, "I predict that the Pentagon will have a finding for the President soon on that two trillion-dollar accounting debacle."

"Tom Rogan! Prediction!" demanded McLaughlin.

"John, I predict ISIS will overrun Bagdad if America doesn't send troops to Iraq for a counter offensive."

"And I predict," said McLaughlin, "that the President will win reelection with the most popular votes ever! Bye, Bye!"

The commentators' voicing of opinions on the President's State of the Union Address speech continued for months.

President Cotti, however, didn't care what the commentators were saying about him. He now was only interested in getting reelected. He was running unopposed for the American Family Freedom Party and was way ahead in the polls, beating both Democratic and Republican opponents by a wide margin of nearly sixty percentage points.

In a Gallop poll, the President was ahead of the Democratic frontrunner, Al Gore, by fifty-six percent; the Republican front runner, Rand Paul, was losing to the

President by a whopping sixty-three percentage points.

The President's reelection campaign was running smoothly. All the needed paperwork had been completed and turned in for his reelection bid. The American Family Freedom Party had reaped hundreds of millions of dollars within just the last few months from the big donors, including one hundred million from the energy CEOs at a donor dinner that Rove had set up… with the President as the honored guest.

The President believed the CEOs gave him money out of fear: fear of losing their freedom and maybe their lives. During the dinner, they tried to find out if he was really serious about his threats of jail.

"Is it your intention, Mr. President, that you would like to see us all in jail?" asked a worried gas company CEO.

Cotti just smiled, refusing to answer their questions concerning their future, and went back to eating his meal. Soon after, he left the dinner party. "Thank you for your support," he told them and then left the room.

These were the only words the President uttered throughout the dinner party. He didn't mingle; he didn't have to. They weren't friends to him; they wanted something from him. Probably a promise that he wouldn't have them thrown in jail. And the President wanted something from them: money. It was a two-way street, and the President understood that. It was nothing new in the world of politics. This was how the game was played. And President Cotti played the game better than most.

***

After the President returned to the White House from the dinner party, he went out into the crisp winter air for a short walk in the garden behind his temporary abode. Smoking his cigar, he looked up into the clear dark night. There he saw a bright, shining light that moved in many different directions at unbelievable speeds before hovering over an area not far from the White House. The President watched the object for a good five minutes before it disappeared in a blink of an eye. He wondered what the hell he had just seen. Then he remembered back to his days in China and all the talk of UFO sightings.

The President believed the sphere of glowing white light was from another world. But he wanted more information on the subject. He had asked Rove about UFOs before but had forgotten about it, until now. The next day, he ordered Rove to bring him an expert on the subject of UFOs. Then the President had an idea, one that would kill two birds with one stone. He mentioned it to Rove.

"Karl," said Cotti, "bring me that general that told me to 'go to hell!' I'll let him tell me not only about UFOs but also about his use of profanity. Let's just see what this guy has got to say."

Rove nodded. "Sure, Mr. President. You want Major General Walt Borske. He's Assistant to the Chairman of the Joint Chiefs of Staff. I just hope you know what you're getting yourself into. Not many Presidents have made war against the Pentagon."

"Don't worry, Karl. I know exactly what I'm doing. ***Forget about it!***"

***

It was nearly two months later, just after the President returned from the campaign trail, that Borske showed up in the Oval Office.

The President was very cordial with the man, shaking his hand, thanking him for his service, but not mentioning the man's outburst during his State of the Union Address speech. Once Borske had taken his seat, the President offered him a drink and cigar, and he accepted both.

Cotti came around his desk as Nino handed the general a scotch on the rocks (the general's favorite drink) and a cigar, which the President lit for him.

The President then returned to his chair and came right out and asked the general about UFOs.

"General, I called you here today because I saw a bright glowing object in the night sky a few months ago that moved around strangely. I'm wondering if it was extraterrestrial or one of ours."

The general thought for a few seconds, taking a few puffs from his cigar, and then answered, "I don't know, Mr. President. I didn't see it."

"General, I'd like to speak with you about this subject at length. Do you bowl, General?"

He nodded. "Yes, I bowl. In fact, I'm in a league at

Washington Bowl."

"Would you like to bowl a game or two in the White House bowling alley while we discuss UFOs?"

"That would be fine, Mr. President."

The President, his guest, Nino, and two other bodyguards walked down the two flights of stairs to the two-lane bowling alley, which was adjacent to the swimming pool.

After Nino handed out bowling shoes to the general and the President, the two picked out their bowling balls.

While the two leaders bowled and talked, Nino and the other bodyguards stood nearby, awaiting any orders from their boss.

Nearing frame five, Cotti asked, "What can you tell me about UFOs, General?"

"They don't exist," the man replied as he rolled his ball down the lane for another strike.

As the general turned to retrieve his ball and just before bowling another frame, he noticed that on the floor, just thirty feet to his left, lay a large twenty-by-thirty-foot piece of twenty mil plastic and a Queen Victoria press back chair sitting in its center.

The general stared at it for nearly a minute and wondered why it was there.

The President knew what the general was thinking and said to him, "They're painting tomorrow."

"Oh!" the general said, but then turned his attention back to bowling and rolled his sixth consecutive strike. He was having a great time, to say the least.

As they neared the tenth and final frame, the general had the chance at a three hundred game, which had never been done before on those lanes. He was giddy as a six-year-old kid in a candy store.

But before he could roll the ball, the President motioned to Nino. As the general was standing at the line concentrating on the pins, Nino sneaked up behind him and cold-cocked him in the temple with the butt of his gun, knocking him out. The other bodyguards dragged him over to the chair that was sitting on the plastic tarp, stripped him of his clothes, and then hog-tied his hands and feet to the arms and feet of the chair. An uncapped bottle of amyl nitrate was held just under the general's nose to awaken him. It worked like a charm.

Once the general came to his senses, he saw that he was nude and that his hands and feet were hog tied to the chair. He began fighting, trying to break free of his bonds. But to no avail. Even so, he refused to give up and continued his feeble attempts to escape until Nino stopped the nonsense by zapping him with a taser that emitted fifty thousand volts to his chest area.

"Augh!" he screamed but kept fighting to escape.

Nino tased him again.

"Augh," he cried, and then he began laughing.

The general was tased again. He laughed even harder. This went on for a good five minutes. Then Nino took a ten-minute cigarette break before returning to his torturous ways. Nino was just warming him up for his boss.

The President didn't exactly explain the reasons behind the little extracurricular activity that he had planned for the general, but Nino knew his boss's ways very well. When he was ordered to place a plastic tarp to one side of the bowling alley floor with a chair in the center, Nino knew exactly what it would be used for. The why? That was another matter and was irrelevant. Nino only took commands from his boss—he never asked questions.

The President motioned to Nino to cease and desist. Smoking his cigar, Cotti walked over and stood directly in front of the general, staring down at him with piercing eyes. He said, "I want a few questions answered, and I want the truth. Capiche?"

The general spit back, "Is this how you treat a general in the United States military, Mr. President? You ***fucking gangster*! *You wop***!" he shouted.

"Until I get the answers I want, yes!" Cotti retorted.

"So, what the fuck do you want from me?" the general yelled, sweating profusely.

The President told him that he wanted to know everything there was about UFOs. "And don't leave nothing out."

"I told you, they don't exist!"

"Nino, do your work," Cotti demanded.

Nino took out a pair of pliers from his jacket pocket, placed their open jaws to the general's ear lobe, and closed the jaws—***hard***.

The general laughed. "I've been trained to withstand pain," he said, "especially from torture. You can't hurt me."

"Quit being pig-headed, General," Cotti barked. "I just want information on UFOs for my own personal reasons. The Chinese President, Zing Ping, seems to think there are UFOs. Funny thing is, though, he wondered if they were extraterrestrial or ours. Imagine that. He thinks we have flying saucers. Well, do we, General?"

"I told you, they ***don't exist***!"

"Tell me the truth about them, and I'll let you live. Don't, and you'll never tell another President to 'go to hell!'"

"Is that what this is all about?" he whined. "Because I got pissed off over your accusations and stormed off during your speech? Well, I'm sorry!"

"General, you disrespected me and the Office of the President of the United States, and in front of my constituents. ***Forget about it***!"

"I apologize!" he shouted. "Your speech was months ago. Why are you doing this to me now?"

"I was busy before. Now, I have the time. So, what about UFOs, General?"

The general remained silent, refusing to speak.

Cotti motioned for Nino to continue his work.

Nino took his pliers, clamped them around the general's balls, and squeezed.

It didn't faze the general. Nino squeezed again. Again,

nothing. No cries of pain. No cursing, no whining. Nothing. To say the least, the general was one tough hombre.

The general looked up at Nino and said, "I told you, you can't hurt me. I've been trained to withstand pain. And anyway, my nuts were replaced with Teflon balls, just for this purpose. So, take a shot. I also have no feeling in my nut sack, a casualty from my training." He laughed.

Nino became angry. He set down his pliers in favor of another implement used in the art of torturing ones' enemies: an ice pick with a velvet handle and eight inches of blade. Nino then stuck the tip of it into the general's ear canal.

"Say the word, Boss!" Nino waited patiently for his boss's order to end the general's life.

"Come on, General. Tell me what I want to know, or Nino will surely put an end to your amazing career."

Nino slowly pushed the ice pick deeper into the ear canal. This got the general's attention, and he sang like a songbird that had just eaten marijuana seeds.

"Wait, wait a minute now!" he yelled. "All right, I'll tell you everything I know about UFOs. FUCK!"

"So, let's hear it," Cotti replied, allowing Nino to keep the ice pick in the general's ear until he was satisfied with the answer.

The general cricked his neck back and forth, around and around, even though the ice pick was still in his ear canal. Then he answered, "Yes, Mr. President. There ***are***

UFOs, and most of those seen in the skies are extraterrestrial. The others are ours, developed after reverse engineering crashed UFOs. But that's all I know. If you want to know more, contact Bob Lazaar, he's a rocket scientist and one of the people that have reverse-engineered UFO technology. Or you can read information on Ben Rich, the former CEO of Lockheed Skunkworks. He talks about some unbelievable things. Whether it's true or not, I can't say. As for what you saw, Mr. President, it could be extraterrestrial or one of ours. I don't know. And that's the truth!" The general gave a look of surrender to his President.

"How can I get a hold of Ben Rich?" Cotti asked him.

"You can't! He's dead. He wrote a letter on his deathbed spelling out what he knew personally about UFOs and UFO technology."

"Okay," Cotti replied, blowing his cigar smoke into the general's face, "we'll leave it at that. But that was just one of the questions I want answered. The other is about money. The two trillion dollars that's still unaccounted for from the Pentagon's budget. The subject that I was so rudely embarrassed by when my military leaders had the gall to walk out in the middle of my State of the Union Address and tell me to 'go to hell.' So, I want to know how you guys are skimming money off the top, 'cause I know that's what you're doing. I've already found you and your peers guilty of that crime. You guys have more scams than the Mafia. You guys are the Military Mafia!" Cotti took a few puffs from his cigar and then continued, "And I know that for a fact. A couple of your generals who gambled at a casino that I'm part owner in—off the books, of course—lost big time and ended up owing us a lot of money. But instead of paying off their debt in dollars, they paid us back in goods, like truckloads of automatic and semi-automatic weapons and tons of ammunition, new tires, batteries—hell, sometimes they even threw in the new trucks that they delivered the shit in; you name it, we got it, at least two to three times a month… and all purchased with taxpayer dollars in return for the VIG owed. We did this quite often. We also got goods from other military officers who sold the shit on the black market. And when they tried to screw us, we hijacked the load. ***Forget about it!***"

The general thought for a minute and then answered, "You could be right about that, Mr. President. I know some of my peers use doctored documents for invisible soldiers, called ***stealth soldiers***, that aren't really there but are on the payroll. I'm told that there are more than two divisions of ***stealth soldiers*** and that the money collected is divided among the many generals on the payroll."

"Are you one of those that get a cut from these ***stealth soldiers***?"

He looked at Cotti with somber eyes. "No, sir. I wanted no part of it."

"Oh," Cotti exclaimed, "you're an honest soldier!" He laughed. "How many other scams do you guys got going on to screw the taxpayers? Huh? How many?" he yelled.

Cotti motioned to Nino to apply pressure. Nino complied and stuck the ice pick into the general's ear far enough to hit the ear drum.

The general tried to get loose from his bonds but finally gave up and whispered, "Dozens!"

"Name some," Cotti ordered.

The general refused. "I can't!"

"You will, or you will pay the consequences."

"You won't kill me," the general surmised. "I'm a general, and my people will be looking for me. They won't stop until they get answers. You ***fucking wop***!"

"I'll give you one last chance, General," Cotti reiterated. "I want to know about the other scams that your people use. And I want to know now!"

The general remained silent as he looked at the floor.

Cotti just shook his head in disgust. "Okay, General. I gave you your chance. Now it's my turn to tell you to 'go to hell!'"

"I told you what you wanted to know. Don't kill me," the general pleaded. "I have a family!"

Cotti laughed while puffing on his cigar.

That made the general angry because he knew what was coming. "Fuck you," he yelled.

"Kill him, Nino," Cotti ordered.

Nino did as ordered, and pushed the eight inch blade into the general's brain, killing him instantly. Only a single drop of blood spilled out of his ear canal. But the facial expression that he made as the ice pick went deep into his brain was unforgettable to all involved. It was an expression of sheer terror and shock. His eyes and mouth were wide open, his neck muscles stiffened and frozen. He was a fright to see—that is, to anyone other than Cotti's boys. This was nothing new to them. They were used to facial expressions showing shock and awe. They'd seen them many, many times on many different people, including women, while doing Cotti's dirty work. And they always carried out their boss's orders with excellent precision.

Cotti gave them one last order for the night before heading upstairs to his bedroom to make love to Toni.

"Take the general to Charlie's!" Cotti told Nino. "He's got a new way of disposing of bodies. I'm told he doesn't need to dump them in the ocean anymore."

Nino and his boys nodded.

As Cotti left the room, the boys cut the bonds from the general's body and rolled him up in the plastic tarp. They usually dismembered the body first but, this time, they decided against it. They would let Charlie take care of that.

However, one of the bodyguards did give his opinion about the incident to the others. "Nino, man! This is bad! His crew is gonna be looking for him. And they've got two million members. We can't win a war against the United States military. They got the best snipers in the world. Charlie better make him disappear forever!"

Nino and friends drove the general's body, as ordered, to Charlie's which was thirty miles outside of D.C. in a very secluded rural area where the nearest neighbor was more than a mile away in either direction. They dumped him there. Then, with Charlie's help, they began dismembering the body before dragging the pieces to a wood-chipping machine that protruded just over a large pond full of piranha.

As Charlie began feeding one of the general's legs into the chipper, he ordered Nino and his two boys to burn the general's clothes completely. Then he added, "And take any metal, like medals, ribbons, and buttons from the general's uniform and melt them down with my acetylene torch. You'll find it in the garage. I don't want one thread of clothing, or any evidence, for that matter, left behind. Capiche?"

Before following that order, they first watched in amazement at the reaction of nearly a thousand piranha as they swarmed and fought each other to get at the tiny bone fragments and minute pieces of flesh; some even jumped out of the water to get first bite of the human food.

Even though it was night, under the full moon you could see the water in the pond change to an even darker color. It was as if Moses had stuck his staff in the water and changed it from a blue to a blood red. It was a sight to see: one Nino and his boys had never witnessed before. This was one story that they couldn't wait to tell their peers.

Charlie read their minds and told them in no uncertain terms that they couldn't tell anyone.

"You boys can't tell a soul about what you saw tonight.

If anyone opens their mouth, it'll be the last thing they talk about. Capiche?"

"***Forget about it***!" Nino told him.

After burning the clothes and plastic tarp and melting down the metal, they took the ashes and other evidence to Charlie for his okay. Then they buried it three feet deep next to the pond.

All three wiseguys returned to the White House and the crime scene. They wiped the chair and surrounding area with bleach so as to leave no evidence of the crime committed. When they finished, they returned to their White House duties of protecting the President.

Chapter 14

Well, it seemed Cotti's bodyguard's premonition came true. Two weeks after the President's meeting with the general, two of his peers came to the White House looking for answers as to the General's disappearance. But they got nowhere fast! Cotti refused to get into a shouting match with them, so he ordered them out of his office.

"We'll be back!" one of them shouted.

"And you better hope that he shows up… alive!" said the other as they stormed out of the Oval Office.

The officers' threats had no effect on the President. He had heard them before, many times, from a number of powerful people. But look where he was now. In the White House, and the most powerful person in the world!

Cotti, however, had other worries. He not only had problems with his military leaders over the disappearance of their friend, but he also had a big problem with his wife when she came to the White House one very early morning to surprise him. And boy, did she surprise him.

Cotti's wife was hosting a charity event on this particular day and brought to the White House the two dresses that the President and Vice President had used to leave the house without the Secret Service noticing. She wanted the two to sign a notarized document explaining what the dresses had been used for.

The President was still sleeping when she arrived and, without waiting to be escorted to his bedroom, she placed the dresses on a chair and rushed in to wake him. But to her big surprise, Cotti wasn't sleeping alone. Next to him was his White House secretary and girlfriend, Toni Ryeburg. To say the least, Maria was livid at the sight and at the lack of loyalty from her husband. She screamed ***bloody murder***. ***Forget about it***!

She grabbed her husband's shoulders and began shaking him, yelling, "You motherfucker! Wake up!"

Both he and Toni awakened at the same time to see Maria standing over them with a contorted expression on her face.

"Oh, my god," whined Toni as she jumped out of bed and threw a robe over her naked body. She left the room, letting the President fend for himself.

"Get up, you sorry sack of shit!" she yelled in Italian.

Cotti wiped the sleepiness out of his eyes and slowly slid his naked body out of bed.

Maria stood there with her hands on her hips, looking as though she either wanted to kill him or put her foot up his ass. Either choice would have sufficed.

Cotti put on his robe and asked his wife why she was so angry.

"We were just sleeping, honey," Cotti quipped.

"Yeah, but it's before the sleeping that concerns me," she retorted.

"Why didn't you tell me you were coming?" he asked her.

"I wanted to surprise you. And I guess I did!"

"Okay, you surprised me," he said as he lit a cigar. "So why are you here?"

She told him the reason, and he obliged her with his signature on the affidavit. She would get Napolie's signature later.

"Thank you, honey," she told her husband before leaving for the charity event.

"I hope everything goes well," the President replied with a sigh of relief as she left the room.

The President didn't see his wife again until after the election. Once the charity event was over, she returned to Queens and kept out of sight, knowing that, all the while, her husband was bedding down with his secretary.

***

But the President's problems didn't end there. Two weeks after that episode, Dick Cheney's people came to see him, begging him to help Cheney.

It seemed that Dick Cheney had been visiting friends in Europe when he was arrested and taken to the World Court to be prosecuted for war crimes. His supporters wanted the President to send military troops there to free him and bring him back to the States.

Cotti was sympathetic to their cause but refused their request for military action—or any action, for that matter—and explained his reasons.

"I'm sorry, fellas. I can't help you. I wouldn't interfere with our courts, and I'm sure not gonna interfere with the International World Court. Dick Cheney will have to get out of that mess without my help or intervention, and without the help of the United States military."

The men hesitated briefly, then, figuring that they didn't have anything to lose, asked him, "What would it cost us to get Dick out of jail? We'll pay you whatever you want. Just get him out of there. If you don't, he'll die in prison."

Cotti got mad. "Quit whining," he told the man. "And quit begging. If Cheney's innocent of the charges, then he'll go Scott free. If not, he can ***rot*** in jail as far as I'm concerned. I didn't like him when he was Vice President, and my opinion of him hasn't changed. However, I will give you a price for intervention. Not military might, mind you. But I'll see what I can do with my connections overseas. My price is one hundred million. From what I've been told, that's a pittance compared to what the guy is worth. But that's the best I can do. ***Forget about it!***"

They didn't give the President an answer right away.

"We'll have to think it over, Mr. President," the group's speaker replied, adding, "Can we get back to you on that?"

The President nodded. "But you better make it soon. One more week, and I have to get back on the road and see my constituents."

To put it mildly, Cheney's people were quite

dissatisfied and angry over the President's refusal to help. They stormed out of the White House, cursing Cotti's name as they went.

A few days later, however, those same gentlemen wired the hundred million dollars to a Cotti-friendly bank. They placed the money into an account under an alias controlled by Cotti.

But Cotti gave them nothing for their money. And when these gentlemen saw that nothing was getting done to get their friend released from the bonds of the World Court, they returned to the White House and ***demanded*** action. Cotti spewed words they didn't want to hear.

"I'm sorry, gentlemen, but I can't help you at this point in time. Dick Cheney will have to bite the bullet until after the election."

Cheney's friends didn't want to hear that. They had paid big money for the President's help in Cheney's release, and now the President wouldn't do anything until after the election. To put it mildly, these powerful men were livid with rage, feeling that they had been ripped off by the President of the United States, and vowed revenge.

Cotti laughed at their threats. He took them like he took all the others: with a ***grain of salt.***

The conventions were over, and the election was less than a month away. But these men didn't want to gamble with Cheney's life, especially if the President lost the election. Then the power that the President wielded would dissipate immensely—he would be in no position to change the opinion of the judges' minds who were sitting on the Court Bench. So, Cheney's friends wanted action now!

Cotti again refused their requests. "Not until after the election," he told them, adding, "I'm leading by a wide margin over both my opponents, so my reelection is in the bag. I'll wield more power than ever. And if military action is necessary to get Dick Cheney out of the mess he's gotten himself into, I would have the power to use it then. So, gentlemen, there's nothing more to say. You'll just have to wait!"

Again, the men were disgusted and angry over Cotti's refusal to help. And again, they stormed out of the room, making threats to the President's health and cursing the Cotti name as they went.

Cotti just sat back in his chair, smoking on his cigar and smiling. He was one hundred million dollars richer, and never lifted a finger to make it.

Somehow this story and others leaked to the press and were blasted on the nightly news.

Fox News' commentators were all taking the low road in their opinions of President Cotti. They expanded on their name calling; not only were they calling the President an ***unstable dictator*** and an ***unstable communist dictator***, but now they called him a ***coward*** for not taking action for the release of Cheney. To top it off, Cotti was the main suspect in Major General Borske's disappearance and possible homicide. They believed him guilty even though there wasn't one shred of evidence connecting the President to the alleged disappearance.

It didn't help matters when it was found that many of the security cameras in and around the White House had not been functioning during that time period. There were no recordings of the general entering or leaving the White House, and there was no record of the general being signed in for that particular meeting. The only evidence that a meeting might have taken place was a notation in the general's appointment book. But reasons to the contrary were given by the President's Press Secretary, Bobby Legend.

"Yes, it is possible," Legend explained to the Press Corp, "that General Borske and the President had scheduled a meeting for that particular day, but the General never showed up at the White House. For what reason, we have no idea." He left it at that, refusing to answer any more questions from the Press Corp.

***

John McLaughlin and his political pundits had more to add concerning the President and his problems.

"With the election only days away," said McLaughlin, "will the recent problems concerning the President hurt his reelection bid? His DEA Director and Secretary of Housing have resigned and General Borske and a number of Congressional politicians have disappeared. Will that hurt Cotti at the polls on election night? I ask you, Pat

Buchanan!"

"I don't think so, John. His polls numbers are still way ahead of Gore's and Paul's. He's leading both by over twenty percentage points. And Las Vegas has him picked as a five-to-one favorite to win. I think he will win on Tuesday. And John," he added, "your prediction was wrong about the President picking another running mate as Vice President."

"Why break up a winning team?" exclaimed Mort Zuckerman.

McLaughlin jumped into the conversation and changed the subject. "Do you think the President should help Dick Cheney get out of jail? I ask you, Eleanor Clift."

She shook her head. "No, John. What good would it do? And I'm told that the people who wanted this done wanted to basically break Cheney out of prison using our military, like a black ops operation."

"I heard they paid the President a very large sum of money for his promise to help," Said Tom Rogan.

"I don't believe it," Clift retorted. "You don't bribe a President. That's just crazy."

"It could be true," exclaimed Buchanan. "After all, the President was once a mobster and might still have that mobster mentality."

"What about the President being caught by his wife in bed, naked, having an affair with his secretary?" McLaughlin asked his pundits. "Will that hurt or help him?"

They all snickered at the question.

"It hasn't seemed to hurt him yet, John," quipped Clift.

"That's between the President and his wife," exclaimed Buchanan.

"And his girlfriend," Zuckerman joked.

"John," interjected Rogan, "I think that the twelve-trillion-dollar debt reduction will put President Cotti back in the White House. That was a bigger coup than when Nixon went to China to visit Mao."

"As I've stated before on this program," McLaughlin reminded his pundits, "I believe the President will win reelection on Tuesday night. And that's all the time we have for today," he added. "Bye, Bye."

***

The political news commentators weren't the only ones talking about the President. Others not in the news business were also concerned about some of Cotti's recent antics. Among these were the FBI agents in the New York City Field Office.

"You know that motherfucker Cotti murdered Borske and made him disappear," Agent Keith Brunson told the others in his group, "because Borske embarrassed him during his State of the Union Address."

The other agents in the room agreed.

"Someone is going to kill that guy," interjected Agent Greg Meadows. "Whether it is Borske's friends in the military, Cheney's friends who asked for his help and were denied—and possibly ripped off—by Cotti, the assassin hired by the Russian mob, or one from the Mafia: somebody is going to get that guy sooner rather than later, and hopefully, when they do, he'll stay ***dead.***"

"You forgot someone, Greg," said Agent Ken Lundy.

"Who?" asked Meadows.

"Me!"

"You? Why you?" Meadows asked him.

"I hated that motherfucker even before he ran for President," Lundy replied angrily. "Remember, I was on the surveillance team that followed him damn near twenty-four-seven. I know how that guy thinks and acts. Sadly, we just couldn't get the evidence needed to bust him and put him away for a thousand years. I just hope that, soon, someone puts him away for eternity. Or I might have to take it upon myself to do the job…"

"I wouldn't say that too loud, Ken," suggested Brunson. "Someone above might not think you're kidding."

Lundy snickered. "Who said I was kidding?"

***

The disparaging comments were still flying on Election Day, but they failed to hinder the President's reelection bid. Political commentators called the election just after midnight on election night. President Cotti won by a landslide. He won in every state but two. His two opponents each won one of those states. Gore finally won his home state of Tennessee, and Paul won his home state of Kentucky. No President had won a reelection bid by such a large margin except Nixon. President Cotti set a new record for most popular votes in a Presidential election.

After listening to the concession speeches of his two opponents, Cotti and Napolie had a closed-door meeting concerning the Heads of the Five Families. Cotti had promised Napolie nearly ten months before that he would hold a meeting after the election to talk about the crackdown on the Mafia.

"Johnny, contact the Heads of the Five Families and tell them that limos will be there to pick them up this afternoon to bring them here to DC for the party. Tell them the trip will take about three hours, so if they want to bring extra clothes for the party, they should do so."

Once the meeting was over, Cotti returned to the stage to say a few words and to thank the crowd for all the tireless work they had done for the American Family Freedom Party, which now had more members than either the Democratic or Republican Parties.

As the President stood on stage listening to the rousing applause and popping of champagne corks, Vice President Napolie and the Congressional Representative from New York, Jack Cotti Jr., joined them, along with the President's wife, Maria, Karl Rove, and the President's other children.

The President had only a few words to say before leaving the stage. He looked to the audience and yelled,

"We did it again. And it was all because of you! Thank you! I'll see you all at the party later on tonight!"

He and Napolie waved to the crowd as they left the stage to go their separate ways. Cotti's wife and kids rode the Presidential helicopter back to Queens, taking off fifteen minutes after the President said goodnight to the crowd.

That morning, the conservative morning talk show hosts were livid and disgusted by another Cotti victory.

So were many FBI agents working in the field against organized crime, in which arrests were at an all-time low due to the crackdown on the Mafia nearly a year before. They still hoped to bust the President for crimes he had committed while in Office, but because of the leaders controlling the crime-busting departments within government, the field agents' hands were tied. Nothing was done without authorization from higher-ups, mainly Attorney General DomAchelli or FBI Director Arms, who they knew were in the President's pocket. So, they just waited patiently, prayed, and hoped the day would come when President Jack Cotti, the 'Godfather President', would slip up and fall into their hands.

They could soon get their chance. Cotti had put his plan in motion, and sparks were sure to fly. If something were to go wrong or not work out as envisioned, someone could die an unintentional death. If, however, the plan worked out, there would be no direct evidence against the President to show that he was involved in the deaths of the

Heads of the Five Families.

***

Early that morning, two limos and two SUVs left the White House garage for New York City to pick up the Heads of the Five Families; nobody else was coming—no Underbosses, no Capos or soldiers, only the Dons. They didn't like that their bulldogs weren't allowed to travel with them, but they had reluctantly agreed to the trip. The Heads of the Genovese, Colombo, and Bonnano Families rode in one limo, while the Valoppi and Lucchese Family Heads rode in the other. One SUV full of Special Secret Service Brigade Agents led the group to DC, and the other SUV, also full of Cotti's special agents, followed behind the second limo.

Napolie came to the White House later that morning, around eleven, to speak with his boss about the meeting. More importantly, Cotti had something to speak with him about.

While Napolie was being escorted to the living room, Cotti and Cantelli were there, waiting. They had already decided on a plan long before this meeting. Nino knew it so well that he had started to think about it when falling asleep, instead of counting sheep or the people he had killed.

Napolie entered the room and took a seat on the sofa next to Nino.

"Hey, Mr. Napolie," said Nino.

Napolie nodded and replied, "Nino," as Cotti handed him a brandy and cigar. "Thanks, Jack."

Napolie lit his cigar and took a swig of brandy before speaking up. "So, what time is the meeting set for?"

Cotti didn't answer right away. He sat back in his plush seat, smoking his cigar, seeming not to have a care in the world. He took a sip from his glass of brandy and then answered his childhood friend.

"Johnny, I have something special I need you to do for me tonight."

"Whatever you need, Jack."

Cotti explained to Napolie about the hits he wanted done. "Nino will go with you and help," he added. "But I want them cocksuckers' dead before my party ends."

Napolie couldn't believe his boss's order. "You want ***me*** to whack ***them?*** Jack, this is insane! You can't just whack the Heads of the Five Families and hope to get away with it. Hell, you even want me to whack our own Family Don who replaced you."

"Yeah," Cotti replied, "it's so crazy that I'll control organized crime from coast to coast. Johnny boy, after tonight I'll have monopolized the Mafia. And I'll be ***Capo di tutti i Capi***, Boss of all Bosses! Except there will be only one boss—me! And Johnny, you'll be my Underboss."

"But Jack!" Napolie looked to Nino for support.

Nino just shrugged. It was an order from the boss; nobody disobeys an order unless they want to be the ones getting whacked and then fed to the fishes. "He's the boss!"

Nino reminded him.

Chapter 15

Around seven that evening, the limos pulled into an unused Teamster-owned warehouse where the five wiseguys could wash up and change clothes.

But when they rolled out of the limousines and saw that they weren't at the White House, Tommy Talluchi spoke up. "What the fuck are we doing here?" he barked, looking to his driver for an answer. "Why weren't we taken to the White House?"

The driver told him the reason and then added, "So when you're finished cleaning up, we'll get you over there as quickly as possible. But you don't have to hurry, the party doesn't start for almost an hour."

But the wiseguys were still disgusted and felt disrespected at not being taken directly to the White House.

While the wiseguys were doing their "thing," the Special Secret Service Brigade went outside and drove to a small building adjacent to the warehouse to eat, drink, and smoke a butt or two. And while the bodyguards were doing their "thing," the President was doing his. Rove entered the Oval Office and gave him a message.

"What's up, Karl?"

As Rove took a seat, he said, "I've got some good news for you about another Wall Street CEO who we were looking for."

Rove stopped speaking and was trying not to sneeze.

"Yeah? So, go ahead, spit it out!" Cotti ordered.

"Ah, Choo!" Rove sneezed. "Sorry, sir," he said as he wiped his nose with his handkerchief.

"You were saying?" Cotti asked him.

"Yes. As I was saying, it seems Jay Hooley of the State Street Corporation was found dead and dismembered in an alley behind a gay bar just outside of Rio, Brazil."

Cotti puffed on his cigar and smiled. "Good!" he remarked. "Only a few to go!"

"Don't worry, Mr. President, we'll get them."

With that said, Rove left the room. Seconds later, Napolie entered, hoping to talk some sense into his boss.

Cotti, seeing Napolie, called out to Nino, who was standing near the door. "Nino, come and join me and Johnny. Take a seat." He pointed to an empty chair.

As they got comfy in their chairs, Napolie spoke up. "Jack, can't we do this another time? It's the night of our party, for Christ sake."

"Johnny," Cotti answered, "the Dons are already here in DC. They're changing their clothes in a warehouse and waiting for the limo ride to the party. But they're not gonna make it. You're gonna take care of it. And I'll have Nino go along with you, just in case you need some help."

Cotti sent Nino along strictly to see how Napolie would react to the order. If needed, Nino could help Napolie with the hits—or Nino could whack them instead.

And in case something out of the ordinary occurred, Cotti and Nino had devised a plan B. So, all was a go.

Nino and Napolie left the White House strapped to the hilt. They each carried a fifteen-shot semi-automatic forty-five caliber pistol and three extra clips fully loaded. Nino knew the directions to the warehouse, so he drove them there in one of the security team's SUVs. It was just a short distance from the White House. During the fifteen-minute drive, Nino wanted to test Napolie to see how loyal he was to the President and the Family.

"Cotti's going crazy!" Nino barked. "I want off this merry-go-round. How can he order the deaths of the Heads of the Five Families? I mean, he even ordered the death of Tommy Valoppi, for Christ sake! The Don of his own Family!"

Napolie turned to him and asked, "Would you work for me?"

"Huh? Yeah. What do you want me to do? Whack the boss?"

Napolie snickered. "You're not far off," he said sarcastically.

"What?"

"Okay, listen," said Napolie. "We're gonna turn the tables on Jack. We're gonna kill him tonight, and then I'll take control—not only of the country as President, but of the Family too. I'll send Pauli DeVito with you to the White House."

"What do you want ***me*** to do?"

"Go into the Oval Office and tell Jack that we did it, that all Five Dons are dead. Then, when he's gloating, let Pauli whack him. And then, you whack Pauli so that you can say you were trying to protect the President. You'd be in the clear, and then you'd be ***my*** number-one bodyguard."

"Sounds good, Mr. Napolie. Is there any reward for doing this piece of work? I heard the Russian those CEOs hired to assassinate the President was paid sixty million dollars. What's in it for me?"

"How does two hundred and fifty grand sound? Plus, I'll make you Underboss for the Family, and I'll give you the same position as you have now. Protecting the President. What do you say? Are you in?"

Nino nodded. "Okay, I'm in!" he exclaimed.

"Good! How much longer to the warehouse?"

"It's just around the corner."

A few minutes later, they arrived at their destination.

As they entered the building, they saw that the Dons were dressed in Tuxes and ready to go to a party. But they were more anxious to talk with the President about certain "things."

When the Dons saw only Napolie and not the President, they became angry and belligerent.

"What the fuck's going on, Johnny?" asked Talluchi.

"Where's Cotti?" Cantano barked.

"That's President Cotti to you, Cantano," Napolie angrily replied. "And there's been a change in plans."

As Napolie explained the situation to the Five Dons, Nino and Pauli DeVito left to take care of business. Was Nino playing possum, or had he really changed sides? It seemed that Nino was ready to sacrifice his life for wiseguy heaven. Why would he do it? Was it the money promised him after the evil deed was done or the power associated with taking out a boss? After all, assassinating the President right in the Oval Office took "brass balls." But if he refused the order, he would be the one killed... and possibly his family. But then, Nino knew who his real boss was.

Before leaving the industrial area, Nino had Pauli turn into a dark alley so they could make sure their weapons were loaded and ready to fire. As Pauli checked his weapon, Nino fired his: two shots right into Pauli's right temple. He died instantly. Nino kicked him into the alley, jumped behind the wheel of the car, and sped away back toward the warehouse to really take care of business.

But Nino didn't know that the Five Dons had already left the building. Napolie had them leave the city because he didn't want them involved in the President's assassination. They left in such a rush that they didn't wait for their drivers to return; seeing that only one limo had the keys in its ignition, they all loaded into it. With Tommy Valoppi driving, they sped away, heading for Queens.

As the Five Dons were hurrying out of the city, Nino returned to the warehouse, unaware that the Dons had fled. Only Napolie and two of his bodyguards were in the building. When Napolie heard a door shut, he looked to see who it was and noticed that Nino had entered.

"Everything go as planned?" Napolie asked him.

"Where's everybody?" Nino wondered.

"They had to leave. Where's Pauli?"

"Dead!"

"And the President?" Napolie asked, lighting his cigar.

"Well, the President…" Nino suddenly pulled out his gun and fired four quick shots. Two in the chest of Napolie and one each in Napolie's bodyguards, killing all three.

Suddenly, the limo drivers and the other bodyguards came running into the building to see what had happened.

"Let's get these bodies out of here. ***Now***!" Nino shouted to his men. "We gotta get 'em to Charlie's."

***

As Cotti's boys were placing the bodies in large plastic tarps, the limo carrying the Five Dons was going down the highway like a bat out of hell. Just about twelve miles out of town, they ran into a little problem. Or should I say, a big problem: a semi-tractor and its forty-foot trailer filled with cement blocks. The semi came up to the rear of the limo too quickly and hit it hard enough to make it flip over and over again, throwing its occupants like rag dolls around its interior. The tractor-trailer suddenly horseshoed and tipped its load directly on top of the limo. This would have instantly killed any occupants that weren't already dead from the roll over.

What Nino had started out to do, a freak accident ended up doing it for him. But was it a freak accident, or was it plan B? It was definitely plan B. Cotti had predicted that the wiseguys would make a run for it. The semi driver was a Valoppi Family member and a professional truck driver for more than thirty-five years. This wasn't his first trip to the rodeo—Cotti had used him in many accidental-looking deaths. These were planned murders using a loaded semi instead of a loaded gun.

***

The boys cleaned up the big mess at the warehouse, scrubbing the floors with bleach before carting off the carcasses to Charlie, who would burn all of the evidence and feed the bodies to the fishes. Soon after, the boys returned to the White House for the party.

Nino went directly to his boss and told him about his failure to kill the Five Dons.

"I'm sorry, Mr. President," he whispered, "but the Dons weren't at the warehouse when I went to hit them. I was only able to get to Napolie and two of his bodyguards. I failed you, sir."

The President thanked him and patted him on the back. "Well done, Nino," he said.

Cotti was a little disappointed, but he believed plan B would work out. So, he returned to the celebration and partied like it was nineteen ninety-nine (1999).

***

And how right he was!

The news about the accident and the deaths of the Five Family Dons didn't break until the following morning. And it was big news. Luckily, nothing was said connecting their deaths to the President. But many agents in the FBI's New York City Field Office knew better. They believed Cotti was the man behind the deaths.

The disappearance of the Vice President didn't ring out over the news stations until a day after the news about the Five Dons. Was it coincidental that all these Mafia leaders were either dead or had disappeared? The Feds in New York didn't think so. They believed the Vice President had been killed just like the Dons, and they also believed that Cotti was behind it. But they couldn't prove it—not yet, anyways.

The political commentators didn't know which way to go with the story. They commented that it was a good thing that these staunch criminals and wiseguys were dead. But didn't know how to react to those supposedly accidental deaths or who to blame for Napolie's disappearance.

"Was it a Mafia hit?" Chris Wallace of Fox News Sunday wondered.

"Is the Vice President ***food for the fishes***?" asked Fred Barnes.

"Did the President have anything to do with the Vice President's disappearance as some people have suggested?" George Will asked.

They had their suspicions but no evidence to point to the President. But the accidental nature of the Five Dons' deaths was now questionable due to the fact that, a few weeks after the collision, it was learned that the semi driver was a Valoppi associate. But he wasn't talking, and he pleaded the fifth when questioned by the police and FBI.

***

The questions asked by reporters concerning the disappearance of Vice President Napolie came fast and furious. So, to protect President Cotti's reputation, Bobby Legend had to give answers to the Press Corp concerning the Vice President's disappearance.

"We don't know what happened to Vice President Napolie," Legend told the reporters. "Attorney General DomAchelli, FBI Director Arms, and their agents are working diligently to find an answer to this question. They will report any information gleaned from the investigation. But for the time being, work on important issues is moving forward in Congress, whether the Vice President is present or not."

"What about a tie in Congress?" asked the ***New York Times*** reporter. "Who will oversee the tiebreaker? We have no Vice President."

Legend was quick to respond. "Luckily, in the four years that President Cotti has been running the country, all the bills that he's proposed have passed with overwhelming support from Congress. So far, there has been no need to vote on a tiebreaker. However, President Cotti is in the process of putting together a list of possible replacement candidates for the Vice President slot. So, if and when it's decided to replace Vice President Napolie, President Cotti will inform Congress and the public. But at this time, the President is gearing up for the visits of Presidents Putin and Xi Zinping."

But due to the current troubles, the visits were cut short. President Cotti met President Putin at the UN and held a meeting there. President Zinping visited the White House and met with the President just long enough for a quick brunch and photos. The two happily agreed to another trillion dollars in debt reduction in return for a military application being delivered to the Chinese government. That piece of news pushed Napolie's name from the headlines to the back pages and had the agreement between Presidents Cotti and Zinping in its place.

The media loved that news. The political pundits were stepping all over each other's shoes to comment on the new deal between the United States and China, especially the McLaughlin Group.

"Well, you all heard the news about the deal made between our government and China," McLaughlin told his pundits and viewers. "This story has taken over the story about the Vice President's disappearance. Is the country's debt more important than the Vice President's investigation? I ask you, Pat Buchanan."

"Evidently, John, it is! Vice President Napolie's

disappearance is old news. To some of the political commentators, Vice President Napolie was nothing more than a thug. They didn't like him then and don't care about him now."

"I agree with Pat, John," exclaimed Clift. "Many of the television news commentators believe that the Vice President is dead and, most likely, ***food for the fishes***. So, his disappearance is really a non-story to them. The big story today is the trillion dollars in debt reduction. That's a total of thirteen trillion of debt that the President has wiped out in four short years. Imagine what he'll do in his next term as President."

"John," said Zuckerman, "it seems President Cotti and President Zinping are very good friends and are helping each other's countries with their incredible deals. And as far as the Vice President is concerned, Bobby Legend stated that the President is considering appointing someone new to the position. I have faith in my President."

"Yes, John," added Rogan. "I agree with the panel. The President is a superior negotiator with the leader of China. It seems right now that Vice President Napolie's disappearance isn't as important as the debt reduction."

"Well, we're out of time," McLaughlin told his pundits and viewers. "We'll talk more about the President and the ongoing investigation of the Vice President's disappearance in the weeks to come. Bye, Bye!"

***

More than a month had passed, and there was still no word on Vice President Napolie. The investigation had stalled due to the fact that no evidence or witnesses to his disappearance had been found. The Feds were searching half-heartedly for a man they believed to be dead, and if true, would never be found; it seemed that Napolie's life of crime had finally caught up with him.

So, just days before Christmas recess, President Cotti appointed his son, Representative Jack Cotti Jr., as Vice President Napolie's replacement. He sent the appointment to the Senate for confirmation, which was granted just days after it was received.

There would be a problem now if, for some unknown reason, the Vice President suddenly showed up. But by the time Christmas vacation rolled around, Napolie was still missing. And because of Charlie's great work in the disposal of bodies, he would never be found. The President knew that and was confident that his son would fill the void left by Napolie's absence.

***

These were happy times for the President; times of celebration. Christmas was near, and the President was full of Christmas spirit as he left Washington and headed home in the Presidential helicopter for his Christmas vacation. On that cold and brisk morning, after landing on the heliport behind his home, President Cotti was in a joyful mood.

Just as he was stepping out of the Presidential

helicopter, an unfamiliar whizzing sound was heard in the distance. It came closer until it was right on top of them. Looking up into the sky, the President and crew saw that it was a weaponized drone fit with an automatic pistol. Before anyone could react, six shots rang out in succession: Pop, pop, pop, pop, pop, pop. Four of the shots from the drone found their target with precision before the machine flew away. When the President's bodyguards checked on his condition, they saw that he had been hit in the chest in four different places. But he was still breathing.

"The President has been shot!" one of the bodyguards yelled into his walkie-talkie. "I repeat, the President has been shot."

The President's surgeon, who was traveling with the President, took his vitals while trying to stop the bleeding. Two of the wounds were in the center of the President's chest, and two were in his right upper torso. There was no time to waste, so Cotti's bodyguards loaded their boss's limp and bleeding body into the helicopter and had him flown to New York-Presbyterian University Hospital of Colombia and Cornell, which had already been set up for just such an emergency.

When the President's helicopter landed at the hospital, hospital staff was already there waiting for them. As they put the President onto a gurney and wheeled him into the room which was only used in Presidential emergencies, the news commentators of television and radio came on with breaking news.

"This just in," said a shocked Lester Holt. "The President has been shot. I repeat, the President has just been shot. No word yet on his condition. All we know so far is that he has been shot and is still alive." Holt listened to the words coming from his earpiece and relayed them to the viewers. "I'm getting word now that the President has four gunshot wounds to his chest and upper torso. The doctors are urgently trying to stop the bleeding as his pulse is weakening. We still have no word on how bad the President's condition is—whether it's dire or stabilizing, we just don't know. We'll keep you updated when we get any new information. NBC Nightly News is responding and has sent a crew to the hospital to keep our viewers informed on the President's condition. We have not heard who shot him and if a suspect is in custody. We just don't know. I'm sure that information will be forthcoming in the minutes and hours to come. We'll stay on the air until we know the outcome of the President's condition."

***

All the news stations were talking about the President's latest assassination attempt. So were the FBI agents in the New York City Field Office. They had already heard how the President was shot and how many wounds he had sustained. They just didn't know who had piloted the drone. If they did, they would have given that person a medal.

"Three strikes and he's out!" Brunson cried happily.

"It couldn't have happened to a nicer guy," quipped Meadows happily.

Then Meadows thought about Lundy and how happy he'd be at this moment hearing about the shooting.

"Hey, guys," he said to his peers, "where is Lundy today? He should be here celebrating with us."

"He told me," replied Brunson, "that he had something to do that couldn't wait."

"Well, he's missing a great celebration," said Meadows as he handed out glasses of Apple cider and homemade peanut butter cookies to all his buddies in the room.

Then Agent Adam Butler spoke up because he felt differently about the situation. Usually he was the quiet one of the bunch and didn't say much. But today he had something to say.

"Come on, guys," he barked. "He is our President! What we should be talking about and asking ourselves is who shot him!"

Delahant spoke up. "It had to be planned," he surmised. "I mean, we know he was shot by a drone armed with an automatic pistol. The pistol had to be loaded with armor-piercing bullets because those bullets penetrated his Kevlar body armor. I want all you guys to check on the streets with your confidential informants."

"I think it's the guy," said Brunson, "who was hired by that Russian in Amsterdam for those Wall Street thugs. He'd be on the top of my list."

"Yeah, but we don't have a clue to who that is,"

acknowledged Meadows.

"What about someone in the Five Families?" Delahant wondered. "I mean, they've got to be pissed that their bosses are dead. And they probably know who is responsible for their deaths. So, let's get a jump on our surveillance of these thugs and see if we can't learn something."

"Yeah, but if Cotti dies," said Meadows, "it will all be moot."

"Not really," replied Brunson. "Cotti's son is now Acting President as soon as Christmas vacation is over. And he may be President very soon."

Their joy suddenly subsided when they were reminded that another mobster would soon be running the country.

"Let's get back to work, guys," ordered Delahant.

Dejectedly, they did as ordered.

***

Press Secretary Bobby Legend gave his own Press release. He said, "President Cotti, the Godfather President elected to a second term, has again been cut down in his prime. Only prayers will help him now."

Many around the world were hoping and praying for Cotti's recovery. But the outlook seemed bleak. Four bullets to the chest was no cakewalk, and this was the third time in four years that the President had been at death's door.

Then word came over the tube that President Cotti was

alive—but barely. Lester Holt's latest news was that the doctors believed the President had no chance for recovery. "Although they operated on him quickly," he reported, "and took out all four bullets and fragments from his body, his pulse was slow, and he had blood loss of more than fifty percent."

"We'll be watching the President's condition closely," he added. "The next twenty-four hours will be crucial. Only time will tell if the President can pull out of it for a third time. Our prayers are with you, Mr. President."

The End

Epilogue

Now who tried to kill the President? Was it a hitter from one of the Five Families? Was it someone from the military, who holds the President accountable for the General's disappearance? Did his kid have something to do with it? Maybe Vice President wasn't good enough? Or maybe it was his wife? She was jealous over the girlfriend? Or someone in government? Not wanting Cotti to have another term. Or was it the assassin hired by Oleg Brakinov? As Services rendered?

You'll have to read ***The Godfather President Part 3—The Dynasty Begins*** to find out what happens to President Jack Cotti.

www.ingramcontent.com/pod-product-compliance
Lightning Source LLC
Chambersburg PA
CBHW020326030826
48979CB00020B/309

* 9 7 8 0 9 9 9 1 8 1 3 1 7 *